CARRY ME THROUGH DARK COUNTRY

LEONIE NEEDHAM

Published in Australia by Leonie Needham

First published in Australia 2025
This edition published 2025
Copyright © Leonie Needham 2025
Cover design, typesetting: WorkingType (www.workingtype.com.au)

The right of Leonie Needham to be identified as the
Author of the Work has been asserted in accordance with the
Copyright, Designs and Patents Act 1988.

This book is a work of fiction. Any similarities to that of
people living or dead are purely coincidental.

ISBN: 978-1-7640828-5-3

ABOUT THE AUTHOR

Leonie lives on the coast in South West Victoria. Her early years in Melbourne, residing in funeral homes, gave her valuable insights into matters of life and death. Working for an airline gave her a taste for travel. Moving on to work in the welfare sector kept her grounded.

She has completed several writing courses and a master class in novel writing. Leonie's work includes: *Port Fairy ~ a likely story!* a brief, informal account of early settlement in Victoria.

For the Journey, a book of poetry and short stories: and two plays; *Mythology, Madness and Mayhem~The Four Horsemen Ride Again* was staged by a local theatre group at a Short Play Festival held annually.

OTHER TITLES BY THE AUTHOR

Port Fairy ~ a likely story!

For the Journey

Mythology, Madness and Mayhem

*To my children and their children, to my friends,
and all of us who take a tumble, brush ourselves off,
and stand to face the wind.*

Sketch by Belinda Needham

ACKNOWLEDGEMENTS

I would like to extend my thanks to my early readers who gave me positive reasons to believe that I had an engaging story to tell. To Mike Nicol, writer and tutor, who loved my characters. To Jo Canham at Blarney Books who loved the humour. To my daughter, Belinda, my competent, exacting proofreader. Most importantly, my thanks to Liz Monument and Kath Harper for their invaluable editing assistance.

CONTENTS

CHAPTER 1

2004 — Arrival

The thought that she was now a widow before her twenty-ninth birthday struck Celia as utterly absurd. Widow, the word sounded so archaic. It rattled in her head. It had to be true, she knew, but the word fell short of expressing the dislocation she felt. Living in limbo here in a dingy, upstairs bedsit in the house of her cousin, Charlie. She sat staring at the documents on her desk. A scrap of coffee-stained paper clung to the back of a gas bill. She prised it loose. As she deciphered the smudged, handwritten words she recalled the day she'd written them; on the day before she locked up her house and left.

The yoke of loss grips firm around my shoulders
In my imagining I watch you stepping from the sea
Beneath the Weeping Cherry tree above the basalt boulders
I remember tasting the salt on your lips that day
You took my hand and we lay there lost in wonder
As the cherry petals showered from the tree...

More lines captured the memories of a holiday with Clive at a beach house, ending with the sadness of today. Wiping her tears Celia read the words over and over, as if to convince herself of the truth of them. Copying the poem into her notebook she placed it to one side and reached into a cardboard box by her feet. From the jumble of stationery she retrieved a roll of sticky tape and moved to fasten the most urgent bills to the windowsill.

Standing there for a moment she gazed pensively through the fly specked panes, thinking of the difficult trip from Bannockburn. She had almost wiped out a small family of ducks crossing the road in front of her...thinking of Clive, feeling hurt and angry about the way he'd left her. How could he do such a dreadful thing.

Hitting the brakes hard like that had sent her old Corolla slewing sideways, groaning with the weight of the load. It was a wake-up call and fortunate that the country road was deserted. She wanted no further heartache, not on these roads, not anywhere.

Her anger still simmered as she threw the roll of tape back into the box where it promptly bounced out again. As she bent to retrieve it she exhaled the useless anger from her chest, remembering Clive's warmth and compassion. Ambivalent feelings about Clive tormented her.

In recent months, before tragedy struck, her mother had joined the household. Failing health prompted the move. Her life was now changed immeasurably. Celia thought about it every day. Ruth was living with advancing dementia at Summerleigh Community Care.

Mortgage payments and memories deemed it impossible for Celia to keep her family home. Charlie's mother, her Aunt Eula, had passed on his offer of the bedsit. Why he didn't contact her directly was puzzling. Maybe, like a lot of others, he felt awkward, didn't know what to say under the circumstances. Confirming her arrival date for early April Celia was mindful of his closing words.

'On a temporary basis of course...until you get back on your feet.'

Accommodation in her cousin's house would incur no rent. At least Charlie had been clear about that.

The mundane requirements of daily living gave structure to her day. Here there are boxes to unpack, cleaning and dusting and dirty washing to be done, food to find.

Her computer sat to one side of her desk, the screen perched on top, dark and silent; waiting for life. Charlie was arranging for an electrician to check the power point which kept shorting out. Or was it the motherboard, or some other stupid problem.

Her thoughts strayed to the kindness of friends who had cocooned her in her time of greatest need. To focus on the here and now Celia tended to her three favourite indoor plants, all she could fit into her overloaded car. They sat on the kitchen bench where the light was poor.

A lush philodendron and a croton with richly coloured leaves were both looking droopy. The third was a nameless grey succulent, a sturdy survivor. Filling a plastic jug with water she gave each one their required allowance and moved them to a windowsill while she pondered how best to proceed with living in this unfamiliar town.

On the day of Celia's arrival her aunt had come to visit, bringing a supply of fresh food. Charlie stored the containers in his freezer and promised not to touch it.

Over a cup of tea in Charlie's kitchen Aunt Eula had introduced her to a brief history of Appleton, 'rooted in the orchards first planted long ago by our European ancestors and still flourishing today. The climate suited them, close enough to the coast for holidays and distant enough from the salty sea air.'

Charlie questioned the number of visits they'd taken to the beach, he said he didn't know there was a beach, or an ocean until he was ten. His mother didn't rise to the bait.

'You must try the cider.' Eula advised.

Celia soon needed to stock her own pantry and cook for herself. She gave a half-smile as she added the brand of cider to her shopping list. Sudden shouts from the street below caught her attention. Glancing from her top storey window she saw a boy lying on the road. His bike lay in front of a small sedan.

Bystanders were assisting when she forced herself to go down the stairs and out onto the street. Her heartbeat thumped loud in her chest.

With a shock she recognised the teenager as Robert Schofield, the boy who had helped carry her bags upstairs when she'd first arrived. Someone was speaking. 'An ambulance is on the way, and the police...' Sirens drowned out the man's voice. She recognised him. He worked at the bank on the corner where, yesterday, she had paid two urgent bills.

Somebody was performing CPR. The boy stirred. Celia could see his legs move slightly as his trapped foot was released from the pedal.

Her heart was still pounding. She averted her eyes and stepped back, leaning against the window of The Ice Cream Shop next door. Lifting a hand to her chest she pressed against it, as if to calm the wayward beats.

Celia watched as onlookers moved aside when paramedics arrived. They checked his vital signs, immobilised the boy's neck, and carefully placed him on a stretcher. A young policeman was speaking to the driver, an elderly man who appeared visibly shaken.

Autumn leaves scattered in a sudden breeze as light rain started to fall. Turning towards the window Celia could see Sally Doyle serving a customer inside the shop. She noticed her own pale reflection, her washed out face darkening her eyes to the colour of blue-grey slate. The ambulance departed and she turned to glance at the driver. He looked in need of someone to drive him home.

Untidy strands of auburn hair blew across her face. Her thoughts flew back to the day she had run from the house to Eddy, laying in the driveway. Brushing at her windblown hair, as if to brush away the memory, she didn't notice Sally emerge from the shop until a steady hand took her arm and escorted her inside.

'You need a sugar hit, come in, my love. I'll bring you an ice cream.'

Celia was grateful. She had begun to feel very wobbly. She sat trying to steady her breathing. The tables were pretty; white lacy paper over a pale pink underlay. On the walls mirrors were set into carved white frames, reflecting the colours of home made ice cream. Local fruits from the orchards that had given the town its name were pureed to create a great-tasting treat.

Sally returned with a double header in a cone and stroked Celia's arm.

'I think Robert will be okay, I'll ring the hospital in a little while. Maybe you could give me your number and I'll call you with any news.'

'Thanks, I'd appreciate that.' Celia took the ice cream. 'And thanks for this. The accident unsettled me.' Her tongue slid around the cone, licking the melting creamy edges.

'Is it peach or mango? Whatever it is, I feel much better.'

The door of the shop opened and Mavis poked her head inside. Today she was wearing a multi-coloured headscarf. Whenever Celia visited the shop she'd noticed this odd woman with her animated mannerisms and a voice sounding like sandpaper rubbing on wood. She had asked if the woman worked there or lived upstairs. Sally had laughingly answered.

'I don't blame you for thinking that. No, Mavis runs Marvellous M, a vintage clothing store further up the road. She seems to live on ice cream, and comes in twice, or sometimes three times a day, often reciting strange predictions that no-one understands.'

Today, true to form, Mavis grinned at them before uttering another mysterious missive.

'Poor kid did a skid. Stars conspire, beware the fire.'

With that cryptic remark she hurriedly retreated. Sally shook her head.

'Silly old biddy with her riddles and rhymes. Most times we don't know what to make of it, but today at least, some of her words made sense.' Celia asked if Mavis had always lived in Appleton.

'No, she arrived here in the seventies. When the mood takes her she talks about her gypsy past, disowned when she married an outsider, a gadjo, who formed a band of travelling troubadours. Her Romany name was useful for the stage but didn't do her any favours when the gadjo died. Tired of endless questions Morvessa became Mavis.'

Celia was fascinated with the tale.

'Left with nothing but trunks of regalia, Mavis used the props and costumes to start her vintage clothing store.'

Celia thought she sounded like an enterprising woman.

The weather had cleared by the following morning and a shaft of weak sunlight fell across Celia's desk. Flipping through a collection of papers she found the rental agreement for her house. With a reluctant sigh she picked up her pen and signed it, shoving it into the agent's self-addressed envelope, placing it in her bag ready to post.

The musty smell of the bedsit seeped into her throat. Had she brought anything, any bleach, polish or sweet-smelling oils? She had no idea what her friends had packed in the box they'd placed in her car at the last minute. She would need to find it.

For now she could only open a window. There were two facing the street. After a tussle she prised one of them loose and chocked it open with an old breadboard. The other wouldn't budge.

Charlie was not at home. He was just out. That's all he ever said. Celia never enquired further, she sensed it would only irritate him if she did. The change in him was mystifying. She remembered a cheerful, carefree cousin when she had come to stay; always teasing, sometimes aggravating. Celia had given as good as she got in those days.

He was often noisy in the mornings. Pent-up anger could be heard in the ping of the cutlery hitting the sink. She wished that they could talk as they had when they were younger. Celia had heard little about her cousin in recent years. She was surprised to learn that he was Sally Doyle's landlord at The Ice Cream Shop. She knew he worked in the dairy industry, inspecting properties for compliance purposes but details of his private life had not yet come to light.

The wall beside her suddenly vibrated as the front door banged shut. Charlie must be home. She frowned, pondering the man Charles had become. At thirty one she could see he had the slim, toned body of a runner. His light brown hair was a straggling mess and he was adopting the careworn stance of an older man. Celia would like to know why.

Sally rang as promised. Robert had sustained a serious head injury and a broken leg. Celia gave a deep sigh. She'd fallen asleep last night thinking of Robert and wondering how the driver was coping.

When she woke she resolved to clarify her precarious financial situation and that would involve finding a job. She was a qualified teacher but since having Eddy in 2001 her hours had moved to part-time and money had been tight.

*   *   *

Too often, thinking of Eddy took Celia back to that February morning. The weather was threatening rain. Celia figured later that Clive spent a few minutes in the old garage, attaching the cover on the tray of his ute. Enough time for Eddy to climb onto the small tin trunk inside the back door of the old weatherboard cottage and lift the door latch.

'Daddy, daddy, I coming, I coming.'

Celia heard him, jumped from her bed and ran, but Clive did not hear. The car radio was on and the noise of the engine drowned out the child's cry. Clive finally stopped when he saw Celia and heard her screaming. How do you recover from such a tragedy? She tried to talk to Clive, begged him not to blame himself.

He refused to listen; he shrugged off any attempt she made to comfort him. She needed him. She knew they needed each other, but Celia saw a haunted man, beyond reach, in a place where grief and guilt rained down on him like a destructive typhoon. His whole being was disintegrating and Celia could only watch in despair.

Two weeks after Eddy's death Clive drove along the Great Ocean Road, over the cliff's edge and into the sea. How could he leave her like that? His death had shaken the very foundations of her being.

Up in her attic room the day was nearly done. Rays from the setting sun caught the diamonds in her pearl pendant as she lifted it gently into out of its box. It had been a wedding present from her husband, designed by his best man, Rohan Collins, a beautiful soul, who had promised to visit her in July. She took it out and cradled it most nights. This ritual was strangely comforting. Tonight she could almost feel Clive's arms around her as she lay in her bed, her thoughts drifting to happier scenes from the not-so-long ago.

Waking early Celia sat up with a start, remembering she was in her cousin's house in Appleton. She was tempted to stay in bed and pull the covers over her head but that wouldn't solve anything. Reluctantly she swung her legs out of the bed and walked quickly to the antiquated shower stall, sandwiched into a corner on the landing. After her morning coffee she felt ready to tackle the jobs at hand and spoke aloud to herself.

'Tidy this desk, get some order happening here, work out your priorities, girl. Charge your phone. Look for work.'

She had been so comfortable in the folds of her old life; self-absorbed and complacent, never dreaming of the sorrow to come. The house at Bannockburn will soon be rented; the estate agent had advised that a sale may take some time. Renting it would provide ready funds. Prospective tenants were on his waiting list.

There were no vacancies at the local primary school. Celia left a resume with the office staff who said no doubt something would come up.

She made a list of phone numbers. After being on hold for some time she spoke with only two service providers. They'd give her an extension, but what good would that do? The third call was to the local Community Centre to make an appointment with a Financial counsellor. She needed to visit the Post Office and buy some folders for this stuff. She threw on a scarf and went for a walk.

There were no vacancies at the local primary school. Celia left a resume with the office staff who said no doubt something would come up.

Loneliness was a mean companion. On her return she would visit Sally and buy an ice cream to stave off the lunchtime hunger pangs. Sam's Bargain store was packed with household and personal items from Fly Sprays to Fancy Dress.

Celia purchased her stationery and wandered out into the sunshine. The Post Office was two blocks north. A longer walk would be good exercise. Passing the theatre she saw an advertisement among the movie posters. In large black letters it read,

PART TIME BOX OFFICE CLERK REQUIRED.
3 NIGHTS & 2 AFTERNOONS. Apply within.

The gracious old building was closed at this time of day. She would call back with a resume. Sally was cleaning tables when Celia arrived.

'Robert's doing well,' she said. Celia asked if she'd heard anything about the driver.

'Not much. Only that the poor guy lost his wife a couple of months back. The police haven't laid any charges yet. I don't think they're keen to do that. Robert was careless by all accounts.'

Taking a seat at one of the tables Celia felt heartened by the ambience here.

'I'm going to apply for a job,' she told Sally, outlining the details she'd copied from the advertisement.

'That could be just the thing for you right now. Make sure that old Hendricks pays award rates, he's known as a bit of a scrooge. By the way, talking of scrooges, Charlie came in earlier, he's going to have a look at the horrible hoarding above the shop. That's progress. I think maybe one of the councillors has had a quiet chat.'

'Oh, a pleasant surprise,' Celia replied. 'I wouldn't hold my breath, Sal. From what I've seen lately I think he might be a serial passive resister.' Sally swept one hand through the longer brown strands of her newly acquired urchin cut and winked.

'I'm forming a lobby group to urge the local Council to draft new planning laws that do away with tacky, modern signs on our old buildings, they're an eyesore.' she said.

'Good work, Sal. Maybe that's why Charlie is more inclined to pay attention. Very commendable of you.'

A message on her phone informed her that Clive's sister was planning a brief visit from Perth. Celia called her.

'Dad hasn't been well lately. I think a visit may lift his spirits.' Katherine said. 'I'm grateful that he has Magda. She's encouraging Dad to sell up and move in with her on the Peninsula. I'm hoping to see you when I come over.'

Caught up in her own sorrow Celia had given scant thought to her husband's family. Feeling guilty she made a call to Frank. Since the funerals in February she had spoken to her father-in law only once, each of them not knowing what to say. She didn't know him well. Limited time and distance had contributed to that during her marriage..

Celia promised she would visit as soon as she was more settled. She didn't like to say, as soon as I can afford the fuel. He sounded pleased, expressing an eagerness see her.

Whenever Celia reflected on the shocking events of the recent past, time played tricks with her mind. She often found herself wondering how she had managed to live through these last few months. She needed to bridge the distance between herself and Clive's family. They too were grieving the loss of Clive and Eddy.

Her own father had been a distant figure in Celia's early life. When he died she had been studying in Melbourne. Her two older brothers inherited the farm. Celia received seven thousand dollars and some shares that weren't going anywhere.

Her mother had been apologetic, even embarrassed and confided to Celia that she hadn't had the courage to leave the marriage.

CHAPTER 2

2004 — Opportunities

From her upstairs window on a dreary Thursday in May Celia spied Katherine climbing out of a boxy rental. She hurried down the stairs to welcome her. It was so good to have someone here that she knew and loved. Someone who needed no explanations.

Charlie had moved a camp bed upstairs. They cried a lot that night, finding consolation in each other.

Her grief was always present, sometimes overwhelming, sometimes contained; pushed back when she needed to function each day. Having Kath here made her aware of the need to comfort another. Aware of her own need. Memories of Clive and Eddy would remain a part of her. She strove to recall their faces, determined that their features would not fade.

Although it hurt to look, she carried her notebook with photos tucked inside and recorded every memory that came to mind... Eddy's baby blonde hair, curling in fine ringlets at his neck. His funny little mannerisms, pulling her earrings or her hair... the way his blue eyes twinkled with merriment. Clive's even temperament, a smile lurking at the corners of his mouth and strong hands holding her. These things she would remember always and know that she had been loved.

To alleviate her despondency after Kath's departure Celia ventured out on Saturday and headed towards the Cinema. Each time she walked these streets she discovered something new; hidden laneways and arcades housing specialty shops and eating spots, some no bigger than a caravan. She sat in a tiny nook and ordered a spicy Tom Yum soup before she continued to the theatre where she found Percy Hendricks, a man in his early fifties, Celia guessed. She introduced herself and handed him her resume.

'Oh right, thanks. I'll have a look at it and give you a call.'

A whiff of disinfectant jostled with the stale odour of Percy's clothing as he stepped into the foyer. His eyes flickered from her face to her feet, and languidly back again, like slats moving on a venetian blind. She felt distinctly uncomfortable but thought she could handle him if she got the job. Two days later Percy phoned and offered her a couple of trial shifts. She agreed when she had confirmed the correct pay rate.

'Wouldn't expect ya t' work for nothin.' replied Percy.

The small amount of savings remaining needed to keep her afloat until she managed to earn a living. Visits to her mother, Ruth, at Summerleigh in Geelong would be limited to coincide with the government Newstart allowance each fortnight. Newstart, she gave an ironic grimace. Yes, make a new start. Simple...lose your family, brush yourself off and step forth to a new beginning. How will I do that? she asked herself.

With the prospect of a job Celia decided she could afford to visit her mother. Hoping her ten year old Corolla would make the distance to Geelong Celia set off the following morning.

Outside in the gardens at Summerleigh they strolled along the pathways. Ruth spoke as if they were wandering around the old family farm.

Celia took her mother's hand. As they walked, Ruth seemed more confused about the recent past, sometimes remembering that Clive had died, or remembering Eddy, asking where he was. Or thinking that Clive had visited her yesterday.

A chance meeting in Melbourne during Celia's student days had brought the three together. Ruth and Celia were having lunch; the place was crowded and a young man was looking for a seat. She could see them now, in her mind's eye, as her mother in her obliging way, indicated the empty chair beside her. It was an auspicious meeting, a life-changing moment, unlike the brutal life-changing moments in February that had impacted her so immediately.

* * *

Before starting her first shift Celia decided to visit The Ice Cream Shop. She was pleased that Sally was now serving coffee and cake. A gleaming new coffee machine sat proudly in the centre of the counter, a timber bench taking its weight between the glass covered tubs of ice cream on either side.

The place was humming. She found a spot at the front window where Sally had recently installed a bench top and stools. Sally's greeting was interrupted in mid sentence as the tin hoarding from the top of the building came crashing down onto the pavement.

Rusty screws, bits of masonry and timber splinters bounced up on impact, clattering on the plate glass window. A narrow canvas awning shading the window collapsed on one corner in a sash of stripes. A child's parked pram sustained a substantial dent in the hood. Luckily she saw the baby suckling contentedly inside the shop. Nobody else seemed to be hurt.

Celia was still too stunned to speak. The State Emergency Services were arriving as Celia prepared to leave. She noticed the guy from the bank, pulling an SES vest over his shirt. Celia greeted him.

'Wearing a different hat today?'

'Hi, Celia, bit of a shambles here.' He introduced himself.

'I'm Marcus. How are you getting on? Settling in alright? Haven't seen you since Robert's accident.'

'I'm managing. Sorry I can't stay to help, I'm off to start work at the theatre today.'

'Well done, see you soon.' Celia stood looking after him as a Council truck arrived. Sally stepped outside to survey the damage.

'A nasty little mess alright,' she said, with hands on hips. 'It seems being slow off the mark has worked in Charlie's favour this time. Hmph.'

Feeling slightly apprehensive Celia had arrived early. Percy had not opened the building. As she stood waiting, her gaze took in the shiny decorative circles set above sculpted clean lines; a 1930's architectural style. From the outside Celia noticed extra windows on either side, covered in a white coarse scrim. She couldn't recall them being part of the cinema complex when Percy had shown her around. She wondered what was behind those windows. Percy would know.

Celia fumbled through the rolls of paper tickets in the box office. Percy stood a little too close, his hand moving on her shoulder as he explained the ticketing system. The movie screening today was 'Driving Miss Daisy.' The computer was slow. The few patrons in the queue were mainly middle-aged or older. They smiled at her with resigned benevolence.

After the fifth sale she mastered the EFTPOS machine and breathed a sigh of relief when Percy left for the projection room. She had been distracted and any thoughts of asking him what lay behind those windows had flown from her head. She opened the doors to the auditorium and collected tickets, hoping her smile didn't look too forced.

The business of adjusting to life in this new place occupied Celia's time. She kept moving relentlessly from task to task, fearful that to stop would see her succumb to the hypnotic pull of the dark abyss lurking just outside of herself on the fringes of her busy-ness, waiting for her to falter and fall headlong into that swirling black mire. So how to tread this fine line...to grieve for these two most loved...give way to the pain of loss, cry for them without losing yourself too, swept away on a current of grief, anger and guilt.

Give Grief its due...survive its demands. Slowly she was learning to tuck her grief into a special place; to take the sodden lump from the back of her brain and move the weight of it from the middle of her chest. Capture those beloved faces and wrap them in imaginary coloured silk scarves. Maybe she should see a bereavement counsellor as her doctor had urged her to do. She would think about it.

The help of a counsellor would be a wise move. Deep down Celia knew it because anniversaries would be very tough. There would be two to live through next February, with birthdays, a wedding anniversary and Christmas in between.

Percy was reading the newspaper one Friday evening when Celia arrived. She noticed an item on page two, about the CEO of a large retail store being sued for a bucket load of money over a sexual harassment issue.

'There you go, Percy,' Celia said, pointing to the article and smiling at him. 'That got him where it hurts, didn't it. I've brought you a coffee, do you take sugar?'

'Thanks, very good of you.' Percy was beaming at her. Celia pressed her advantage.

'By the way, I noticed that this building has extra windows to the street that don't relate to the cinema. What's behind them, Percy?'

'Oh, a couple of old musty shops. The owner of the place wasn't interested in keeping them open. He's an absent landlord, overseas half the time.'

'How do you access them?' Celia asked.

'The doors are on either side of the foyer, hidden by the advertisements. You would have noticed the movie posters on the screens.'

'Oh, yes. Coming attractions and headshots. I noticed Johnny Depp and Mel Gibson, I'm looking forward to seeing 'Pirates of the Caribbean: Curse of the Black Pearl.'

'That's right.' Percy nodded. 'Won't be here for a while.'

'I can wait.' Celia laughed. Her mind was pondering the possibilities. A coffee bar, or maybe a wine bar in one of those rooms would be a winner. Hiring a room for art classes or yoga. The building was under utilised. She would approach the owner sometime, he might pay her a management fee. It gave her something to think about.

The following Saturday evening, Marcus McFadden, man

with two hats, Celia thought, sauntered up to the box-office and bought a ticket.

'Hi, Celia, I'd like to talk to you after the movie if you're free then. Would you come for a drink? I've a suggestion I'd like to put to you.'

'Sounds intriguing, Marcus, okay.'

After the show Marcus was waiting. They walked to The Cosy Cat Bar in the next block. Celia observed the small dimensions and the cat themed decor. Near the open fire a large black cat lay curled up on a fat red cushion. As they sipped a warming red Marcus explained that he was a friend of the Schofield family and proceeded to outline the message he'd been asked to convey.

'Robert's returned from re-hab after his accident. His parents are worried he's behind at school, he's not cleared to return to classes yet. They wondered if you would be interested in giving him some tutoring...you having teaching experience and all that.' He was embarrassed, but continued.

'Of course they would pay you if you agree to take him on. If he's on top of his schoolwork it would be a step in restoring his confidence.'

'Oh, I see, how did they know, or you, for that matter, that I was a teacher?'

'Oh, well, you know how it is, people talk, especially when...,' he was embarrassed again. Celia broke in.

'You mean, especially when someone like me, a newcomer, moves into town carrying such a shocking story.' Her eyes teared up as she struggled to continue. 'I know people feel uncomfortable talking to me...or not talking, as the case may be.'

'Oh, Celia, look, if you'd rather we leave it for another time...'

He touched her arm in a gesture of comfort then withdrew it as quickly, not knowing how to respond.

'Marcus, it's okay, you're not shying away and I'm grateful for that. I hope it will get easier to talk about, and I don't want people to feel as if they're treading on eggshells around me. Parents have lost children in many different ways since time immemorial. I'm not the only one. I just need to learn how to navigate through this somehow. There's no particular rulebook. Now let's have another wine and talk about you.'

'Before we get to me, will you give the proposition some thought?'

'I will, seriously, I will.'

Celia did give the matter some thought and decided to arrange a meeting with Robert and his parents to assess whether she could be of help. On her next visit to the bank she put her suggestion to Marcus and gave him her number. He asked if she would like to go somewhere for lunch the following Sunday.

'Thanks Marcus, that's very kind of you, but I need to visit Mum.'

To be asked out by another man was quite confronting. Celia didn't think of herself as a single person. Waves of panic started rising in her throat. She grabbed a tissue from a pocket and blew her nose. 'Gotta go, maybe I'm catching a cold. Bye.'

She had to admit, it was a rather appealing thought to be with someone and share a meal. He was easy to be with...and quite attractive in an unconventional sense, although not quite as tall as Celia. On the other hand she didn't want to start something that might become awkward. The eternal problem...men and women...a friend who wants more, or a friend who remains a friend, no question.

Somehow she didn't think the latter would be the case with Marcus and she wasn't ready for that. When she was discussing the topic with her good friend and fellow teacher, Sandy Paynter, she could hear the third member of their share house days in the background. Now married to Sandy, Liam wanted a word. Sandy put her on loudspeaker.

'You're young and beautiful, Celia, this is going to happen. Have a think about ways to deflect these guys, work out a considered response. Be prepared. Maybe I'll write one for you.' Liam laughed. 'Good luck, we'll see you soon.'

His words made her smile. These two special people had brought comfort and care in the blurry days immediately after her loss.

*   *   *

On a drizzly Monday in the middle of June Celia was searching through a box of documents to take to the Financial wizard when she received a call from the local hospital. Charlie had been admitted after falling down a mineshaft. Celia tried to control her shaking hands as the phone crackled. 'Yes, I'm here,' she said. 'I'm listening'… at work on a property near Killaura…a broken leg and severe abrasions, the voice said…not critical, but could she come in.

Her stomach felt like she'd swallowed a cup of vinegar. She reached for her coat, where are my keys, my bag. Celia took a moment to think. Her bag was hanging on the door knob, the usual place, and her car keys were in it.

A fire siren sounded in the distance as she drove to the hospital. She wondered briefly where the problem was, if she was to be diverted. But no, she arrived without incident and found her way to the ward where Charlie lay looking forlorn. Lacerations marked his face. His leg was suspended in a hoist.

'I'm sorry Celia, Mum wasn't answering, so I asked the staff to call you.'

'I'm glad you did. How are you feeling?'

'A bit achy, my back hurts more than my leg.'

'I hope they're keeping up the pain management. Speak to the nurse, Charlie, if the pain gets too much for you. I'll call in to your mother's on the way home.'

'I don't know how long they're going to keep me here.'

He seemed at a loss to know how to continue and was close to tears. Celia told him to take it easy, she assured him she would be there for him.

'We'll take it one day at a time. I'll speak to someone who might know, see when we can get you home.' The charge nurse was no help.

As Celia drove away her mobile rang. She pulled the car off the road. It was Sally.

'I'm the bearer of bad news I'm afraid.' Celia caught her breath.

'Oh, dear, what now?' she asked.

'There's been a fire at the theatre, Celia, not many details yet but there was no-one in the building at the time.'

'My God, no! I'm in the car, see you shortly.' Beware the fire! Mavis's warning words rang in her ears. How odd. She needed to know more about that canny woman.

Celia drove on to Eula's place where she stayed only long enough to reassure her aunt that Charlie would make a full recovery. When she arrived at the shop Sally ushered her out onto the street again, away from inquisitive ears, and told her the police had been looking for her.

'Am I a suspect? Heavens above,' she exclaimed in horror.

'I doubt it, Celia, but I guess they have to follow up lines of enquiry, shall we say. An officer said they would call back later today.'

Marcus caught sight of them and crossed the road.

'Glad I saw you.' He turned to Celia. 'We heard about the fire, bad business, alright. The Schofields would like to engage you to tutor Robert. They'd be happy to meet with you. I hope the small fee will help.' He handed Celia a slip of paper. 'Call them when you're ready.'

'Thanks, Marcus, I will.'

No news was forthcoming on the cause of the fire until an investigation was completed, according to Leading Senior Constable Harry Bolitho. He knocked at the door at ten minutes past five removing his cap in a gesture of courtesy. She ushered him inside, He was friendly enough, asking her the usual questions...her whereabouts the previous night, could she throw any light...oops, excuse the pun. Did she know anything that may help the investigation.

Celia told him she had heard the siren on the way to the hospital and no, she wasn't aware of anyone with arson on their mind, if that's what it was, except Mavis, of course. Celia saw his brown eyes twinkle with amusement as she related Mavis's grim prediction.

'Sounds like she has a clairvoyant flair for rhyming revelations. She could be helpful in the policing business.' He winked and broke into infectious laughter as she saw him out onto the street.

'I'll keep you posted,' he called. Celia watched him drive away and smiled as Aunt Eula drove into the space the constable had vacated. She hurried over to help as Eula retrieved supplies from the back seat. She had wasted no time after visiting Charlie.

'He expects to be home before the end of the week,' Aunt Eula informed her. Celia told her not to worry about his house, she would take care of it. With no job at the theatre she would have the time.

On Thursday a patient transport vehicle brought Charlie home. Their first conversation was a little strained. He seemed reluctant to divulge any details about the accident.

'It was a silly mistake,' was all he said.

When Celia defined it as a workplace accident...that he may be able to claim compensation, he replied tersely,

'Don't think so.' She tried again.

'Well, perhaps you should seek legal advice.'

He had grunted in reply to that. Aunt Eula was back on Friday morning. Celia left him with his mother and his grumpiness and went upstairs. She would join them at lunch for a slice of Eula's cottage pie. There was a message from Alan Schofield on her phone asking her to visit the family at her earliest convenience.

When Eula was about to leave Celia suggested they meet up soon to discuss her concerns regarding Charles. Although his injuries were healing Celia was sure there was something ailing his soul. They arranged to have afternoon tea the following Sunday.

CHAPTER 3

2004 — Hard lessons

Dark clouds were gathering in the west as Celia drove home from the Schofields house. Winter, in this year of her grieving, seemed long and dreary. When it wasn't raining the skies filled with brooding clouds. It wasn't only the weather, she couldn't shake off a sense of foreboding. She told herself it was just her state of mind; her emotions were tacking like a tub in a stormy sea.

It had been decided that Celia would give Robert Maths and English lessons on Monday and Wednesday each week. With four children to manage, the Schofield household seemed to be run like clockwork. While Celia was there the older girl prepared a salad. The younger two, a boy and a small girl, quietly set the table. When Celia commented on their earnest efforts, Donna Schofield replied that she worked part-time and liked to be organised.

Celia knew Alan was a manager at an engineering works not far out of town. From remarks dropped by Marcus she gathered he had a reputation as a hard task master. She was curious about the diminutive Donna, who had said no more when Celia brought Robert's lesson to a close.

As she alighted from her car Sally Doyle called to her. In view of the fire, she wondered whether Celia would be interested in working at The Ice Cream Shop, until there was further news about the future of the theatre.

'That's really kind of you, thanks, but my skills on a coffee machine are zilch.' Sally insisted that it wouldn't be a problem.

'You'll get the hang of it in no time.' Her words were encouraging.

'And don't think for a minute I'm offering a job just to be charitable. I'm a practical business woman and I need another employee. Somebody like you, who is personable, and reliable. Give it some thought, Celia. We would love to have you as a member of our team. I'm expanding the menu. We've graduated to toasted sandwiches and wraps.'

'The food will be popular. I could manage that! I'll sleep on your offer and let you know tomorrow. Thanks again, Sal.'

It would be foolish not to accept Sally's offer. A busy life in Appleton was just what she needed. It was disappointing that her ideas for those hidden rooms at the theatre had gone up in smoke.

When Celia arrived for barista training on Friday, she carefully skirted two ladders that were erected outside. Looking up, Celia saw painters at work on the facade where once the horrible hoarding had obscured attractive details. A row of diamond shapes, fashioned from black metal, adorned a narrow balcony.

Sally's excitement bubbled over as she welcomed the new trainee.

'Yes, the building is starting to look super cool! And now we're going to make a barista of you. This machine is not an enemy, that's the first thing to remember. He is your friend and you will grow to love him. We call him Ricardo and he's a maestro. You can have the first latte you make and perhaps a cappuccino at lunch. Aren't I the benevolent boss? Careful with the milk, it has to be just right.'

Celia loved the sound of the milk frother gurgling and pulsing. She pumped the jug under the stream of steam, breathing in the heady aroma of ground coffee beans. At the end of the day Sally told her how impressed she was.

'You've done well. I knew you would.'

By the following Friday Celia had worked four six hour shifts, washed clothing, changed the bed linen for Charles, cleaned his ensuite, helped him manage to shower, much to his embarrassment, prepared meals and kept her tutoring appointments. When the shop closed at five she was feeling the strain and looked forward to putting her feet up.

Charlie's house, a two storey Georgian style building, was set back from the pavement with a low front wall on either side of the path. Celia surveyed the wrought iron entry gate lying to one side, tethered to the ground by weeds. She noticed the untidy patches of dead grass, shrivelled shrubs on the borders and ivy growing up the wall.

On the opposite side, gravity would soon have its way with the fence palings that were coming adrift. The front door needed sanding and painting, the number 70 could barely be deciphered. She vowed she would do some work out here very soon.

A laneway on the right gave access to the rear yard where there was an outdoor wash house, as her grandmother used to call it, and parking space for two or three cars. This area could do with a shrub or two, she would pitch it to Charlie that gardening would be her way of repaying his kindness.

While rummaging for her house key a male voice startled her. At first she didn't recognise Harry Bolitho out of uniform. Today he was dressed in running shorts and navy singlet. She invited him inside, not sure how she should address him.

'Please, call me Harry. I won't come in. I'm too sweaty today. The boffins from Forensic have concluded that there is evidence of the fire being deliberately lit. We're compiling a list of suspects and talking to the building's owner, as soon as we can locate him. I'll have more on that next week and pay you an official visit.'

A young woman called to her as Harry continued on his run. She came from the house across the laneway and introduced herself as Yvette. Apologising for taking so long to meet her new neighbour, she said she'd been away in Melbourne exhibiting her art.

The intricate green beading and braid work on her head put Celia in mind of tiny caterpillars clinging to her scalp. Celia introduced herself and shook Yvette's hand.

'Lovely to meet you, I hope you had some success in the city.'

'Yes, I'm happy enough. Are you coming to the market tomorrow? I have a stall there.' Celia said she hadn't heard about it. 'I love markets. I'll make an effort to get there.' Yvette enquired after Charlie. Celia explained about his accident.

'I've been working all day and need to see if he's been eating. Thanks for the info on the market.'

Charlie was on his crutches stirring a lamb curry when Celia went inside. He asked if she would like a serve as he'd prepared enough for both of them.

'Thanks, it smells yummy.' He appeared to be in a better frame of mind. She told him she'd just met Yvette.

'Quirky girl,' he replied, and suggested she pour a wine for herself.

Although Celia had been helping Charlie with personal tasks she had not spoken at length with him since her arrival in April, except for superficial chat during the lunch that Eula had served. Over dinner the conversation skipped around the work being done next door, local news, his work situation and a reminiscence on their earlier years.

As Celia collected the empty plates Charlie's voice took on a different tone. It seemed to catch in his throat as he spoke.

'Look, I don't know what to say, you know, I feel sick when I think of what you must be going through. I'm sorry I haven't been doing what I should, I don't know how.' Celia took a moment before replying.

'I know it's hard, Charlie. You're not the only one. Don't stress about it. What happened to my family makes people uncertain about the way to...to talk about it. It's the elephant in the room. I'm planning to see a bereavement counsellor. I'm sure I'll learn something helpful...how to put other people at ease. I suspect your life hasn't been easy. Can we talk about you some time soon? I want to ask you about the garden too. You would be doing me a favour if you'd let me put in some attractive plants. Very good therapy for grievers.'

The market was in full swing when Celia arrived. The morning air was crisp. Hellebores flowered beside the pathways. Produce stalls were busy and variety stalls were loaded with colourful gifts, handcrafted goods and clothing.

Yvette was chatting to customers when Celia located her stall. She moved closer and drew in a sharp breath. The paintings were not what she had expected.

These were not pretty commercial landscapes, or scenes of a

bucolic countryside. They were confronting...and captivating at the same time. Most featured dark arresting skies, with swathes of diffused light. Koalas, echidnas, emus and wombats, barely discernible, peered from partly burnt tree trunks.

Another painting captured her gaze. Within the crevices of the variegated cliffs three or four nudes, men and women, were partly visible. Celia peered into the painting. It was mesmerising, and skilfully executed. Perhaps Yvette could capture the spirit of Clive and Eddy.

A Scottish pipe band was warming up. The sound of the caterwauling pipes filled the air before a kaleidoscope of random notes fell into place and transformed into a stirring tune. The band stepped out to march in unison through the park. Celia was moved to tears. She reached for her sunglasses and a tissue.

At three o'clock on Sunday Celia joined Aunt Eula for an afternoon tea of appetising scones, jam and cream, a caress to the soul as well as the stomach. The conversation soon turned to the topic of Charles and the likely source of his unhappiness.

'You might guess that it concerns a relationship. He was very keen on an Indigenous girl who worked at his solicitor's office.' was Aunt Eula's opening remark. As Celia listened to the story she began to understand the change in her cousin. She had considered that a thwarted affair of the heart may have been at the bottom of his miserable moods but hadn't anticipated the complex situation outlined by her aunt.

Work at The Ice Cream Shop and tutoring sessions with Robert kept Celia busy during July. Today Alan Schofield had been abrupt and disparaging towards Robert when the boy was doing his best to understand the correct use of verb tenses in his essay. Celia was fuming at the man's tone. She tried to keep her voice level.

'These are new concepts for him, Alan, and they take time to learn. I know Robert will do well.' Alan turned on his heel and left the room. Donna appeared at the end of the lesson, anxiously waiting to serve the evening meal.

Celia cleared the dining table. Robert picked up his worksheets for the following week and saw her to the door. As Celia reached her car she heard hurried footsteps behind her.

Alan Schofield caught up and stood there, staring. At first she thought he may want to apologise, or at least talk about his unhelpful interjections. How wrong she was. He pushed her into the side of the vehicle and planted his lips on her neck, sucking violently at her skin. With a grim expression on his florid face, he hissed into her ear.

'I'll thank you not to buy into what goes on between me and my son.'

His menacing voice spurred Celia to action. She raised the hand which held her keys, thrust the longest one forward and prodded the tip of his nose, threatening to shove it up his nostril.

'You have a choice,' she said, in the coolest voice she could muster. 'Step away from me now. I can report you for this assault. You would face criminal charges. That would mean the end of our tutoring arrangement and your son would be the loser.'

Alan stepped further away as Celia held the key at his nose. He waved a clenched fist back and forth, brushing her right ear. She stepped sideways and continued speaking.

'It was my understanding that you wished to employ me to assist Robert to keep up with school requirements and increase his self-confidence. You are undermining that goal by the way you ridicule the boy's efforts. Can you explain the contradiction?'

Alan uncurled his clenched fingers and let his arm drop. He seemed incapable of forming a reply. Frowning, he turned to stare back towards the house as if trying to get his bearings. Celia addressed him again as she opened the door of her car.

'I'll thank you,' she stressed the word, you, 'to stay out of my way. Your bullying behaviour is not acceptable and I won't tolerate it and I won't be returning to this house. I'll make other arrangements. You can let me know if Robert is to continue with lessons. You have my number but if there's any further trouble from you, a police report will follow. The evidence will be on my neck.'

Swiftly she stepped inside and slammed the car door shut. She watched for a moment as Alan retreated into the approaching gloom.

Celia took off with a burst of speed. The accelerator felt like it was undergoing an epileptic seizure as her shaking foot would not maintain an even pressure. Her whole body was trembling. She could hardly believe what had just happened. I should reverse back over the bastard, she thought.

She was sobbing with shock and fury when she found Charlie in his sitting room. He started to rise when he saw the state she was in.

'What on earth...'

'I'll tell you in a minute, I need to make a cuppa.'

Charlie grabbed his crutches and followed her to the kitchen.

'Are you alright?' Alarm was written all over his face.

'I will be shortly, when I debrief to you. I've just had a horrible experience with Alan Schofield, very scary.'

When Celia finished her story Charlie gave her a warm cousinly hug.

'It's okay, I'm okay,' she assured him. He asked her if it was wise to continue with the tutoring.

'I don't want to leave Robert in the lurch, and what would I tell him? Why should he be punished for the sins of the father? We'll see if his father responds.' Charlie turned to her as she said goodnight. Wobbling on his crutches he put both hands on her shoulders.

'Celie, girl, listen to me, I'm here for you too, you know.'

'Thanks Charlie, it was good that I could talk to you tonight.' He called to her as she ascended the stairs.

'Come down if you need me.'

How she wished that Clive was here to hold her, but he wasn't. She would have to learn to live without that comfort. But could she do it? This life felt like an endurance test set by an unknown protagonist. She resolved that she would find a suitable grief counsellor.

Celia's mobile was running hot next morning. Senior Constable Bolitho wished to call on her later in the afternoon. She sent a reply asking if he could come after five o'clock. A message from her brother's wife, Gwen, that one could wait until later. Celia felt wrecked after the assault the previous evening.

Sally was appalled when she heard the story and had plenty to say about it. She gave Celia an extra break that afternoon and joined her in the upstairs staff room. She extended an invitation to Celia to share a meal with her and her husband that night.

'Thanks, Sal. Could we make it another time? A police officer wants to see me after work to give an update on the fire. I should stay home with Charlie until his plaster is removed. He needs the company and I need to return a call to my sister-in-law.'

Harry Bolitho duly arrived ten minutes after Celia had scurried upstairs to freshen up. He was taller than she remembered, or maybe his height was accentuated by the small Georgian door frame. His leather boots clunked loudly on the wooden stairs and creaked a protest as he sat at her kitchen table.

'This certainly is a garret, just the place for an impoverished artist. I don't think you are one, are you? Can't see any easels,' he joked, putting her at ease.

'You're right, that's not one of my talents, Harry, but there is an accomplished artist across the laneway.'

'Yes, I've spoken with her at the market.'

'I discovered the market last week, thanks to Yvette, and I'm going to see her next Saturday. I have an idea for a painting I'd like her to do. It concerns my family, or should I say, the family I no longer have.'

She felt safe with Harry and decided she owed him an explanation after that remark slipped out. She wasn't sure if he'd heard anything about her, so she gave him a brief outline of the events that had changed her life. He hadn't heard, but he was an experienced police officer and showed no sign of awkwardness while he listened. At the end of her story he took her hand in both of his.

'It's a difficult road for you, Celia, only you know what you need to do.'

'Are you married, Harry?' She didn't know why she had suddenly asked him that question, but she felt the need to change the subject. He hesitated for a moment before replying.

' No, I'm not married. I have a friend who likes a break in the country. She works in Melbourne a lot of the time. It's complicated. Am I committed? I'm not sure about that.'

'Oh, I'm sorry, I didn't mean to...,' She felt her cheeks flush with embarrassment.

'Hey, no need to worry,' Harry assured her.

He stayed for almost an hour informing her that the owner of the theatre was top of the list of suspects, not Percy Hendricks, who loved the place.

'This guy's not a local but we can prove that he was in the area not long before the fire. The investigators are delving into his financial affairs. He has interests in other dubious business pursuits and owes more money than a third world country,' was the way Harry put it.

'The place is likely to go on the market, so I don't fancy your chances of getting back to work there this side of Christmas, or the next. Sorry to be the bearer of bad news. In this town it may take a decade to find a buyer. Percy's not a happy man.'

'Oh damn, that's so disappointing. At least I have other work, although one job is looking a bit precarious.'

Celia hadn't heard from Alan Schofield. It might be wise to let Harry know about the assault. She had covered her neck with a roll top sweater and as she related the details she pulled it down to reveal the dark purple-black bruise.

'Celia, this is serious. It would be risky business to go back to that house. I realise you have concerns about the boy, but something else needs to be worked out.'

'I'll discuss it with Robert's mother. Marcus will have her number, do you think that's safe enough? ' Her question hung in the air. Harry was thinking about it.

'I don't know the guy well but he has come to our attention.

Minor stuff: a trivial report about a break-in at his work, no evidence of one. At the time it crossed my mind that he was covering himself. With your permission I'd like to follow up, pay a friendly visit.' A text notification sounded on Celia's mobile.

'Well, what do you know,' Celia smiled as she read the gist of a text aloud.

'It's from Alan. He's sorry about his late reply, unavoidable, trouble at work. Then a lukewarm apology. Just forgot himself momentarily, won't happen again. Continue with lessons.' she concluded.

'What a loser,' Harry scoffed. 'Alan is not to approach you, I'll make that clear.' She let out a long sigh.

'I'm relieved. Thanks Harry, a friendly visit might work.'

Celia found Charlie in his kitchen preparing a salad.

'Sliced beef to go with this, if you want some.'

'You're the invalid, I'm supposed to be cooking for you, but I'll gladly accept your offer. I'm famished.'

'Tell me what the lawman had to say, couldn't help overhearing some of it; Harry's got a loud voice.' Celia filled in the blanks for him.

'I'm glad you're going to stay away from the Schofield house, I was worried about that guy, wouldn't trust him. You could tutor Robert here in my sitting room, for that matter.'

'Oh, Charlie, that's very generous of you. Let's wait and see how this plays out.'

Good heavens, my cousin's becoming more like his old self every day. I like it! Celia thought. She was tempted to pursue the touchy subject of his personal life but thought better of it, reluctant to prick the bubble of his cheeriness.

Speaking to her sister-in-law that evening Celia was relieved to know that Gwen thought her mother was quite happy, settling in well at Summerleigh. Celia promised to ring Beth, her oldest and most difficult friend who was working in Canberra. She was also Gwen's younger sister. A note of disapproval, or was it resentment in Gwen's voice had surprised her.

She felt hurt that Gwen was not more supportive. She suspected it had to do with her move to Appleton.

CHAPTER 4

2004 — Disclosures

From the fruit shop across the road a booming baritone filled the surrounding thoroughfare. The bold operatic voice floated up like a lover's serenade to penetrate Celia's sleepy head. She turned to reach for a lover who wasn't there. Fully awake now she threw her pillow across the room, got out of bed and switched the jug on.

Glancing around her bed-sit she thought there was a serious need to improve this space. The amenities were not wonderful. A hotplate and toaster sat on an old bench with a double cupboard below. Her clothing hung on a rack at the end of her narrow bed. There was no television set. Her clock radio on the desk provided some comfort in the vacuum of a lonely night. At least the faulty wiring had been fixed.

While sipping her tea Celia remembered that Charlie needed her to transport him to an appointment at the hospital this morning. It would be an opportunity to book an appointment with a counsellor at the nearby clinic.

Opposite the hospital a nature reserve offered a place of respite for patients or visitors, away from the busy wards. On the perimeter a covered picnic area provided shelter where you could sit and listen to the sounds of birds, the croaking of frogs, and watch the ducks gliding on a man made waterway. As they sat sipping coffee Charlie stared pensively into the distance, tapping one finger against his crutch.

Celia sat with half-closed eyes, and imagined herself floating down into a forest of kelp on the ocean bed. It was one of those days, not a diamond or a pearl. She couldn't help thinking about Eddy. Charlie finally spoke.

'With a bit of luck this plaster will come off in about two weeks.' He paused. 'You know, while I was in the waiting room I thought I saw a woman who meant a lot to me at one time, well, still does, if I'm honest. She passed the door and disappeared by the time I could get up to look.' Celia opened her eyes and turned to him.

'So, who do you think it might have been?' He took a deep breath before continuing.

'Oh, where do I start? Her name's Lauren, I met her at the legal firm. I was...am a client.' He spoke with a passionate intensity as he related almost the same details that Aunt Eula had relayed to Celia. He confirmed what Eula had said...that the young woman in question had given birth to a girl. He wondered if he was the father. He told Celia that it worried him considerably.

'Why did she suddenly cut all ties with me? We'd been seeing each other for months.' He had been shocked at the unexpected rejection. Celia saw the hurt in his eyes. She asked about the girl's family.

'The parents came here from the Torres Strait Islands some years back. I'm not sure if they're still in this country. She's secretive about her family. I was never invited to meet them. She said she lived with her older sister whose husband was a white guy. I got the impression she didn't like him much.'

But there was something more and it concerned his fall down the mine shaft. Revelations that Celia found quite alarming. When they returned to the car Celia showed him the handouts she'd been given by the Counselling service.

'These might have some helpful information for you too. You know, it's a form of grieving that you're dealing with as well. What a sad and sorry pair we are.' She gave Charlie a rueful smile as she started the engine.

'I'll do dinner tonight. What would you like?'

While Celia prepared a simple pasta meal she spoke to Charlie about the ideas she'd had for the disused rooms at the theatre.

'Dashed to dust because of a wretched fire.' she said indignantly.

'Yes, maybe so. How would you have benefitted though? A different matter if you'd owned it.'

'Mm, that's a point. Fat chance of that now.'

*   *   *

Several early birds were at the Saturday market when Celia arrived. She pitched her idea, asking Yvette if she was interested in creating a similar painting of the cliffs, with Eddy and Clive half hidden, as if playing a game of hide and seek.

'I can give you photos,' Celia said, as she related why she would like this painting. Yvette nodded, placing her hand on Celia's arm. She invited Celia to come for dinner one night soon.

The plant stall was packed with variety for the keen gardener. Celia picked up three pots of low growing shrubs, ready to make a start on the front garden. In a newly erected bandstand a string quartet was playing a lively composition in the extravagant Baroque style. A crowd was gathering and she moved closer to listen.

Someone tapped her on the shoulder. She turned to find Harry standing there, smiling at her, noting that he was dressed in casual gear today.

'Hi, this is a great addition,' she remarked, pointing to the bandstand. 'A day off for you, is it Harry?'

'Not the whole day, unfortunately, but I'm off tomorrow. Would you like to do lunch then?'

'Lunch? Um, I'd like to do lunch, but I need to visit my mother, she's in care, over two hours drive away.'

'I see, well, how about I do the driving and we can grab a bite somewhere.' Celia hesitated for a moment.

'Y'know what, I'll take you up on that offer, some company would be great. Thanks.'

Mavis was sitting inside The Ice Cream Shop enjoying a sundae with her friends when Celia took up her post behind the counter. Pushing back her chair Mavis turned, waving her whimsically decorated fingernails. Coated with dark red polish and embossed with pearly half moons, they were at odds with her faded, navy wool jacket. She peered with a squinty eye in Celia's direction.

'Doves a'cooing, spring's renewing, watch your step at the waning of the moon, and for you, my dear, a visitor and a windfall, coming soon.' She spoke loud enough for the other patrons to hear, ending with an enigmatic smile. Celia glanced up, holding a jug of frothy milk and called to her.

'Hi, Mavis, you should set up a stall and charge for these little gems.' Her companions laughed and nodded in agreement.

Sally was introducing the newest recruit, a young lady named Brianna, who radiated enthusiasm as she took the arm of a smartly dressed woman with her white hair swept up in an elegant chignon. Mavis suddenly appeared in front of Celia as she reached into an ice cream tub.

'Now I've something to tell you,' Mavis gestured as if she was hitching a ride, 'and I think this may be of interest to you. That smart lady over there is about to retire from the Catholic primary school. She says they're looking for a relief teacher. I told her you have a teaching background and I mentioned your work with Robert after his accident. When you've got a moment she's happy to give you the details.'

'Oh, thanks, Mavis. I'll bring the orders over myself, won't be long.' Celia glanced at the cluster of chattering ladies. The scoop she was about to plunge into the fruity depths hovered uncertainly in her gloved hand. She hadn't considered applying for work at the Catholic school, thinking that her views would be at odds with that community.

Celia's disenchantment with religion had taken hold when a litany of abuses had dominated the daily news. Did it really matter what she thought?

Sally wanted a word at the end of the day. 'I've been very lucky. I'm renting part of the large garden space on the property next door. The owner will remove the hedge so we can be seen and accessed from the street. An outdoor dining area will give us an edge. It should be popular come summer.' Her words spilled out in a rush and her enthusiasm was infectious.

'Wow, when did all this happen?' Celia asked. 'Sounds like a great idea. You might need extra staff.'

'Finalised the lease agreement last night, and we'll probably need another part-timer in summer. You can work more hours, Celia, if you want. I'm going to approach Charlie about converting one of the windows on that side to a door. I'd be happy to contribute to that, but he may not agree.'

'Well, his mood is improving, Sal, although I'm not sure that he's progressed to expansive gestures of co-operation when it comes to knocking out bricks and mortar.' Celia was highly amused at the idea. 'You can only ask, I suppose. I'd wait until his plaster comes off. That's not long now, he might be more amenable when he can drive again. I'm really pleased for you, Sally.' Celia took a tentative breath. 'I need to tell you something.' Sally suggested they go upstairs and sit in the staffroom.

Celia could hear herself. Her voice betrayed the guilt she felt.

'I feel bad because you've been so good.' Sally was looking at her, drawing her brows together, wondering what Celia was trying to say.

'Hey, what's wrong, is Charlie alright?'

'Yes, he's fine. It's just…I might be teaching again.' Celia explained how the opportunity had come about.

'Only relieving, so I'd still be available, nothing is settled yet. I need to drop in a resume.'

'Is that all? Well, of course you should teach if there's an opening there for you. We can work it out, never fear.' Celia felt a wave of relief.

Harry arrived soon after nine the next morning. Conversation flowed easily between them as they drove through dairy country and on past golden crops of canola. He told Celia that he had called on Alan Schofield at his work.

'It was a private conversation in his office, although I'm sure other staff could observe the defensive body language through the glass. He had little to say, trying to make lame excuses. I told him there's no justification for causing the injury to your neck. He says his wife will make sure Robert gets to his lesson. You can let him know where that will be. Now let's talk about something else, tell me about your mother.'

Celia gave a brief outline of her mother's life, privately concluding at the end of her summary, that there wasn't much to tell...kids, drudgery, a moody husband, and finally, early onset dementia. Architects of our own destiny? The philosophical assertion popped into her mind and raised a lot of questions.

She wasn't inclined to pursue them today and changed track, thanking Harry for dealing with Alan Schofield. She felt happier about continuing Robert's lessons, knowing that Alan had been put on notice.

Celia spent almost an hour with Ruth, while Harry took a walk. These days she noted how easily her mother tired.

The anniversary of what would have been Eddy's third birthday was creeping closer. She didn't mention her own unremarkable birthday a few days previously but told Harry about Eddy's. Her appointment with the grief counsellor was scheduled shortly before Eddy's birthday anniversary. She hoped she might gain some ideas on how to get through the day.

'Whatever you do I guess it won't be easy,' Harry said. 'Plan something beyond that day too.'

'I know what I'll do on the day, I'll plant something, and plan as well. I'm not going to work...' The rasping voice of Jimmy Barnes rocked out from the radio, interrupting Celia's train of thought. Harry lowered the volume.

'An orange tree, it might have to be an ornamental one. I'm not sure that orange trees grow here. Too cool. I'll plant it in a tub that I can take with me, wherever I might live. I'll use the day to work on Charlie's front garden. An orange tree beside the front door will add character to the house.'

Harry told her a little about his girlfriend. 'She's a career woman. Living in the country doesn't really do it for her. We met at a conference a couple of years ago. She works in Police Forensic Services. It's not a satisfactory arrangement. Well, it might be for Helen, she'd be happy to keep up the FIFO routine. It's not working for me.'

'The what?' Celia asked.

'F. I. F.O. Fly in, fly out, you know, like the miners, or the guys working the oil rigs. I feel like I'm being mined,' Harry laughed, 'precious resource that I am.'

'Oh, of course you are.' Celia laughed at his facetiousness.

A Lamborghini was parked at the front when they arrived at Number 70. Celia asked Harry to come in and meet Charlie. He said he knew of the guy with the car, everyone did, it was so distinctive. Dominic Romano was a friend of Charlie, an extrovert, a stand up comedian and restaurateur.

He told them he had trained as a chef with the sole aim of owning a restaurant just to fulfil his comedic ambitions. 'When I set up Capers restaurant I realised I had to accommodate other performers or suffer over-exposure. Anyway, I couldn't keep up with the demands of writing new material; comedy is an insatiable beast.'

CHAPTER 5

2004 — Quandary

In the waiting room of the clinic Celia was feeling stressed about her imminent session with a counsellor. She need not have worried. This smiling woman introduced herself and soon put her at ease. She had read the referral from Celia's doctor and started the session by asking Celia what she did every day.

Outlining the busy-ness of the last few months, Celia finally drew breath.

'Have you noticed how tiring it is?' the counsellor asked.

'I hadn't thought of it like that.' Celia admitted. She confessed that her anger about the way Clive had left her complicated her grieving.

'Such a deliberate act,' she said. 'It's impossible to comprehend, and yes, I am feeling exhausted.'

'Give it time. That conflict between anger and understanding will gradually resolve. Choose to daydream a little more; of what you may want, where you would like to be and who you like to be with. Thinking of these things can help with your decision-making into the future.'

*   *   *

Too soon the day of Eddy's birthday anniversary arrived. Sally helped Celia to unload the orange tree, the bags of potting mix and an attractive tub. She got to work, systematically clearing the borders and digging over the soil. Settling the tub into position she filled it with potting mix. The lush green leaves of the orange tree smelt as bitter sweet as the memories of her little lost boy. Celia was gradually coming to accept that he was not away somewhere, as she had liked to imagine .

Being busy in the garden kept her from unravelling like a piece of rotted wicker. Her counsellor had given her a clearer perspective. Celia would continue to see her. While systematically pulling out weeds she daydreamed about travel, about returning to teaching, about the type of house she would like. Disconcertingly, Harry kept appearing in the rooms.

She lay back against the cool, white wall of the house. Closing her eyes the memory she had been trying to ignore rose to the forefront of her mind. When Harry had driven her to visit Ruth she could admit it now, there had been moments when she had had to suppress the almost irresistible urge to kiss him passionately; on his lips and all over his tanned face.

She wanted to roll with him in warm sand. She wanted him to run his fingers over her face, her neck, her shoulders and down, down, over her breasts, her tummy. She wanted him inside her. There, now she had owned her feelings.

She sat in the dirt and daydreamed about Harry. The attraction had thrown her into a quandary. Since then she had kept her distance. It was too soon for both of them and it muddied the waters. Harry was sorting out his relationship with Helen.

47

Sudden desire had caught her by surprise. Was it just a reaction to her need? Was he feeling sorry for her? How often did people who were struggling with grief throw themselves into inappropriate, even ruinous relationships?

She had known Harry for a total of nine hours, she'd calculated, hardly time to know a person. There was a risk that she could be using him as a mere distraction. She would have to tread carefully. Sally interrupted her daydreams with a coffee. While she sipped Celia made a long overdue call to her oldest friend, Beth, who worked in Canberra.

Reception was patchy but Celia gathered that Beth was enjoying her job in the Public Service sector, although once more coming to terms with a broken relationship. She was planning to come home at Christmas. Celia couldn't help thinking that Beth's life was punctuated with failed relationships of all kinds.

'We've got a lot of catching up to do,' Celia told her. 'I really want to see you. Promise me you'll come and stay for a few days. Oh, sorry, Beth, I've got a call coming through. Bye.' It was the Sacred Heart primary school asking her to come in for an interview.

As Celia crossed the laneway for her dinner date with Yvette on Friday evening she felt a tentative confidence. The steps she'd taken since she had first arrived in April had been worthwhile and she would continue to play it safe.

Standing on Yvette's porch she stared at the varieties of the Monstera plant creating a verdant ambience on the tessellated veranda floor. Vines trailed from beneath its corrugated iron roof. Celia could see herself swaddled in greenery, in a cottage of her own. Yvette opened the front door and ushered her inside. The passageway ran a close parallel with the lane. Watercolours arranged on the wall added softness to the horizontal boards.

Entering a sunny extension the changing light contrasted sharply with the dimness of the hall. A young woman was chopping at the kitchen bench. Yvette introduced her.

'This is my partner, Simone.' Celia felt a vibe of surprise, recovered her composure in a beat and shook Simone's hand.

'Hello, can I be of any assistance?'

In spite of its purpose, the evening was a lively affirmation of shared womanhood. After dinner Celia passed over her photos. Yvette promised to do them justice.

'It's a lovely idea to have them playing in a rugged landscape. I'm looking forward to starting work on it.' Celia looked thoughtful before commenting.

'Yes, it suggests to me how tough the world can be, and at the same time how beautiful it is.'

On Saturday morning Celia caught sight of Rohan Collins, Clive's best man, as he parked his car on Mountside Road. She had been anticipating his arrival, he'd messaged her two days ago. She watched as he came in from the street. Was he the visitor that Mavis had predicted?

He looked different; dressed in patterned board shorts and a polar fleece hoodie. She had not seen him since the funerals. His fair hair was longer, tied back in a ponytail. She ran down the stairs to greet him.

Celia felt his body shaking with emotion, felt his tears, damp and warm on her cheek as he threw his arms around her. Rohan sighed as he pulled out a handkerchief. Wordlessly, she cradled his head and led him inside.

Like a flat stone skimmed on a pond, Clive's death had cast

far-reaching ripples, encircling each life caught up in its wake. He told her he knew something of how she must feel and it was bloody dreadful.

Rohan spoke briefly about his travels in Europe, marketing his designs with some success. He stroked the pearl pendant at Celia's throat. She sensed that he was going to cry again.

'It's beautiful, Rohan, it comforts me. I thought I should wear it today. You did a wonderful job. It can't be kept hidden in a drawer.'

Charlie agreed to join them for lunch.

Smiling fondly, Celia slipped an arm through each of theirs. Charlie was still sporting a slight limp, but Dominic's restaurant was not far away. In the late afternoon they sauntered back along Mountside Road. Rohan was returning to friends on the coast. Charlie bade him goodbye and left them at the gate. Rohan held her close. Letting go, he turned away and ran to his car. It was a short minute later when Celia cried.

Clothing was Celia's first concern on Monday. She stood in her bathrobe surveying her limited choices. Jeans and T-shirt was not a good look for an interview. A pair of navy pants and a plain white shirt, the best she could do, made her look drab.

Sighing, she pulled out a cinnamon jacket she hadn't worn in years, and patiently combed off the pilled balls of fluff. Pinning a peacock on a lapel, she shrugged into the coat and ran downstairs. A pleasing result, said the mirror in the hallway. Charlie agreed as he came to the door to wish her luck.

The Sacred Heart school stood on a rise, nestled inside old limestone walls. Celia parked her car inside the gates and walked along the curved driveway, nodding approvingly to a bank of shade trees edging the playground, their leaves turning bronze as a late winter chill stole their green robes away.

Her eyes travelled across the spread of buildings marking the eras. Claiming first place, the original school of sandstone rubble with its steep iron roof, red brick quoins, and tiny porch stood in eminent contrast to the featureless hodgepodge surrounding it.

Her interview was no more than a brief and brisk chat with the Principal who was eager to 'get cracking' and show Celia an arsenal of the most up-to-date tools and procedures for the betterment of little minds and bodies. Here's a woman who has certainly found her calling, Celia thought, as she was guided around what sounded to Celia like the greatest little seat of learning this side of the Vatican.

Harry called into The Ice Cream Shop the following day. Celia had not seen him since their road trip over six weeks ago. Sally glanced at her with a shrewd eye, inclining her head towards the window where Harry sat. Celia peeled her gloves off and joined him.

Harry's manner was respectful, restrained. He was not in uniform this morning. His freshly washed hair, released from the flattening constraints of his cap, bounced free and curled at the ends. She wanted to run her fingers through the thick darkness of it.

When he told her that Helen would not be returning she tried to submerge a sudden throb in her ribcage and bury it below the ache of her self-imposed resolve. The internal wiring of her signal box was shorting out, itching for her to press the green button.

Celia reined in the recalcitrant urge and told herself she wouldn't do it. When Harry asked her out for dinner she said that she wasn't ready for serious dating, she said they needed to talk. Harry momentarily closed his eyes as he rested his fingers on his forehead.

'Oka-ay,' he drawled the word. 'If that's what you want I'll pick you up later, would that suit? Text me when you're ready. Let me show you my place, we'll get fish and chips on the way.'

'That'll be fine. See you then.' she said, as she moved from her seat.

Robert came for his lesson at four thirty that afternoon. The new routine had been working well but Celia anticipated that it wouldn't be necessary for much longer as Robert had recently returned to school. She redirected her concentration several times during the lesson.

The style of Harry's house was not what Celia had expected. Sitting on a generous block the pale cream brick presented a sleek face to the street. The front entry sat beyond a corner window on the left and flush with the window and wall on the right.

Trimmed with white wrought iron the place screamed sixties. Harry glided his Pajero into the wide carport fixed to the side wall.

She found the interior decor even more astonishing. A print of the Cahill Expressway by the Australian artist, Jeffrey Smart, dominated one expansive wall of the living area. Below the print stood a Scandinavian teak sideboard where a pewter cat sat crouching, his hind legs extended, his slinky tail pointing towards the print.

Next to the cat a silver trimmed lava lamp released eerie blobs of moving colour inside a glass cylinder.

'I love your house. I never would have guessed you were a bona fide retro man,' Celia told him.

'Yeah, I have a lot of fun chasing up pieces of paraphernalia, it's a nice distraction from the job. I don't often find originals but I'm not fussed about that,' Harry replied. He ushered her to a chair at the white laminex table.

'Oh, you have a real cat.' Celia smiled as a large, black cat came snooping around the table.

'That's Jethro,' Harry said, as he freed the fish and chips from their paper wrapping. He reached for a bottle of Pinot and held it up to her.

'Yes, please.' She watched as Harry opened the wine. Her stomach felt as unsettled as the moving waxy blobs in the lamp.

She tried to eat, waiting for the right moment to launch into her list of reasons why it was inadvisable to be seeing each other, all the while thinking how much she would have enjoyed spending time here.

'Go on,' said Harry. 'Tell me what's on your mind.'

'I'm worried about this.' Celia sighed. 'It's just...it's lovely...that you've asked me out, I enjoy being with you, Harry, but it's too soon, and it's not fair to you that I'm in such a muddle about it. I need time. It's only eight months since I lost Clive. I'm not used to thinking I'm single. I carry a lot of baggage...I don't want to burden you with that.'

Celia recited her reasons, outlining the dangers and further hurts that might result when a person was in the midst of the grieving process. She didn't want to be responsible for causing distress; to herself or anyone else.

When she had finished Harry leaned back in his chair and reached into a kitchen drawer for matches and a pack of Winston

Blue. He pulled a cigarette from the pack and placed it, purposeful and slow, between his lips. Seconds passed in suspended delay.

Then, with a sudden flick of his wrist he struck the match. Igniting the papery cylinder, he drew in a lungful of smoke. Opposite him Celia sat mesmerised as he blew three perfectly formed smoke rings into the air. His eyes followed them as he exhaled.

'You smoke!' she exclaimed.

'Only on occasion, and this is one, I think. Do you mind?' She shook her head. 'No, no, I don't mind.' Harry bent to pick up the cat, silently stroking it for a long minute.

'If you're wanting me to shoot down your defences, I'm not going to do that, they are all legitimate concerns,' was Harry's considered response. 'I'd like to say just one thing. Life...the business of living is a risk you can't hide from. You would know that as well as anyone, I imagine. I'll be here... if you want to take a chance when you're ready. No pressure.' Celia nodded.

'Thanks, Harry, you've made me feel better.' She'd not been aware of it, but the instant she heard his words Celia realised that she had half expected him to do exactly that...to downplay her reasons, consider them trivial. Instead of sweeping them aside, Harry had deferred to her anxiety, while exposing her internal narrative for what it was.

Fear...of going against convention, of being hurt or hurtful, of being seen as fast and loose, of being a user, of damaging her self esteem. The man was disconcerting to say the least. They sat in silence a little longer finishing their drinks, until Harry rose and removed the remainder of their meal to the bin.

'Come on,' he said quietly. 'I'll drive you home.'

There were too many conflicting notions to deal with. Celia climbed into her narrow bed that night and watched the waning moon, its pared down crescent shape matching her own shrinking morale.

Mavis again. There were no cooing doves but a pair of pigeons were murmuring to each other somewhere close by. On the edge of sleep Celia remembered a lizard of long ago with a missing tail. Smiling, she recalled the comforting words of her mother who had reassured her that, given time, the lizard's tail would grow again.

CHAPTER 6

2004 — Reconnections

It had been on Celia's mind that Charlie had done nothing, as far as she knew, to clarify the matter of his suspected paternity. She raised it with him over a leisurely meal on Friday night. He sidetracked her question at first, asking about her visit to Harry's house. She gave him the barest details and prompted him to update her on his own progress.

'I've been thinking about it,' Charles replied. 'I spoke to my solicitor, who informed me that, in this country, a DNA test can't be done without the consent of the mother, unless there are extenuating circumstances. He would have to check with a Family Law expert for detailed information and get back to me.'

'Hm.' Celia thought for a moment. 'Sounds like you might need to find a carrot to dangle. I know it's not in your nature, Charlie, but could you utilise the circumstances surrounding your fall? You told me you suspected it had something to do with your ex-girlfriend, Lauren.'

'Yes, you're right. I might have to bring that altercation into the daylight. I'll think of something.'

*   *   *

A ladybird was the only spot of colour on the orange tree as Celia tended the watering. Opening its tiny tangerine wings it flew away at the first spray. Celia wished that she could fly so easily from her sadness, that aching loss embedded in her being.

At the counselling session the day before Celia had confided that she was conflicted about a growing attraction to another man so soon. The counsellor had assured her that some people get lucky.

'It's a compliment to the previous love,' she'd said. 'And only natural to want to experience the same again. There's no reason to think that we are incapable of a number of genuine loves in our life. Timing is only an issue if you make it so. It's going to happen sooner or later. The nature of love is not exclusive and time will tell if a new love is right for you.'

Celia was still determined not to rush headlong into an intimate relationship with Harry, even though she would like nothing better. She felt guilty even thinking that; disloyal, diminished. She decided to take a short break. It was time to visit her father-in-law. His birthday was coming up next week.

The estate agent called her, saying he'd answered a general enquiry and had included her house with other prospective properties for sale. He would prepare a valuation. She felt better about missing a few shifts in view of this heartening news, although she knew the enquiry might come to nothing.

It had not been practical for Celia's brothers to take on Ruth's care. Celia understood their reasons. Bradley had taken a mining job in the West and Nathan's house was busting at the seams with three teenagers still at home. It would be a sad but necessary day when her house was sold.

The piercing sound of chainsaws disturbed the street as Celia hurried into the shop. Workmen were busy removing part of the hedge in preparation for the outdoor garden. Sally buzzed back and forth, instructing the men to mark a gateway to the street.

Celia busied herself with coffee orders, waiting for a convenient moment to broach the matter of her intended trip.

'Your timing's right,' Sally said. 'You'll be back before the grand opening. Well, who knows how grand…but you won't want to miss it.' It was always a pleasure to be around Sal.

'Thanks, Sally, I appreciate it.'

Celia departed for the peninsula on Wednesday morning. It would be a long trip despite booking the ferry from Geelong. It was late afternoon when she located Magda's house.

Feeling slightly nervous Celia rang the front doorbell. When Frank opened the door she held out a potted plant wrapped in shiny red paper.

'Hi Frank, happy birthday,' she said brightly. 'It's good to see you.'

'A Polyanthus, lovely colour, thank you.' Frank studied the plant, reading the label thoughtfully. 'I'll try not to kill it. Come in, we've been waiting. I thought you were lost.' He put his arm around her and guided her through the hall. After setting the plant on a side table he kissed her cheek. Celia smiled at him. 'I can smell coffee.'

'Yes, and Magda has baked a sponge.' Magda came from the kitchen to greet her, kissing her on both cheeks.

She gazed at Celia, smiling and chatting. Celia had the feeling that Magda was sizing her up as if she was in need of reinforcing. Frank collected the steaming coffee pot from the range. Magda beckoned her to a glass atrium where her sponge sat invitingly on the coffee table. Frank spoke as he poured the coffee.

'My sixtieth birthday prompted me to do some thinking. I could see myself as a cobweb-covered male version of Miss Havisham, and I had no great expectations that things would change unless I did something about it. Here at least, I'm entertained by Magda's preposterous tales of her childhood.'

Magda recounted stories of her early life in Poland. Her family had been flower sellers in the markets of Warsaw, She had married to escape the hardship of that life, then fled to escape the marriage. Frank took up the story again.

'Magda's an expert textile restorer, her credentials opened the doors of international museums and galleries. I met Magda at the National Gallery in Melbourne; I have a longstanding contract with them. Magda's doing less restoration work these days. I'm still providing print services.'

Celia tried to speak but the lavish cream and jam filling was oozing from the corners of her mouth. Magda passed her a napkin.

'You are one excellent sponge maker, Magda.'

'Thank you, sometimes they rise, sometimes they fall, er, fail, I mean. Lucky today, not always so lucky.' She ended by telling Celia that needlework was a more predictable pursuit. Frank was smiling as he refilled the coffee cups.

It was good to meet Magda and to see Frank again, connecting with him on a deeper level through the shared bond of loss. She knew the marks were there, indelibly etched in both of them. There had been tears interspersed with laughter around an open fire. Clive and Eddy made their presence felt, as Frank and Celia pulled remnants of comfort around each other, like the threadbare strands of a child's security blanket.

On the second day of her visit Celia felt the need for solitude and took a jog to the beach. Summer was playing for time, but she couldn't resist the chance of a swim. A school of tiny silver fish scattered from their tight unity, freewheeling in the shallows, as Celia's feet disturbed their domain. She strode further into the icy waves feeling the brisk stinging shock of cold water.

It was time to leave. Frank told her he could see courage and a sense of purpose as she struggled to regain her footing. Celia said she thought he'd made the right move, coming to live with Magda, a wonderful person to temper his loss. Boarding the ferry, she looked forward to a night in Geelong with Liam and Sandy.

*   *   *

At breakfast on Saturday morning Celia was enjoying eggs on toast when her mobile sounded.

'Hi, Charlie,' she said, sounding pleased to hear from him. As she listened her face changed and her voice rose in consternation. Wide eyed, she jumped from her chair and looked at Liam, seriously alarmed.

'Harry's been shot! He was out on a run and someone shot him. Shot him!' she said, incredulously as she took in the enormity of this news. She pressed the phone closer to her ear.

'Charlie says he's conscious and on his way to a hospital here in Geelong.' she relayed. 'Charlie, are you there? How do you know this?' Celia felt sick and cried out as she swayed against Liam's shoulder.

'Oh, my God. Charlie heard the news report and rang the station.' Sandy rushed from the study to find out the reason for the commotion.

In the early evening they received word that Harry had been transferred from theatre to intensive care. Sandy said they would be unlikely to see him. Celia insisted on going anyway.

The sanitised corridors of St. John of God Hospital seemed never ending as they hurried from the reception desk, turning this way and that. Locating the room, Celia tried desperately to catch a glimpse inside as nursing staff came and went. She managed to extract brief details from a nurse when the woman recognised Celia's distress.

The bullet had splintered a rib, necessitating the removal of several fragments of bone. He might have to undergo further surgery depending whether any slivers were yet to be detected. She was sorry that visits were restricted to immediate family. No other visitors were in sight.

Celia was longing to touch him, to let him know that she was here. The only thing she could do was to leave a message at the nurses' station where a hollow-eyed nurse nodded briefly as she took down Celia's name and number; her message would be relayed when the patient woke. Celia realised she knew very little of Harry's family.

During their road trip he had mentioned a younger brother. Where they lived she couldn't remember. She thought it was somewhere in the Eastern suburbs. How ironic that she was here, so near and yet so far. She felt powerless and totally pissed off.

As Sandy convinced her it was time to leave two men in

suits came striding towards them. Detectives, certainly. She remembered too well the practised empathy of the investigators who came when Clive's body had been discovered. Men and women who must deal daily with destruction, violence and death.

All the same, you could smell the unmistakeable gust of self-importance puffing from beneath every snap of their shoe leather as their feet hit the hard floor. It dawned on her that there'd be a barrage of people descending upon Harry. It might be days before she could see him.

'Never mind,' Sandy said. 'If you call the hospital tomorrow they can connect you to his room. I'm sure you'll be able to speak with him.' Celia wondered about Harry's cat as they drove home, mulling over various other contingencies, a frustrating and futile exercise.

She was guessing that Harry hadn't carried any personal items. He was unlikely to have his phone if he'd left his house wearing only his running gear.

Somebody at Appleton Police Station might know more. She was annoyed that she hadn't met even one of his colleagues. A recorded message advised the caller to ring triple 0 if the call was urgent. She knew the station was manned until late. Where were they?

She left her details and asked for a call back. Liam had prepared a light supper.

'No more coffee for you,' he said, encouraging Celia to drink two glasses of water first. She had been running on adrenaline all day and could barely stay awake to finish her meal. It was far too late to hear from anyone at Harry's station. Everything would have to wait.

The clock radio in the guest room showed seven minutes past six. Celia thought the alarm had woken her, then realised that someone was calling her mobile. She didn't recognise the number.

'Morning,' said the caller. She didn't recognise the hoarse voice either.

'Yes, hello, who's speaking?'

'It's me, Harry.' Celia sat bolt upright. Her heart was flying about in her chest like a damp towel in a tumble dryer.

'Celia, are you there, can you hear me?' She heard a faint cough.

'Yes, yes, I'm here Harry, I'm here. Oh, my God, you sound terrible!'

'So would you if you'd had a tube stuck down your throat for hours.' She heard him give a wheezy laugh.

'It's great to hear your voice, scratchy or not. I tried to see you but...'

'Yes, I know, I received your message.'

'How are you feeling? Can I see you?'

'Oh, I'm ecstatic,' he said miserably. 'Come and make my day.'

She wanted to wake Sandy and Liam. She wanted to dance outside on the damp grass. She wanted to swing through the branches of the old ghost gum in the yard.

This time Celia did run her fingers through Harry's thick, tangled hair while monitors clicked and flashed, measuring the effect of her presence. She sat on the bed on his left side, opposite the drip inserted into his right arm.

Leaning her face into his cheek, she kissed him gently. She felt his mouth seeking hers, responding in hungry accord as he pulled her firmly into his chest.

'Now I really am ecstatic,' he sighed. 'I'll be out of here today and into a ward, as long as you don't send my blood pressure up!'

He smiled, and his brown eyes danced again showing some of the old spark as he regarded her affectionately.

'In my wildest imaginings I did not picture our first kiss happening in an ICU! Who did this to you, Harry? Have you any idea?'

'No, none whatsoever, but the guys are working on it.'

'I spoke to your Sergeant this morning. He said they have someone checking your house, and Jethro is fine.'

'That would be Barnesy, he's sending my stuff. How come you're in Geelong? Charlie told me you were on the Peninsula.'

'Mavis would probably say the universe had arranged it, and maybe that's true.'

She told him about Liam and Sandy and tried to describe Magda. That made him laugh. She felt bad because it hurt.

Celia made the long journey home the following day. Work on the summer garden was almost completed. She parked on the street, admiring the changes and entered through the open gates to join Sally sitting at one of the new tables. She had been away a day longer than she'd intended.

'Am I pleased to see you,' was Sally's heartfelt greeting. 'I can imagine it was difficult to tear yourself away. How is Harry? What a business! Do the police know anything yet?'

'No, Sal, Any number of people might hold a grudge. No point in speculating. Police are worried about his safety when he comes home. There's still a shooter out there somewhere. The bullet the surgeon dug out of his side is all they have. They think it came from a Glock 19 Luger.'

Sally shook her head as she handed Celia a new peach coloured apron. 'There's a choice of colours coming. Are you ready for work this afternoon?'

Driving down the laneway to park, Celia saw a short barrel of a man peering into Charlie's yard. He skedaddled when she pulled in. Charlie was clearing weeds behind the old laundry. He set aside the hoe and gave her a warm welcome home. 'I've missed you. Bit of a shock about Harry. I'm glad you saw him.' He raised an eyebrow and gave her a quizzical look.

'Yes, Charlie, we'll talk tonight.' Celia gave him a cheeky smile. 'I saw a man poking about near the gates. He looked like he might be trouble.' Celia described him. Charlie looked shocked and hurried her inside.

'Oh, God, that's a worry. Think I know who it might have been. Let's have a cuppa.'

'Yes, you can tell me about this guy before I start work.'

'While I remember, I have a message for you from Yvette, she has some sketches ready.'

Charlie walked slowly back and forth in front of the wood stove. He stopped pacing and poured boiling water into their mugs. Watching him, Celia could see fear in the quiver of his bottom lip.

'On that morning at Killaura, the bully who hit me was shouting obscenities at me. I thought I heard Lauren's name somewhere amongst the stream of abuse. It wasn't long before she contacted me, confirming that my attacker was a family member and begging me not to go to the police. She refused to say more, wouldn't answer my questions. She was nervous. It was a hurried call. I got the impression she was under some sort of threat.'

*   *   *

Celia was walking to the shop when the Sacred Heart school sent notice of upcoming work in November. Rewarding though it was to be part of the school scene again, Celia thought that juggling two casual jobs might get awkward.

A mini bus unloaded a stream of elderly people who filed in soon after Celia arrived. The Ice Cream Shop had supplanted the Bowls Club with its stale, pale brewed coffee, and was now the favourite venue for the Senior Citizens Haymakers Club.

Mavis took a turn about the room and came to a stop in front of Celia as she worked the coffee machine.

'I've joined the Haymakers, Celia.' Mavis lifted her arm and flicked a thumb across to the right.

'That gentleman in the beret took a shine to me here last week, talked me into signing up.'

'Good idea, Mavis, they look like a fun bunch.' Mavis did a little do-si-do with an imaginary partner, then leaned in with a conspiratorial pronouncement.

'Fsss, steam heat, feet on the beat, the kid means no harm, no intent to cause alarm.'

Good heavens, Mavis and her rhymes were getting more cryptic by the week. Celia raised her eyebrows.

'What does that mean, Mavis?'

'Dunno, just comes to me from nowhere, always has.' She gave a hearty laugh. 'Takes me by surprise every time.'

Over dinner Charlie told her about his plan, the carrot he would dangle. If Lauren agreed to a DNA test he would not report the shellacking he received from the man Lauren had referred to as a family member. Charlie stabbed his fork in the air.

'In fact, the bastard's married to her sister,' Charlie stated, vehemently. 'If my paternity is proven,' he told her, the mention of inheritance might flesh out the carrot.'

'How brilliant, Charlie, you've certainly given the matter considerable thought. How did you find out that this bloke is a brother-in-law?'

Charlie put his head in his hands, then leaned back in his chair.

'At first I thought it might have been her father, but my solicitor knew more. The reason why he took to me with a plank is a matter for conjecture and what I'm thinking is, at worst, a very nasty thought. At best, he's just a control freak, the self appointed bouncer keeping undesirables from the family door.' He paused for breath and continued with his story.

I don't think his intention was to send me down a mineshaft. I was moving backwards, trying to dodge the waving plank. He must have called the emergency services. Don't think he wanted a body found on his shift. He's had a a couple of minor convictions, I gather.'

'Shit, Charlie!' was all Celia could say.

CHAPTER 7

2004 — Compromise

Celia recognised Harry's voice this time, so sexy he could have been a radio presenter, she told him. He sounded much happier.

'I'll consider that as a future career move. Sounds like a fun idea.' She heard him give an amused chuckle. 'I've got a favour to ask you, Celia, would you consider coming to stay with me? I'm fed up with the hospital routine already. They've found no more bone fragments and the medicos will let me out on Thursday if there's someone at home with me, and I don't really want to ask my mother.'

'I could do that. I'm glad you asked me. I've got a few questions for you. I realised I didn't know much about you …or your family.'

'I'll be happy to give you a complete run down on my boring life. My parents have been and gone, thank heavens. You may get a call from Barnesy, he's co-ordinating security at my place. Just routine stuff, no need to worry.'

Celia felt a warm glow flood her loins. The next two days loomed interminably long.

That same day the real estate agent called. He was confident that the sale of her house at Bannockburn was in the bag. The present tenants had been spurred on by the previous enquiry.

'I'm really pleased, I thought it might take much longer to sell.' Celia did not admit to him the painful stab of regret she felt. She concentrated on the upside. Once the mortgage was paid there would not be a lot left but a few thousand dollars profit would make her financial situation more secure.

Following a patch of cool weather the morning dawned with the promise of a fine sunny day. Celia decided to go for a brisk run around the parkland. She needed to develop an exercise routine. A pair of brightly coloured rosellas flew from a sugar gum in search of breakfast.

There were at least fifteen dogs and their owners trotting around the track. Among them Celia spied Marcus McFadden being led by an energetic Labrador.

'Morning,' he called as he approached, trying to rein in the excited dog.

'Has he been to puppy school? I gather it's a boy,' Celia said with a laugh.

'Yes, he's a boy, his name's Moses and he does need to go to dog training. He hasn't been with me very long. I didn't realise what I was in for.' He stood looking apprehensive for a few seconds then asked if Celia would like to go for a drink. Now she would have to own up about Harry.

'That's sweet of you Marcus, I'm flattered, but I really need to tell you something. It's quite a recent thing. I didn't expect it to happen.' She stumbled on, trying to find the right words. She told him a little about her association with Harry Bolitho.

'I'm sorry Marcus, I really like you, I hope we can still be friends,' she finished lamely.

'Thanks for telling me. I know Harry, he's a great guy. I'll admit to feeling a bit disappointed, so if things, well, you know...' He leaned forward and gave her a kiss on the cheek.

'Of course we can still be friends, and I mean that, so can we go for a drink on that basis, maybe the three of us, when Harry is up and about again?'

'Thanks, Marcus. I'd like you to visit at Harry's place, it would cheer him up. Would you do that?'

'Sure, just message me when you're ready.'

As she resumed her run Celia was conscious of his gaze following her as she waved away a couple of magpies dive bombing her head. It was spring after all and obviously they had young to protect. She felt relieved that she'd got through the awkward conversation with Marcus and would follow up on her invitation as soon as possible.

Yvette had arranged a late afternoon meeting to see the finished painting. The two smiling faces conveying a sense of fun in a playful study made Celia cry. Each appeared more than once, merging in and out from the crenellations of thick craggy cliffs.

Charlie prepared a roast dinner.

'Thought I'd give you a decent meal. You might not come back.'

Charlie said he'd thought about Sally's request for a connecting door to the garden.

'In fact I think it's quite a good idea...not a huge impact on the integrity of the building, or my bank balance. Sally is happy to share the cost.'

'That's great, Charlie, and a door from the shop will make life easier for us poor workers. Any news from your solicitor yet?'

'No, nothing yet, but my legal eagle has asked Lauren to come to his office.' Charles made a wry face.

'Well, tomorrow's the big day Celie, I'm going to miss you.'

'Don't speak too soon, I'm not going for good, Charlie, not yet anyway, and thank you for offering me a place to stay when I needed it.'

'Oh, stop it, Celia, I don't deserve thanks, I was such a grouch. You're welcome to come back anytime. I hope it works out for you and Harry.'

'Will you come and visit? Harry will need his friends around.'

'Sure, I'll be there whenever you want me.'

The sounds of fruit crates being thumped onto the pavement woke Celia on Thursday morning, signalling that she was running late for work. Sally had asked her to do an early shift. The melodic baritone floated up in full throttle reminding her that she would soon be able to reach for a lover who would actually be there.

At two o'clock she hurried home, packed a bag, and threw it into the Corolla. She was about to slide into the driver's seat when she remembered her precious plants. She would have been upset had she forgotten them. Symbols of survival, they were a reminder to Celia to strengthen her resolve when her circumstances got the better of her.

Sergeant Barnes rang as she turned on the motor. He told her that an officer would be on duty at Harry's house today and probably for quite a while after that. She could come over when she was ready.

'I'm on my way,' she told him.

'Harry's due in the late afternoon. Detectives will drive him home, they want to check his house for security.'

'Okay, thanks, Detective.'

'Call me Barnesy, or Bill, no need for the formalities, you're a friend of the force now, Celia.'

Harry's house was a seven minute drive away from the older, more central part of town in an area known as Wombat Glade. Shady trees lined the streets. Celia admired the modern concrete block designs and thought the houses exuded the quiet confidence of middle class complacency.

Harry's front lawn looked freshly mowed. Celia cast her eye over the garden beds. Not a weed in sight. Kangaroo paws sat glowing amber and red in front of a variety of flowering Grevilleas. A red tipped Photinia hedge, neatly trimmed, formed part of the fence-line to the street.

She shivered as she tried to imagine what sort of nameless threat might be skulking in the vicinity of Harry's place, waiting to terrorise and shock the neighbourhood. A fresh faced young man appeared through the carport dressed in work clothes.

'Hi, you'd be Celia then,' he said, as he removed one gardening glove to shake her hand. 'I'm Kieran Huntley, member of the team at Appleton Police Station.'

'Hi, Kieran, you've done a great job on the garden.' He looked pleased as he took Celia's bag and showed her through the front door.

'If there's anything I can help you with, let me know.' Celia asked him if he would like a cup of tea. Once the bed was made up she consigned the dirty sheets to the laundry, prepared the tea, and joined Kieran on the back patio. Jethro came by, sliding his furry body around her legs.

'Well, that's a good sign,' she said aloud.

At ten past four Celia heard a car pull into the driveway. She ran from the house and watched as Harry climbed painfully from the back seat. He was smiling broadly by the time he managed to straighten up and wrap his arms around her. 'The roads are getting worse,' one detective said.

Everyone was smiling now and Celia felt that it was she who had come home. The officers discussed security arrangements. A patrol car would be doing a regular drive by overnight. An extra security camera would be installed. Doors and windows were inspected for any weak points.

It was unnerving to contemplate the reason for all this added security. Harry said he was feeling a bit sore, but he managed to eat a slice of Aunt Eula's quiche. Celia gave him his medication and helped him into bed.

'Right, lover boy, once again this was not what I had in mind. I'll sleep on the couch. All my fantasies are evaporating fast,' Celia remarked dryly.

'Mine are still intact, and no, you won't sleep on the couch,' Harry replied. 'Having you here makes me feel amazing, despite my banged-up body. Who would have thought it would take a bullet to get you into my bed, so come on, hop in and give me a cuddle. Don't worry, give me a week and I'll be almost new again.'

Soon after midnight the sound of a motor bike roared into life; the engine choking in staccato bursts as it accelerated and sped away. Headlights flashed in the window. The patrol car must have been parked in the driveway. Whoever was driving floored it in reverse and they listened as the gears changed up and the engine revved in hot pursuit. Celia and Harry clung to each other in petrified silence. It seemed an age before either of them managed to breathe. It brought home to Celia the enormity of the situation.

'I'm so sorry,' Harry spoke. 'I should not have put you in this predicament.'

'I'd rather be here with you. Life's a risk, remember. I'll make us a very hot cuppa, nothing like it to calm the nerves.'

A short while later they were informed that it was a neighbour heading off to a night shift. It was a huge relief. When Kieran arrived the two detectives left to get some well earned rest. The days passed uneventfully, that is, apart from getting to know each other.

'You really are a precious resource, Harry Bolitho,' Celia said to him. 'Now tell me more about your so-called boring life.'

Harry told her he'd dropped out after two years of a science degree.

'Obviously I had no great aptitude for study. I preferred playing guitar and squandering my time in various mediocre bands. Jobs in the hospitality industry paid my bills. My poor father was despairing. He's an engineer and my mother teaches music. You can see the converging lines of my parentage conflicting to produce the dissolute, aimless meanderings of my youth. I'm very happy being a country cop, in spite of a nasty little bullet wound.' Celia laughed.

Over the course of the weekend Celia met a couple of Harry's neighbours, They came to the door on Saturday morning, expressing their concern for Harry's well-being. She soon realised they were a little anxious for their own safety. Kieran joined her on the porch and Celia watched him put their fears to rest in a demonstration of skilled community liaising.

'You would have to be seriously impaired not to notice the

presence of police officers coming and going,' she said to him when the visitors left. Celia thought the message would soon be relayed up and down the street.

Sure enough, a young lady knocked at the door on Sunday asking after Harry. Kieran was again called upon to demonstrate his abilities. Celia wasn't sure they had the desired effect.

'That young woman was certainly disappointed she didn't get to see Harry.' Celia expressed her opinion to Kieran as the young lady flounced down the driveway.

'I'll be asking Harry about that little lady.'

'I think you have a secret admirer.' Harry poked his head from the bedcovers.

'Have I ? And who would that be?' he asked, giving her an amused grin. Celia thought it was a somewhat self-satisfied one. She enunciated a crystal clear description.

'Cropped, spiky henna hair, gold hoop earrings, wearing ripped blue denims, Doc Marten boots...' Harry chuckled as he reached out for her.

'Oh, that one, she lives in the next street. We have a little chat from time to time, since our first encounter at the servo about a year ago. She was enjoying a bit of shoplifting. The cashier had her in a headlock when I arrived. We sorted it. Yeah, I paid for the smokes and the Caramello bar. Kept the smokes and gave her the chocolate. Pays to keep sweet, I'll give her a call.'

Celia rolled on the bed, laughing at Harry's account of the connection between him and his feisty young fan.

As dawn broke on the following Sunday morning and the last glow of moonlight was fading, Celia woke to the feel of Harry's forefinger lightly caressing her cheek. She sighed with pleasure as two fingers moved like the flutter of a butterfly just where she had wanted them. From her face to her neck and down over her breasts, across her hips and up again.

Cradling her head with both hands he kissed her for a long tender moment, then stoking the fire in her belly he entered her and soon her body exploded like a New Year's Eve firework display on Sydney Harbour Bridge. She could swear that for a few seconds she was propelled upwards to the ceiling where she could look down and observe them in disembodied awe. Harry spoke softly.

'Celie, darling, you are something else, I thought you were going to be gentle with me. I'd have to say that was an unmitigated success. Can we do it again?'

'Your aptitude for wickedly talented lovemaking has me at your mercy, but no, not this morning, too much of a good thing… is, you know, really a bad thing.' Headlights shone briefly as a car turned into the driveway.

'They're back,' said Harry. 'Poor sleep deprived bastards.'

'Have you still got your guitar? I'd like to hear you play, that's another surprise.'

'I think it's around here somewhere, I'll dig it out, you've given me the motivation to shake the cobwebs off.'

Late in the day Celia answered a call from the self described real estate hot shot. A deposit would be paid into her nominated bank account. He would send a detailed summary. Celia danced through the house, calling to Harry who was resting in bed.

'Mavis mentioned a windfall and this must be it!' She danced again and sat on Harry's bed.

'It seems Mavis is not wrong.' he said, as he pulled her down to lie next to him.

'Yes, there have been good things happening, I'm doing some part-time teaching...but the first and best thing for a long time was meeting you, Harry Bolitho.'

She kissed Harry goodbye at eight the next morning.

'I hope you can find that guitar, we'll sing a duet when I get back.'

Helen sent a get-well card and said she was seeing someone, but if there was anything she could do... The flying ducks that Helen had bought for him had been languishing in a cupboard. Harry showed them to Celia, who thought they were charming and told him they must be free to wing their way across a wall.

She had brought him a gift of her own. His thirty-second birthday was coming up and together they were arranging a trip to the coast for the coming weekend. It would be Harry's birthday treat. She told him about her daydream...of being at the beach with him, rolling in the sand, exploring each other's buzz spots.

'I'll look forward to that, sounds very appealing, but no sandy nakedness, mind you, it's a bugger when it gets into your privates.'

The quaint stone cottage by the sea was less than a two hour drive, a convenient romantic getaway. Although the early November days were cool, the sun shone and they swam in the freezing waters. Harry insisted on preparing lunch while Celia browsed through books on the mantel. For Harry's birthday dinner Celia served crayfish on a bed of salad mix, washed down with a chablis. Celia lit candles on an ice cream cake. They sat by the open fire and Celia gave Harry his birthday gift.

When he opened it and saw the simple carving of two lovers entwined in a tender embrace Celia could see that he was touched. Harry took her in his arms and slowly started removing her clothes, kissing her all the while. She lifted his cashmere sweater and ran her fingers over the scar on his side, her eyes questioning. 'Heaps better.' he said.

On the night after their weekend away Celia broached the matter of returning to Charlie's house.

'For how long?' Harry asked. 'I'd like you to be here. Don't you want to live with me?'

'Yes, when the time's right. It's a big step and I won't be taking it lightly.' She didn't want to sound negative.

'I did tell Charlie that I was coming back. I need to give myself, and Charlie, time to adjust.' Celia admitted she had a lot on her plate. The daunting task of disposing of goods and chattels from the house at Bannockburn weighed on her mind.

'A lot of stuff is stored at various places and I need to collect it.'

'Right, if that's what you need to do,' Harry gave her a hug. 'I can help with that, we'll work it out. Don't stress.'

Business was pleasing for Sal but Celia's day had been dogged by minor problems. A mouse was obviously gaining access to the storeroom. It was after five, and she was left to clean and lock up.

Pulling at her soiled gloves she tried to hold her phone while a member of the school staff was verifying prior arrangements, updating her on the relevant subjects, activities and timetables for the classes she would be taking.

The days were skipping by too quickly, the commitment she'd made was now demanding her attention and she was far from ready. Forgetting about smelly mice, her thoughts turned to the preparation she needed to do in record time.

CHAPTER 8

2004 — Revelations

Celia called for quiet as the composite class of Grade 3 and 4 filed into their classroom on the following Tuesday morning, chattering excitedly. Yesterday she'd been thrown into a pool of squirming tadpoles. Navigating this new terrain was challenging. Today would be better. The first lesson was Show and Tell, the kids loved it.

Celia recognised a small boy named Anthony who was jumping about with undisguised enthusiasm, like a little brown beetle caught in a bucket. Because his name started with A, Celia asked if he would like to be the first to get the ball rolling. Anthony eagerly pulled a parcel from his schoolbag, placed it on his desk with a thud and tugged at the waterproof covering. He let out a triumphant squeal as the wrapping fell away.

When Celia saw the gleaming black gun sitting in all its menacing glory, her heart skipped a beat, then skittered like a new-born colt. She thought she could feel it teetering on the verge of a cardiac arrest.

'Anthony,' she said, clutching her hand to her breast, her mind filling with a rush of misgivings. 'Just leave it there so we can all admire it. Follow me Anthony.' She took his hand. Leading him quickly to the front of the room, she addressed the class who were staring at her in bewilderment.

'It's time for a special treat.' she said, brightly. 'Line up at the door, kids, and we'll head off to a party.'

Celia grabbed her bag and herded her class through the door, ushering them in the direction of the canteen. When they were settled with cool drinks and chocolate bars she moved out of earshot and called the Appleton Police Station. Anthony was calling to her. Slipping her phone back into her bag she answered him.

'Yes, Anthony, the gun will be quite safe on your desk.'

Sergeant Bill Barnes arrived in record time. He told Celia he couldn't believe his ears when he got her message. The Principal stood adjusting her glasses and looking non-plussed as Celia introduced Sergeant Barnes. They sat with young Anthony Schofield in the Principal's office while the Sergeant smiled reassuringly, telling Anthony to call him Mr Bill. Celia listened with interest as he spoke in his most casual, kid-friendly voice. She wondered how he really felt as he quietly framed his questions.

'So, tell me, Anthony, you say you found the gun in the rubbish?' His voice took on a note of surprise. Anthony nodded vigorously.

'Yes, Mr Bill.'

'Whose rubbish, Anthony? And where was this rubbish?'

Anthony was only too happy to provide more details.

'Behind the chook shed, Mr Bill, yeah, it was in an old pipe. I whacked a cricket ball. It was a beauty! The ball went right over the chook shed into Dad's rubbish pile. I climbed over but I couldn't find it. And then I saw the broken pipe so I turned the pipe up to have a look 'cos I thought my ball might've rolled in there and that's when the parcel fell out.'

'And did you tell your dad about this, sonny?'

'No, nup, he's been very mean. He belted Robert the other day an' he didn't do nuthin'. Mum says he's been actin' funny and I knew she was a bit scared. Anyway, I didn't find my ball.'

'Out of the mouths of babes,' Barnesy said later, shaking his head. Celia was still astonished at such an inconceivable turn of events.

'Come to think of it, I recall a report that Harry filed some weeks ago.'

'That would have been when he spoke to Alan, after my rather nasty experience with the wretched man.'

Following Celia's revealing Show and Tell class two police officers were sent to the engineering factory and brought Alan Schofield in for questioning. It was a shock to Celia when she heard that Alan Schofield was exhibiting signs of psychosis, muttering venomous threats, incoherent and unable to respond to their questions. He was admitted to the local hospital and placed under guard.

There were celebrations at Harry's house that night. Kieran stayed on. Celia had hurriedly contacted a few close friends. Charlie and Marcus arrived after dinner. The way that Alan Schofield had been found out was the chief topic of conversation and Celia was asked to go over the details ad infinitum.

Fetching his guitar Harry sat on the sofa and played some soulful Joni Mitchell songs, which Celia thought was his way of distracting their guests from the endless questions. Sally and her husband arrived in time to hear a few rollicking sea shanties but when Harry finished playing Celia had to repeat the story again, until she answered the door to Barnesy about nine o'clock.

'At least you know the story,' she said, explaining to him how many times she'd repeated the mesmerising details.

It wasn't until the conversation turned to the unfortunate Schofield family that Celia suddenly remembered Mavis's mysterious words. *The kid means no harm, no intent to cause alarm.* When she told the gathered company they were dumbfounded.

'The woman's a walking Nostradamus!' Harry exclaimed. 'If only we knew how to interpret her riddles and rhymes before the event.'

In the last few days Celia had been feeling a bit flat. The initial euphoria after the arrest was wearing off and reality was kicking in. On Friday evening Celia admitted to Harry how she felt about the consequences of her involvement with the Schofield family which had led to him being shot. 'It sits very uncomfortably inside my head.'

'Oh, Celie, sweetheart, you mustn't think like that. The man was ready to blow a gasket and I was in the firing line, so to speak. It wasn't your fault. I'm proud of you standing up for Robert. And it had the upside of bringing you back to me. We have a lot to be thankful for. We're good together, and I don't want that jeopardised by a bastard like him. Don't let him do it. He's done enough damage already.'

'Alright. When you put it like that I won't let him do it and I don't want to be a misery or you might not stay around.'

'Okay, my girl, let's go play some games, and I will be staying around, you can be sure of that.'

Noisy corellas were feeding on the back lawn when Marcus and Charlie arrived on Saturday. Their antics made Celia laugh as she served drinks on the deck. Marcus handed a card to Harry. It was from Donna Schofield, apologising for the pain caused by her husband.

Marcus explained. 'In one way she was thankful that the shooting had brought matters to a head for her. It's given her and the children the means to escape an abusive relationship. She'll be filing for divorce now that her crazy husband is holed up in custody.'

'Pass on our best wishes to her, Marcus,' Harry said. 'The DPP is ready to charge Schofield with attempted murder. It's not clear yet whether he will be declared fit to stand trial.'

* * *

Harry woke to the sound of distressed screams coming from the rear of the house. He found Celia in the yard crying out for Eddy. She was running distractedly across the lawn, looking in every corner and calling Eddy's name. When he reached her and tried to hold her she seemed not to know who he was and pushed him aside.

Was she sleepwalking? He couldn't tell. He waited, watching her, trying to think. What should he do? He had no idea. Celia was pulling at the shed door, still calling Eddy's name. Harry tried to keep calm. He spoke her name and she turned to look at him, pausing, staring at him before she spoke.

'Harry, what's happening, why am I out here?'

'It's okay, sweetheart, I think you've had a bad dream, let's go inside.' Celia was compliant now.

She appeared totally spent as he took her arm and guided her into the house. Harry was trying to still the beating of his heart as he made two cups of sweet tea.

'Here, drink this, you'll feel better soon.' He gave her Panadol. Celia swallowed the tablets without a murmur. He wondered if she knew what she was doing. Celia said nothing as she sipped her tea.

Suddenly the mug hit the table with a thump and she slumped in her chair on the verge of collapse. Harry swept her up in his arms and carried her back to bed, cradling her until he was sure she was sleeping soundly. He lay awake until sunlight showed through the upper window.

For the first time he had witnessed the traumatic effects of her grief and it gave him a lot to think about. It had been a disturbing scene. Will she get through this? Where do we go from here? he asked himself.

Celia was still sleeping as Harry showered and dressed for work. He was standing in the kitchen staring through the window, waiting for the toaster to pop when Celia's voice startled him. 'Morning,' she said. 'I could smell bacon, it was making me hungry.'

'Pleased to hear it. Give me a sec. Have some toast while I do the eggs. I'll butter these for you, jam or Vegemite?' Over breakfast Harry avoided mentioning the distressing scene in the early hours, except to say that Celia could do with a rest day.

He wasn't sure how much she remembered and there was no time to raise the matter this morning.

Celia agreed to delay her return to Mountside Road for one more day. When Harry returned that evening he advised Celia that he'd booked a van for the coming weekend.

'Great, that'll be another job I'll be pleased to get over and done with. How was your day at work?'

'They gave me an easy time of it, even bought doughnuts for morning tea to welcome me back.'

Harry was feeling glum next morning. He should have left for work by now. Celia left aside her packing and pulled his lips into a smile, laughing as she kissed him.

'That looked more like a grimace, give me a decent smile and get to work,' she chided. 'I'll see you on Friday.'

'I'll be missing you.' Harry put his arms around her. He was still not certain whether to mention finding Celia outside in the early hours, but it seemed she must have read his thoughts.

'What happened the other night, Harry? I know something did. Was I outside?' Harry played it down, telling her that she had probably had a nightmare and, yes, he'd found her in the garden.

'The prospect of having to reclaim your belongings is a bit stressful, we'll make it as smooth as possible. You can take your time to sort it later.'

'I don't care so much about the furniture.' Celia spoke slowly, 'I think we should take it to the auction rooms while we're in Geelong. Most of it came from Mum's place. You might like Mum's double bed for the spare room. It's not very old, just a mattress and base. You could add a headboard, with a suitable retro design, of course,' she teased.

'Sounds like a good idea, I won't say no, the room's been empty long enough. Thanks.'

On her way back to Charlie's place Celia's mind turned to the vexing riddle of the missing motor bike that Schofield was riding when he shot Harry. She'd mused on the mystery for some time. The police had been slack in her opinion. Their efforts to locate the bike Schofield was riding when he shot Harry had lacked imagination.

Sitting here in their midst Celia kept this view to herself. She had surprised Harry, arriving at the station so soon after their fond farewells.

Feeling smug and trying not to show it as she sat next to Harry, Celia prepared herself to dictate her statement. Detective Barnes nodded when he was ready to start recording.

'I decided to take a detour and do a little snooping,' she said. She could sense Harry stiffen and gave him a sharp glance. 'If I wanted to hide a bike where would I put it, I asked myself. The most likely hiding place would be in plain sight, that's what I was thinking. I cruised past the engineering works and parked a few metres away where I had a good view of the scrap metal yard next door. The yard gates were open. I decided to take a look. On the right an old rusted truck body was partly obscured behind a bank of trees. It was the type used to carry deep loads of earth and sand. I climbed onto the chassis. A rusty hole in the tail gate gave me a foothold. When I peered over the top, into the interior, I saw the wheel of a motor bike partly exposed where a faded blue tarp had come adrift.'

They left Barnesy as he prepared to write a formal account.

'Have you thought about joining the police force? We could use you,' Harry joked, and suggested they go for lunch. Celia would read and sign the official document when they had eaten.

'I think you've earned a nice fat cake.' Celia agreed. As they ate she told him she was becoming disheartened to see the theatre left in disrepair for so long.

'It's such a waste, Harry, the town needs it. In fact, I've got an idea, I'm going to write to the local council and ask them about the possibility of turning the place into a space that would benefit the community. A theatre company would be a boost for the town. I'll draw up a proposal. What do you think?' Harry made to answer but Celia was on a roll. 'If they're interested I would volunteer to co-ordinate the venture. Getting the council on board will be the first step. Sorry, you can answer now.' Harry was smiling broadly.

'That's the smartest idea I've heard all day.' Celia gave him a punch on the arm.

'Are you making fun of me? You're so exasperating.' Celia looked indignant.

'I'm not making fun, no way,' Harry protested. 'I think it's inspirational, but you're forgetting one crucial factor, Ariti still owns the building. It may end up being sold but until he's located and faces a court your ideas are going to languish in limbo.' Celia's face crinkled in disappointment.

'Oh, damn, what a nuisance. Trust you to raise it. A minor inconvenience, wouldn't you say?' Harry laughed at her ironic tone.

*   *   *

When Celia spoke with Sandy and Liam they were excited about meeting Harry and took it for granted they would stay a couple of nights. Hurriedly, she gathered up a few clothes and toiletries and headed for work.

Sally was on a high this morning, excited at the success of the Cafe garden. The sunshine had brought quite a few customers and they were filling the tables under the pastel umbrellas.

Brianna was run off her feet and very pleased that Celia had arrived. Gleefully indicating the connecting doorway Brianna swung it open on a clever hinge to hug the outside wall. A grand opening was planned for the weekend and she would miss it.

Celia had pushed the matter of Clive and Eddy's ashes out of her mind. They were being held at the Geelong cemetery and she needed to decide whether to place them in a memorial wall or if she would prefer to have them scattered.

It was a difficult and confronting decision, another step bringing home the reality of her loss. She was uncertain where life would take her in the future, so perhaps it would be best to scatter them, but where? It was too upsetting to contemplate.

She would discuss it with Frank. Until then she would try to forget about it and concentrate on the immediate future.

CHAPTER 9

2004 — Tribulations

Celia was looking forward to some time with Charlie though not so keen to resume life in a lonely bedsit. On the positive side, being there would give her headspace to start work on a proposal to council... a useful distraction on solitary nights.

Charlie was about to relate an interesting tidbit to Celia concerning his mother when Harry arrived. Charlie took a chilled bottle from the fridge and ushered them through to the front room. He filled their glasses and sat to continue his story.

'Yes, I got quite a surprise two nights ago when I called in to see Mum. Would you believe, I found her entertaining a man. She looked a bit sheepish about it.' Celia was all ears.

'You're kidding me, what sort of man? I'm guessing it wasn't the local vicar.'

'No, she introduced him as Guy Stoltz. He sounded American, or maybe Canadian. They were enjoying a wine together.' Harry was leaning forward, a quizzical expression creasing his face.

'She wouldn't be that old, would she?' he postulated.

'Well, I suppose not,' Charlie replied. 'I think she'll be fifty-four next birthday.'

'She's quite attractive, Charlie. Has she ever had a relationship since your father died?' asked Celia.

'Not that I know of.'

'Good luck to her then. What did this guy, Guy, look like?' Celia made a wry face. 'And where did she meet him?'

'Haven't got a clue where she met him, couldn't really ask, not while he was sitting there. He was a pretty confident sort, maybe mid fifties, average height...wore a waistcoat, and I think he had dyed blonde tips in his hair...looked a bit like Liam Neeson. Do you know that actor?' Celia nodded, yes, she knew the one.

'Irish, isn't he?' Harry remarked, inconsequentially.

'This bears further investigation, Charlie,' Celia said. 'He's probably got a wife somewhere. Can I fit in a visit before we leave?' She glanced at Harry. 'Better still, I'll ask her to come for a coffee while I'm at work.'

'Right, do that, Celia. Let me know what you find out. I think I need to keep a closer eye on my mother.'

Harry was in mid-sentence and Celia was smothering a giggle when the sound of breaking glass interrupted Harry's funny story. In the space of a second they were rendered speechless as half a brick flew through the window and landed on the coffee table. The evening's pleasant bonhomie evaporated like water on hot metal. The shock of it launched them to their feet. Shards of glass covered the floor. Moments later the lights went out and the cassette player stopped abruptly, killing Mark Seymour's sonorous vocals.

'Mind the glass,' Celia cautioned. Harry whispered to them to stay low. He was unarmed, off duty. In the light from the street she saw his silhouette bending to pick up a log from the fireplace.

They moved into the hallway. Charlie slid open the drawer of the hallstand and brought out a torch.

'Can I borrow that?' Harry asked him. 'I'm going out through the back door. Lock it after me, just in case.'

'Celia, could you stand behind the front door and let me in when I give the all clear. Whoever it was will be gone, I'm pretty sure.'

Charlie hurried back along the hall and stood deathly still with Celia until they heard Harry's voice on the other side. She opened the door. Harry stepped in quickly, snibbing the Yale lock again.

'Nobody around. I've called a patrol car. Let's see if we've got power. Where's your meter box?'

Down the hall they went again, Charlie leading the way along the outside wall to the meter box. 'This is getting ridiculous,' he muttered. A streetlight near Yvette's house on the corner shone weakly along the fence line. Celia stood in the shadows clutching a spade, keeping an eye out for any suspicious movement.

She could see the outline of Harry's face in the torchlight. She watched as he flipped the power switch while Charlie held the cover open. A light over the back door glowed.

'All good,' Celia called, with a confidence she was far from feeling.

'Get a lock for the meter box, Charlie,' Harry said, as they hurried down the path and into the house again.

A breeze was blowing through the smashed window. Harry examined the damage, removing the remaining shards. Charlie fetched his toolbox, located a roll of tape and used a beer carton to board up the space. He grabbed a bottle of whisky and Celia carried the glasses to the kitchen.

They sat in front of the old wood burning range, still warm, and clasped their arms around one another.

'Is this the work of the man I saw looking into the yard?' Celia asked.

'I could be barking up the wrong tree but it's very likely. Or someone sent to do his dirty work. But why?' Charlie wondered, shaking his head. 'There's something here that makes no sense. If this is the work of Lauren's brother-in-law what's his problem? I haven't reported the assault that sent me down a mineshaft.'

At midnight Celia felt mean about sending Harry home but they would be together at the weekend.

When Celia finished work on Friday afternoon Harry was there to collect her for the drive to Geelong. Celia's belongings were stored in various locations, including Sandy and Liam's garage. As they drove, Celia related what she had learnt from Aunt Eula.

'My lovely aunt came for a coffee with me at lunchtime and told me she had met Guy about a month ago at the supermarket. He was behind her at the checkout and was purchasing a sandwich for his lunch. She offered to let him go first. He declined, but hurried after her, offering to carry her shopping bags, asking if she had a large family to cook for as she had quite a lot of supplies. The conversation went from there. He'd only been in town a few weeks, he said, and was working for a confectionery company, servicing various shops in the area. Aunt Eula asked him if he'd sold any stock to The Ice Cream Shop. He asked if she would like to meet him there the next day. She thought he was personable enough, so she went along.'

'She's been very coy about it,' Harry commented.

'Yes, she didn't breathe a word about him. It must have been while I was away. Her life has been pretty dull for a long while. I got the impression she was quite excited about this chance encounter.'

'I haven't met Eula yet, but I'm looking forward to it. Can we arrange a meeting, a dinner maybe?' Harry asked.

'Yes, good idea, I think it's about time you two met. I'll text her, tell her we'll take her to dinner next week.'

Suddenly the heavens opened and heavy rain made the highway hazardous. Harry kept a firm hold on the steering wheel while Celia's fingers clamped around her seatbelt. By the time they reached Sandy and Liam's house the rain had eased.

It was obvious to Celia that her friends liked what they saw as they listened to Harry answer their questions. He was impressed with the seafood dinner that Liam presented.

'You're setting the bar a bit high, mate. I was keen to impress some guests once by trying my hand at Beef Wellington. Very embarrassing. When they took a knife to it the meat had shrunk away from the pastry...reduced to the size of a couple of pet food pellets. Took a while to live that one down. One person didn't even get any meat, just a piece of hollow pastry.'

Everyone shrieked with laughter at Harry's description.

'Yeah, turns out I should have browned that expensive eye fillet before I wrapped it.'

'Didn't you read the old Margaret Fulton Cookbook, the baby boomers bible? We grew up with it. Everyone we knew had a copy. You see it sitting around in op shops these days. I'm sure I've seen one in your kitchen, Harry,' Celia joked. She proceeded to tell them about Harry's fascinating retro decor.

'You'll have to pay a visit. Harry will have a bed in the spare room soon. Wait, there's a thought, how do we get Ruth's bed home?' Celia looked at Harry. Before he could answer Liam suggested that it might fit on top of their station wagon.

'School holidays start in December, that's not long, so we'll pencil it in. Sandy and I haven't been away for ages.'

'Is there anything you'd like from my motley collection of goods?' Celia asked. This prompted Sandy and Liam to glance at each other.

'Well, we have news...we weren't going to say anything just yet...' Sandy hesitated.

'Don't tell me.' Celia leaned forward as the penny started to drop. 'Are you pregnant?'

'Yes, I am, we are.' Sandy was looking slightly uncomfortable.

'That's excellent news, I'm so pleased to hear that. Don't be hesitant about it, there's no need to be. You've waited a long time for this. I'm really happy for you. Look, I think I know what you'd like. Is it Eddy's bed?'

'Oh, no, we hadn't thought about that. We just thought that we'd like something of Eddy's, we hadn't thought about his bed.' Sandy started to cry.

'Hey, no tears, unless they're happy ones. I think that's a very nice idea. It would be a comfort to me if you would like Eddy's bed. It just seems right.' Celia gave them both a big hug, remembering how good they had been after her loss.

'If I remember rightly, it's with my neighbourly mechanic, George. We'll drop it off tomorrow night.'

Harry picked up a ukulele from a nearby shelf and started strumming *How Deep is Your Love* by the Bee Gees. Celia felt a lump in her throat. A wave of anxious confusion unsettled her.

The skies looked dull but the weather was dry when Harry and

Celia set off just after seven. It would be a big day. Leaving the Pajero in a parking bay at the rental company Harry sorted the paperwork and Celia paid the charges before they climbed up into the van. As the engine kicked into life Harry located the lights and wipers, and adjusted the mirrors.

The grinding of the manual gearbox set Celia's nerves on edge. Harry told her he'd get the hang of it in no time, joking that he wouldn't want to drive this old crate too often. When they arrived in Bannockburn her old neighbours had hot scones and coffee ready. While Harry struggled to reverse the van up the driveway Celia asked them if they would like any of Clive's tools.

In the shed she fought back tears as she ran her fingers over them. She took a deep breath and pushed the memories she couldn't afford to dwell on out of her head. She chose two of Clive's hammers, a set of screwdrivers, two pairs of pliers, and a small drill to keep for herself.

George couldn't bring himself to keep any, telling Celia that tools always sold well. Thelma did show interest in a coffee table and Celia was only too pleased to gift it to her.

'It's not much in the way of appreciation for all that you've done for me. Is there anything else?' she asked. George finally accepted the tin trunk that had been instrumental on that fateful day.

'Thanks, George, I couldn't bear to take the trunk with me.' Celia's voice shook. Harry put his arm around her. Eddy's bed had been loaded first and a pile of boxes were stacked on top.

Thankfully, Celia's brother, Nathan, and his wife, Gwen, had taken other large items. She was grateful for the money they'd paid into her account.

It was a relief to be on the road again. Before they headed for the auction rooms they needed to offload the respective beds at Liam and Sandy's house.

'It's hard to keep track of what we're supposed to be doing. I'm starting to get brain fade now,' Celia remarked.

'It's been a tiring day, that's for sure. How are you feeling?' Harry asked her.

'I would rather have been at Sally's grand opening but I feel happier in a way, and a bit drained. It had to be done. Thanks Harry, I'll be fine after a good night's sleep. I can see Liam waiting for us, I feel very lucky to know at least two fine men, or maybe I should make that three, counting Charlie.'

Celia brushed at her face. Harry leaned over and squeezed her hand as he pulled up in front of the house. Liam opened her door and helped her down. They unpacked the beds into the garage and left a number of boxes on the verandah because they surely would not all fit into the Pajero. The guys at the auction rooms made light work of the remaining furniture.

'Only a few boxes left now and we're almost done.' Harry sounded pleased as he loaded the Pajero, 'I couldn't quite imagine how much stuff we were going to handle today. Liam may have to bring a few boxes next month.'

'And, y'know what? I don't want to collect any more stuff, ever. This might be a lesson for you, Harry.'

CHAPTER 10

2004 – Crime and Uncertainty

November was fast disappearing. On the Wednesday evening after their busy weekend Harry and Celia started on foot towards Dominic's restaurant. Charlie waved to them as he drove from the lane on his way to collect his mother.

The slinky black dress Celia was wearing shimmered under the soft light. In response to Harry's admiring comments Celia twirled playfully along the street.

'Impeccable taste,' Harry said, as he pulled her close.

Celia had never seen her aunt look so glamorous; navy pants paired with a snow white jacket fastened with silver buttons set off her petite figure nicely. Harry rose from his seat as Eula approached and Charlie introduced him.

'Hello, Harry,' she greeted him warmly. 'I'd kiss you on that handsome cheek if you weren't so tall!' Harry obligingly bent closer.

'I'll have that kiss now, thanks,' he said, putting Eula to the test. Instantly he scored a bright red imprint of her lips on his cheek, which Eula hurriedly wiped away with a napkin, much to Celia's amusement.

At Capers restaurant Dominic was in fine form, telling them that he was thinking of changing the decor from the present theme, featuring many and varied caricatures of the most recognisable and outrageous politicians in the country, to a very different one with haunted, and decidedly creepy overtones, based on classic, ghostly literature.

He asked them to submit ideas and pop them into a box at the Bar. Everyone had something to suggest, ranging from Dracula and Frankenstein to tales by H.G. Wells, involving carnivorous squid, blood-sucking orchids, and creepy toys that lurked in the world of children. Celia sat back, frowning, declaring all of a sudden, 'I don't think this new theme will help his business one iota, it's a bad idea. What is Dominic thinking of!' Eula was in solid agreement.

'Imagine the effect on young children, or older ones, for that matter. Families will boycott the place.'

Charles and Harry reluctantly agreed that the women were probably right.

'Yeah, and seafood sales would take a big hit, no more salt and pepper squid, thanks.' Harry's accent called Al Pacino to mind. Dominic would have to be set straight. Eula thought he should be canvassing ideas on dependable literature, books by Beatrix Potter, for instance, or cartoon themes or the tales of Paddington Bear. Celia agreed.

'A much better idea. We'll have a word with him before we leave.'

* * *

Murders were rare in Appleton. When Harry called her Celia could hear the distress in his voice.

'This one's nasty, it's a woman.' he said. 'Bashed and tossed on the side of the road. I've just got back to the office. Detectives are there now.'

'I'll come over tonight, you sound like you might need a hug.'

That evening Celia showed up with comfort food to ease his misery.

'Stay with me tonight?' he asked. Celia nodded. Harry opened the teak sideboard and chose a recording of the *Rumours* album by Fleetwood Mac. They danced. He smiled at her as they glided around the space. Harry sang softly, echoing one of the track titles as they solo'd off and came together again.

'You'd look like the lead singer if you grew your hair and sported a beard,' Celia told him. Her fingers lightly caressed his cheek bone. He took her hand and clasped it against his chest.

'It's tempting to give up the job on days like this and pursue a musical career. Perhaps I can trade on the likeness. Love the vest and black tights. And the apple catchers on the cover of that album.'

Hours later, as the dawn broke, Celia heard the ring tone on Harry's phone. He was sleeping as sound as a piglet in a pile of hay. She shook him awake and handed him the phone. Frowning, she watched as he jumped out of bed and paced the floor. It was several minutes before he finished the call.

'The victim's been identified. Gina Carruthers, married to a Morrie Carruthers. Isn't she...' Harry corrected himself. 'Wasn't she the sister of Charlie's girlfriend, the one who had a baby? Police are trying to locate him.'

'This is awful!' Celia's hand flew to her mouth. 'I need to get over to Charlie's place before he hears about this.' Celia threw on some clothes and ran.

There was no answer at 70 Mountside Road when Celia rang the bell. She banged on the front door several times. It was still early. Charlie must be in bed. Shivering in the grey morning she went to the back door and heard the shower running.

She waited for the water to stop and knocked hard, calling his name. Finally the door opened. Astonishment flashed across Charlie's flushed face when he saw her standing there at this early hour.

Hearing why she'd come his face turned a sickly pale. He looked as if he might faint. Celia took hold of him and led him to the kitchen.

'Sit down, Charlie, you need a hot drink.' She stoked the range and watched him staring vaguely around, as if the kitchen had become an alien place. With a sudden movement Charlie grabbed at the edge of the table.

'Where are Lauren and the baby, does anybody know?' .

'Not yet, not yet. We'll have to wait.' She handed him a mug, adding two sugars with the teabag. 'The water's almost ready. I need to go back to Harry's and shower, my clothes and school stuff are there. I'm teaching today. I'll see you tonight.'

*   *   *

It was almost midday when Celia received a message from Harry. She called him in her lunch break.

'Lauren and the baby were found at a neighbour's house.

Lauren had taken refuge there during an argument.'

'What a relief, Does Charlie know? He's been beside himself.'

'Yes, I've just spoken to him.'

On the Saturday, after their dinner at Capers, Eula was the first customer to arrive at The Ice Cream Shop. Celia had just warmed up the coffee machine. The usual crowd from the Haymakers Club would soon be filing through the door. She finished chalking up the day's menu and joined her aunt who, she could see, was eager to discuss how pleased she was that she'd finally met Harry.

'Charles was right,' she said. 'I think you're in good hands if you stick with that young man, Celia, there's a lot to like about him.'

'I'm glad you think so. Now you can probably see why I'm in such a tizz-wazz about it.'

'Yes, I can. You know, time is meaningless when it comes to grieving. I speak from experience. I miss your uncle every day, he was such good company, but we need to live our lives, enjoy the days, get out and about, have some fun. I'm sorry for Charlie, after that terrible business, he's not having much fun.' Celia sat quietly for a moment.

'He'll be alright. Are you having fun these days, how's it going with Guy?'

'Oh, well, he's very different, a bit of fun, yes, a distraction from the humdrum, at least. He took me out for lunch yesterday, said he had some business to attend to, so he might be away for a few days.' Celia thought she saw a fleeting shadow of uncertainty cross Eula's face.

'Oh, nice, where did he take you?' Eula glanced up at her.

'Well, when I told him about Dominic's preoccupation with

themes he was intrigued and wanted to take a look, so we went to Capers. You'll be pleased to know that Dominic is taking our opinion on his ghoulish ideas seriously. I think it's dawned on him that he might lose customers.'

Celia was about to ask Eula if she could help at the garage sale next Saturday when the door of the shop swung open and the morning rush began.

Charlie called into the Cafe garden later that morning to speak with Celia. He told her he'd received word from his lawyer. After the murder of her sister Lauren was too distressed to make a decision about a DNA test.

'So that's that, I suppose. It's all very complicated. I don't know where she is or what to think. Enough about me, what's happening with you and Harry?' Celia told him how conflicted she was about moving in with Harry.

'It's not even twelve months since I lost Clive and Eddy and I'm not sure what I should be doing.'

'Oh, Celie, do you love him?'

'Yes, I think I do, and that makes me very anxious. I don't want to burden him with my baggage.'

'God, Celia, you're putting up barriers that don't need to be there. You'll cause a lot more problems for yourself by pussy footing around. You might lose out, big time. Where's your courage? Time isn't the issue, except that it's slipping by. Life's too short to procrastinate. Harry's a big boy, he'll cope...but if you keep this up you'll cause him grief too. Have you thought about that?'

'Yes, I know you're right, I need to get over it. I'm just trying to figure out how.'

Towards the end of the day Celia's attention was taken by a young couple dressed in bushwalking gear, in animated conversation with Sally. They had completed the two hundred and fifty kilometre Great South West Walk and were feeling very pleased with themselves. Sally commented to Celia that she had walked a section with her husband a couple of years ago.

'I wish we'd had the time to go further, it's mapped out in sections. Fabulous scenery and the campsites are top notch. It's right in our own backyard and those two reminded me that we need to go back. We wanted to do Discovery Bay.'

'It's hard to get away if you're running a business, but you need to take a break, Sal, and recharge your batteries.'

'You should do it, Celia. A walk like that out in the natural environment has no end of benefits. Go now, before Christmas. You won't regret it. And next year you could look after the shop while we take ourselves off on the next leg.'

'Thanks for the vote of confidence. I see you're intent on stretching my capabilities, aren't you? I'd like to give you a break, but I'd feel a bit anxious about managing the shop. Anyhow, next year's a long way off.'

'It'll come around fast enough. I'm sure you would be fine. In fact, I've been thinking about asking you to be my back-up but I wasn't sure if you'd be settling here. How about it, Celia? I'd train you in all the other aspects of running this business. Give my proposition some thought while you're on that walk!' Sally gave her a cheeky smile. 'Come for dinner on Monday. I'll show you the guidebook and tell you more about the walk. Don't refuse me this time.'

'Trust you, Sally.' Celia let out a deep sigh.

'Alright, I'll come on Monday.'

Mavis entered the shop as Celia was about to leave. She did a little shimmy before launching into another cryptic ditty. 'Quiver, shiver. Snakes alive! Hurry, scurry, the team's arrived.' She bounced away, dancing to a jaunty beat and joined someone sitting at a table.

As Celia approached Harry's front door a tawny frog-mouth swooped past, very close to her head. She got such a fright in the dusky night that she dropped the pizza she had just collected. Luckily it stayed in the box. To make matters worse, she spied a dead mouse on the mat, a gift from Jethro, no doubt. Cursing, Celia banged on the door, shouting Harry's name. When he opened it, she pointed to the doormat.

'Look, here's another problem for you to deal with...and a huge bird made me drop the pizza.' She stepped over the mat and marched into the house, tossing her head. Harry tried to keep a straight face. 'Oh dear, what's been happening to you today?'

'Nothing. Except I don't like mice, dead or alive, or squashed pizza!'

'Right, you go sort out the pizza and I'll deal with this little critter, then we can have a wine and you can calm down.'

Celia's temper turned to self-conscious giggles. 'Sorry, I just got a fright...or two, in quick succession.'

It crossed her mind that here she was, being a wimp, while contemplating a week's walk in nature. She didn't mention the walk to Harry. It might be best to wait until she spoke with Sally on Monday evening, then she would come to a decision armed with all the facts.

CHAPTER 11

2004 — The Wild Side

Boxes were piled high in Harry's spare room, stark reminders of a different time. Celia stared at them on Sunday morning and wished they would disappear. The stacked boxes sat like silent sentinels, each one symbolising her loss. Harry had already left for work and the last thing Celia wanted to do was to spend the day sorting through the past.

She wanted none of this stuff, except Blue Ted, Eddy's favourite soft toy. The rest had to go. Never again would she wear the navy jacket and matching pants, labelled in her mind as the funeral suit. She recoiled at the memory and tore off a number of black plastic garbage bags. Gritting her teeth she set herself against the clock, sorting the contents into categories...op shop, garage sale. Within the hour there were five bags to load into her car.

More boxes would arrive when Sandy and Liam came to visit at Christmas. It was time for a lunch break.

In a phone call with Eula about the garage sale, Celia steered the conversation to Guy Stolz.

'You haven't discovered much about him, then. I'm just concerned for you. There's no way you can tell if he's trustworthy because there's no framework around him, not a soul in this town knows him.'

'You make a good point, Celia, thanks for your concern, and I have thought about it, but as far as I can tell he's not a threat to me. I feel perfectly safe in his company and he hasn't asked for any money yet. That would definitely be a red flag. He'll probably move on at some stage. I'm not too hung up about it.'

'Okay, well, that's good, see you on Saturday.'

Celia also spoke with her father-in-law and discussed what was to be done about Clive and Eddy's ashes. They decided she would collect them sometime during the holiday period and hand them over to Frank for safekeeping.

Her dinner date with Sally and Trevor Doyle was punctuated with travel tales and helpful facts about the Great South West Walk. Sally lent her a backpack, sleeping bag and a torch. 'Practise with this on your back when you go for your morning run this week. Gradually fill it with supplies and see how you go.'

'Good idea, I haven't been hiking since high school days.'

When Celia broached her planned walk to Harry on Tuesday evening he jumped up in dismay, marching in circles around the kitchen table. 'You're turning my hair grey!' he shouted, grabbing at his hair with both hands. 'What are you thinking?'

'Are you throwing a tantrum, Harry? Settle down.' It was the closest they'd come to a lover's tiff. Celia was determined to go ahead in spite of Harry's protestations.

'I'll see you tomorrow,' she told him, as she rose to leave. 'Sally wants me at eight in the morning to help with prepping.'

Harry was contrite. He stood behind her and put his hands on her shoulders. 'Sorry, Celie, I didn't mean to sound so...I'm not cross, I'm just concerned.'

'Yes, I know you are, but life's a risk, isn't it? Now who reminded me of that?' Celia put her arms around his neck and hugged him.

*   *   *

Overcast skies threatened rain as the garage sale got under way. Celia was thankful that a light shower didn't dampen the enthusiasm of the early customers. She briskly handled the dealers who, she knew from past experience, always showed up at the crack of dawn to maximise their chances of finding a rare piece.

She could tell who they were by the way their practised eyes scanned the goods and their speedy hands rifled through the assortment of mundane household items.

By ten o'clock Harry's carport was a hive of activity and the weather had cleared. Keiran Huntley came to help, along with Aunt Eula and Charlie, and just as well. They were run off their feet. It seemed that half the population of Appleton had descended on them, ready to do some serious Christmas shopping.

At five o'clock Aunt Eula called time out.

'Garage sales are exhausting, it's time to pack up and have a cuppa.' Charles couldn't agree more and marched his mother inside, sat her on the sofa and went to find Celia. Harry returned with the signs from the street.

'We should keep these signs and have another sale in the new year. We did alright today,' Harry grinned. Aunt Eula threw a cushion at him, but her arm was too weak to make it go the distance. Too tired for conversation they gathered around the table, enjoying Eula's meat pie until the silence was broken by a loud rapping at the front door.

'Oh, not another customer, surely,' said Charlie, as Harry went to investigate. He returned with a visitor. Aunt Eula certainly seemed astonished to see who it was.

'Guy, what are you doing here?' she asked, incredulously. Harry introduced the others as he ushered Guy to the seat he'd vacated. Celia's expression was wary, taking in the new arrival. Guy explained, addressing Eula.

'Thought I'd surprise ya, take y'out for a drink. I saw the ad in the paper. You told me you'd be helping at a garage sale, so here I am, whaddya think?'

'I'm flabbergasted, Guy, that's very kind of you.' Eula sounded nervous. Celia interrupted.

'We're all a bit wrecked, it was a hard day's work today. How about you make yourself at home and have a beer with us here? Would you like something to eat, there's no pie left but I can...' Guy interrupted her.

'No, no, I'm fine thanks, a beer will be great. Lovely to meet y'all.'

This guy really has chutzpah, thought Celia, as she prepared a plate of crackers and cheese.

Guy's visit had prolonged the evening and when Eula started to fall asleep in her chair the group decided to call it a night. Eula accepted Guy's offer to drive her home and left her car at Harry's place.

It was a tense and miserable Sunday, with Celia's imminent departure weighing on both of them. She suggested to Harry that he could meet her at the end of her walk next Saturday night at the Cape Nelson lighthouse. The lightkeepers cottage provided accommodation. Harry was very keen on that idea. The cottage was available when Celia rang to make the booking.

After returning Eula's car, Celia was surprised to see Charlie waiting for them outside Harry's house.

'I asked him to come over,' Harry said. 'I'm worried, you never know who's on that track and I can't go with you.'

'I don't want anyone with me, Harry, that's the whole idea, I need to be alone.'

'What if Charlie joins you for the first night? He's offered to meet you at the kiosk in Nelson, you'll be leaving your car there. I'd feel better if you agree to that. Let's go inside.' Celia sat facing the two of them. Harry filled the kettle. Charlie stood leaning against the bench, grinning.

'I sense a conspiracy here,' she said. 'What is it with you two, do you think I'm a defenceless woman?' Charlie answered.

'Not at all, a night out there under the stars appeals to me, Celia. I don't mind. I'll be there after work. I'll bring one of Mum's apricot tarts. '

'One night then, I might appreciate it, Charlie, out there in the scary night. I'll cook sausages for our dinner.' She spoke with a hint of sardonic bravado that echoed hollow in her ears. She looked at Charlie. Did he sense how glad she was of his offer? Charlie was looking at Harry.

'I'll check out the other walkers, there's always groups going through at this time of the year. It'll be fine, Harry. Relax.'

When Charlie left, Celia led Harry to the bedroom for a nap. He folded his arms around her and snuggled into her back. Too tired for any other activity they fell asleep in seconds, waking an hour later to the sound of heavy rain on the roof. Celia hoped it would clear before she started the hike. Harry handed her a coffee and sat on the bed.

'I've got something I want you to think about while you're on that walk,' he said.

'Yes, and what's on your mind now, Harry?'

'You must know that I love you. I want to be with you. I'm asking you to marry me, Celia. I know you're struggling with the idea of a relationship with me, so I don't mean anytime soon. But will you marry me sometime? I'll wait, I'll wait for as long as it takes. We can take a break, if you want. I needed to say these things before you go.' Celia blinked as her eyes welled up.

'Harry! Oh my God, you are intent on complicating my life, aren't you? I'm so...I'm elated and dismayed all at the same time. Just know that I love you, whatever happens.'

Ziplock bags were lined up on the table in Harry's kitchen, filled with dried food and nourishing snacks. Celia shoved them into her backpack along with spare socks and undies, sunscreen, and her bikini. Hopefully every other necessity was packed inside. Sally's flimsy tent and sleeping bag were strapped on top.

'It's only six days, you'll be joining me at Cape Nelson. Stop getting so up-tight about it. I love you, but you're giving me the heebie-jeebies!' She dared not let Harry see the apprehension she was feeling.

Before she left Appleton Celia bought sausages and salad and popped them in an Esky. During the drive to Nelson Celia wondered if she would ever get over her conflicting emotions. To distract herself she listened to Powderfinger, choosing their My Happiness album, which she thought was rather amusing under the circumstances. The only opinion she formed was that they were the best Australian band to date.

Her backpack sat on the rear seat loaded with food. How she would manage with so few clothes she couldn't imagine. She would probably starve as well. Even in her straitened circumstances she was unaccustomed to the privations required now. This was austerity on a whole different level.

Celia had to admit to feeling cynical about the healing benefits of trekking in nature. How could it ease her feelings of loss? She had no doubt that if she survived a week in the wilderness her physical body would be rewarded. She supposed that a stronger body and a sense of accomplishment could only be a positive thing.

*   *   *

Cormorants were wading in the shallows as Celia trudged across the wide beach of talc-fine sand at Discovery Bay. After passing through rolling farmland she had checked her bearings and headed west towards the coast. Charlie had joined her in time for dinner last night at the Nelson kiosk. For that, Celia was grateful.

During the evening her nerve had started to fail her; she was having serious doubts about her fitness, wondering if her body would hold up. She should have trained harder. They had camped at the nearby caravan park where Charlie did his best to reassure her that she could do this.

'Just think of the next hour, and then the next until you hit your stride. Pace yourself and take in your surroundings. You'll soon start to build your confidence. Eat lots of chocolate. Follow the signs and read your guidebook. It's not the Nullarbor, you know, civilisation isn't far away.' He smiled and gave her a hug as he said a cheery goodbye. 'Message me when you have reception.' She felt a strong urge to call Charlie to come back. Instead, she laced her boots and strode towards the Bridgewater lakes and Monibeong camp, where she would spend her first night alone.

Watching the cormorants at low tide Celia allowed their calm concentration to settle over her. The birds seemed so at ease, gazing into the clear water in search of a meal.

She had decided to take the slightly longer inland route as her guidebook told her it provided a more diverse landscape with sheltered pockets. Before leaving the beach she took the opportunity to have a quick dip.

It was still early, the sky was overcast but weak rays of sun promised to dispel the grey. Celia took a deep breath and slid under the waves. She thought of Clive...he must have been completely out of his mind to do that dreadful thing, his need to seek oblivion so great. What was he feeling in that moment of descent? She couldn't bear to think about it. A surge of compassion engulfed her, and forgiveness hovered around her heart.

The sun was warming the sand as Celia stepped from the water. Checking that no-one was peeking she located clean undies, pulled on long pants and T-shirt, and tied her wind cheater around her waist. Her confidence grew as she located the track cutting through the dunes.

Within a few minutes she reached the carpark near Nobles Rocks. The swim had made her hungry. Before she started onto the next section she pulled out a ziplock bag and shook a serve of muesli into a plastic bowl, adding a scant amount of long life milk.

Perched on a convenient rock she sat watching a pair of fairy wrens flitting about in a Cushion Bush, the male flashing his bright blue markings while the female, in shades of dull brown, called to him in a rapid shrill trill.

The smell of Coast Daisy sweetened the air. The track rose and fell through dense banks of Turpentine Bush, Beard-heath and Sea Box. Passing along a flat ridge she entered deep shade in a long stretch of Moonah forest, where the trees leaned in on both sides to form a bower. It was time for a chocolate snack.

The track opened up as Celia left the forest, meandering over a wide plain where Sword Sedge and Tussock Grass gave way to a graceful grove of Drooping She-oaks high on a hilltop. From a vantage point further along Celia spotted the vast expanse of Lake Monibeong. Skirting the lake she kept an eye out for snakes. It would be easy to fall foul of one, attracted as they were by the abundance of frogs and insects.

Close on dinner time Celia reached the campsite. Sally's tent was compact and easy to erect. Her shoulders ached from the weight of her pack. She was sitting at a nearby table, sipping hot tomato soup and eating toast, barely browned over a fitful fire as dusk descended. Celia gazed up at the hazy swathe of stars making up the Milky Way. She remembered teaching a class about the goddess, Hera, who, legend had it, sprayed milk across the sky.

She was happy to be teaching again but there was so much uncertainty in her head. Resting her arms on the table she put her head down and dreamed of a massage, preferably from Harry. She did love him, but marriage...Celia quailed at the thought. Missing company and still hungry, she ate a banana covered in custard and choc bits, which went some way towards making her feel less anxious and ready for sleep.

Not far from the Monibeong campsite a jetty extended over the lake. The water was crystal clear and Celia could see Pygmy Perch flashing silver, with speckles of black, flicking their orange tails in the morning light. While she lay on her stomach, stretching her head over the edge of the boards to gaze into the water, Celia thought she heard a faint cry, off in the tall grasses to her right. There had been one other tent a distance away at the campsite last night but she hadn't seen anyone around.

There it was again, a distinct human sound. Celia moved to investigate. Leaving her pack on the jetty she pushed her way through the scrub in the direction of the call. The vegetation thinned, opening onto a clearing where a man lay huddled on the ground.

'Thank God,' he said when he saw her. 'Thought there was-nay a wee body around. Think I've been bitten by a snake.'

'Show me, quickly.' Celia gasped as he pointed to the faint puncture marks just above the top of his right sock.

'Lie still, breathe, relax,' she said, feeling anything but relaxed. Her hand shook as she pulled out her mobile, hoping for enough charge and praying to get reception. Only one bar.

'I'll have to move to higher ground. Stay still, or the venom will travel. I need your scarf.'

She wound it firmly round the bite site and up and down again. She had done her fair share of first aid classes.

'I'll collect my pack from the jetty and bring another bandage. I'll try for mobile reception now.'

Celia raced out of the clearing towards the dunes. Precious time was being lost. Two bars. She faced towards Portland and hit triple O. It rang and dropped out. She had tried to call Harry yesterday and got nowhere. Climbing higher she called his number anyway, not knowing what else to do. It rang... and rang. Oh, God, answer the phone, please. His voice was suddenly on the line.

'Celia, are you okay?'

'Yes, I am, but there's an emergency.' She spoke quickly, afraid the call would drop out. 'Snakebite, can you organise for help?' She gave him the location. 'I've got to go, Harry, I've left him back near the camp. How do we get him out? Text me.'

CHAPTER 12

2004 — Rendezvous

The man's name was Andy McConnell. He looked to be in his early forties, his chubby face was pale under tousled fair hair.

'I'm Celia,' she said, as she sat by him on the damp ground. 'Help's coming, you're going to be okay.'

She plonked her pack down and pulled a roller bandage from her first aid kit, smiling at him, trying to engender confidence. He told her how pleased he was to meet her. I bet you are, Celia thought... haven't met a soul and the first person I come across gets a snakebite!

Nobody had ever been bitten on this walk, according to her guidebook. Oh, the irony of it all. What a stupid idea this was, she thought. Although, it's just as well that I am here, or he might not have been found alive.

A Scotsman and a botanist, Andy told her that he'd come to Australia on a research fellowship to study fungi. Walking from Portland he'd reached the Monibeong camp three days after leaving the Cobboboonee Forest where many varieties of fungi grew in abundance.

'I was careless, I should've known better. Thought I saw a wee potoroo, they like fungi...I was trying to get closer and stumbled on a ruddy rock into the bracken... must have disturbed the bugger.' His brogue was soft and lilting.

'It happens sometimes.' Celia didn't tell him that no snakebites had been recorded on this walk; she thought it might make him feel worse.

'We'll just sit tight. I couldn't find a suitable stick, your leg should be immobilised, but I can mark the bite site.' She pulled her lipstick from a pocket and patted Andy's leg.

'It's important to keep the pressure on until all is well. It was probably a tiger snake but anti-venom is effective for all bites.'

Celia hurried to the dunes again, hoping for a message from Harry. There was nothing. She waited several minutes. From nowhere, a fox appeared and pulled up short to stare at her for a second, so close she could smell him. Goosebumps tickled her skin as he crept off across the dunes. She tried to keep her balance on the slipping sand, her anxiety levels bombing out.

So much for a tranquil hike in wonderland. As she turned to go, a message pinged on her phone. *Police SAR helicopter coming to Monibeong camp, ETA 1 hr. Love you, H.* Tears of relief pricked her eyelids. She had the feeling that a foxy spirit guide was on her side.

It was almost eleven o'clock when they heard the repetitive whirr of a chopper. Celia covered her ears and watched in awe as it hovered above them, a mechanised saviour with wings of spinning steel. A figure in a hi-vis vest hung from a cable. She saw Andy start to shiver as they watched the man being lowered to the ground, one hand reaching up to steady a folding stretcher. Celia walked to meet him.

'G'day, young lady, not a bad day, is it? My name's Chris, sorry we're a bit late, needed to refuel.' Celia introduced herself.

'I'm very glad you're here. He's feeling a bit sick,' she told him, as he followed her to where Andy lay in the clearing. The noise from above occasioned the need to shout.

Chris knelt, pulling a bite kit from his pack. Loudly, he reassured the patient and administered the jab.

'You've done well, girl. Are you two...?'

'No, no, this is Andy... I just discovered him.'

Chris started to wind a fresh pressure bandage covering the whole limb from Andy's foot and up over his knee length shorts. 'Oh, right. Hi, Andy.' He checked blood pressure and heart rate.

'Not bad, heart rate's a bit fast.' Chris was unfolding the stretcher. 'Wanna help me with this?' He gestured to Celia as he clicked one side and locked it into place. She did the same on the other side.

'We'll get him onto it. Are you okay, Andy? We've gotcha now, buddy.'

Andy's leg was placed in splints, nice and secure. Celia saw his eyes drooping as they lifted him onto the stretcher.

His tent was still erected but Celia had retrieved his backpack while they had been waiting. Chris slung it onto his back and fastened his first aid bag to his chest.

'You're going on the tightrope now, buddy. I'll be the safety net and steady you on the way up.'

Celia squeezed Andy's hand, assuring him that she'd see him at the hospital. Chris tapped her details into his phone and told her he would be in touch. Celia watched as they ascended, the stretcher hanging like flotsam in the blue. It was a sight she had never expected to witness. There was something glorious about it. The noise of the blades revved and faded as the sky warrior carried them away.

Mobile reception improved as Celia walked toward open farmland. She needed directions and managed to contact Harry. 'What a great time you're having.' Celia could hear the irony in Harry's voice.

He answered her question. 'Yes, I'm still at work, in the patrol car right now, so I'm free to talk.'

'Thank God I got hold of you this morning. I was starting to panic.'

'You did well, sweetheart, wouldn't be surprised to see you in tomorrow's paper.'

'Oh, no, I hope not. Where am I heading, Harry? I'm stuffed. I want out of here.'

'Ok, chin up, let's see, follow the track from the camp to Windmill Road, crossing Guthrie, it's about a ninety minute walk. I'll send one of the guys from Portland Police to collect you along that road somewhere. I'll give them your phone number. It's about a half hour drive for them. I can come over later, if you want? I'm off at three. Let me know where you'll be.'

'Yes I will, that'd be great, thanks. Bye.'

She trekked on, following the fence line bordering the pine forest, trying to find the road. It was past one o'clock. Celia sat on the track while she put together a tasteless cheese wrap. I'd kill for a coffee, she thought, as she wondered how Andy was faring.

A faint rustling beyond the fence drew her attention. She turned her head and laughed in delight as she spotted a koala with a joey in its pouch, loping towards a bank of eucalypts. The sight of the furry pair gave rise to her maternal instincts. She wanted another child, or even two. She hadn't thought about having more children since losing Eddy.

Standing up with an effort she noticed two leeches clinging low down on her pants. Sally had given her a box of matches for this very reason. Her pants nearly caught fire as she tried to dislodge the slimy, bloodsucking wretches. Her pen knife did a better job. Were there any more where she couldn't see them?

Wearing white socks so leeches would be visible was another good tip. She pulled off boots and pants in a panic, inspecting them carefully. Yes! One was attached below the toe of her boot and one more, just inside the hemline.

'Ugh,' she cried, flicking them off with her knife. Stepping into her pants again she tucked them firmly down into her socks and checked the inside of her boots.

It was a relief to get out onto a better road. Celia hoped she'd found the right one. Her pack felt like a mountain on her back, the straps biting into her shoulders and straining her neck muscles. There was no road sign that she could see. A message came through from Chris. Andy was safely tucked up at the Portland Hospital.

Blisters were starting to become bothersome but she pressed on until she saw what she hoped was a police car heading towards her on Windmill Rd. Yes, a knight in blue and white armour was approaching. The driver pulled up in a shower of gravel. Smiling broadly, he jumped out and greeted her, 'Celia Booth?'

'Hi, yes, that's me.'

How grateful she was to be rid of her backpack and sit in the comfort of a vehicle. Her feet were hurting. If she had learned one thing it was to appreciate the advantages of living in this day and age. She said as much to the young officer, who was keen to know all the details of the rescue operation. Forty minutes later they arrived at the hospital. The officer asked if there was anything more he could do.

'Thanks, I think everything will be fine now. I'm grateful that you came to pick me up.'

He waved her goodbye at the entrance. A nearby coffee shop beckoned and Celia couldn't resist a much needed caffeine hit before visiting Andy. While waiting for her order she browsed a rack of brochures. How funny is this, she thought, as she picked one from the rack. Here's a place called The Portland Retro Motel. A map on the back told her it was only two blocks away. Celia called the number. There was no problem booking a unit. It was mid-week, she even scored a discount.

Andy was very drowsy...not looking so good when she saw him. She would come back tomorrow when she hoped he would be feeling better and they could discuss 'where to from here' for him.

'He'll be okay,' a male nurse assured her. 'It can take a while to recover from snakebite. He'll be in for a couple of days.'

The unexpected change in plan had turned out to be an advantage. She could continue the walk in the morning, starting from the Portland Information Centre. At least she had been spared a further stretch of trudging on sand. She made a call to change her site bookings and the payment was transferred to Mallee Camp. Tomorrow she would be able to explore the mysteries of the Enchanted Forest.

At the motel Celia messaged Harry before summoning the energy to step into a hot shower, laughing to herself at the retro fittings. Harry will love this place. Standing under the comforting warmth Celia thought she would never take this luxury for granted either. Her soiled clothes were left to soak in the shower base.

Wrapped in a towel she plugged her phone in to charge, folded back the striped sixties bedcover and slid down between soft sheets. A loud knocking roused her. She had no idea of the time; daylight saving extended the light until late at this time of the year. That'll be Harry, she thought.

When Celia opened the door, still wrapped in a towel, it wasn't Harry standing there, it was a young woman from the *Portland Observer*. Barely drawing breath she bombarded Celia with questions about the rescue of Andy McConnell. Standing beside her a photographer held up his camera and started taking photos.

'Hey, stop!' Celia protested. 'You can't do that. I'm not even dressed.'

'It's only a headshot, the towel won't show.' he said.

As she stood there feeling vulnerable, a white ute drove in and parked in the drive-thru. Celia caught sight of the driver as he hurried into the Reception office. She thought he looked familiar. It was the way he moved, quick, light on his feet, in spite of his solid body. The way his head sat squat on his shoulders gave Celia an immediate flash back.

The reporter followed Celia's gaze, wondering what had distracted her. Before the woman could ask any further questions Celia held up her hand. She had seen Harry's car turn into the driveway and watched as he proceeded past the ute. Celia crouched further back into the doorway as Harry pulled up. The media hounds soon realised their mistake when he flashed his credentials and asked them to show a little respect.

'Delete the photos or your camera will be confiscated,' he told the subdued photographer. 'That's no way to get your story.' The young woman begged forgiveness.

'I'm really sorry, we don't get much in the way of a good scoop in these parts.' She handed Celia her card. 'Will you contact me, I'd love to hear from you.' Celia told her she would think about it.

'Right now, I need to get dressed.'

Harry shut the door and moved towards the bed, sliding his hand over the sixties design with an approving nod.

'I think the towel will be just fine for the moment, don't you? It blends with the peachy colour scheme nicely.' Laughing, he nuzzled his cheek into Celia's neck.

'Good to see you,' he whispered, wrapping one arm around her waist, brushing his fingers across her collarbone with the other. Celia took hold of his hand.

'Harry, listen, I think we may have more serious things to worry about. There's a guy booking in here that looked familiar to me. He's driving the ute that was parked at Reception when you arrived. I think it's the man I saw snooping in Charlie's yard a few weeks back.' Harry let out a long, slow whistle. 'I'll call Barnesy. If you're right he might need the Portland police. I'll pop over to Reception first. We need to be sure. If it's him it's almost certain he'll be using fake ID.'

When Harry returned he said the investigative wheels were in motion, starting with a trace on the ute's registration.

'I've cautioned the motel owner to say nothing to anyone.'

Celia smiled. 'If those media hounds hadn't knocked at my door I wouldn't have noticed him. What are the chances? The timing was perfect.'

'Things like that happen all the time. Makes you wonder.' Harry said.

'You've lost weight,' he observed, as he stepped into her embrace. 'Would you rather we go for dinner first, or ...' Celia interrupted him by running the tip of her tongue across his lips.

'That's decided then, I was going to say, or go for a drink.' he said, laughing, as he lifted her onto the bed. 'Dinner can wait.'

'Okay, can you massage my shoulders, please?'

'Hmm, let me see.' Harry's tone was teasing.

They chose a restaurant at the Henty Hotel, above the waterfront. While they ate, Harry told Celia that Sally had formed a group aiming to bring a music festival to the town on the Labour Day long weekend in March. They've done a lot of the groundwork already. It will be a modest start for this first venture.'

'What a great idea,' Celia responded. 'I'd love to help out.'

'I'm a bit tempted myself, I must admit. We could have a bit of fun working on that together.'

'You'd be an asset, that's for sure, with your musical background. Are you coming with me to see Andy tomorrow?'

'I'd like to, but I'll need to leave early tomorrow morning.'

'Oh, shame, could you take my damp clothes with you please, and bring them on Saturday?'

When Celia and Harry returned after dinner two police cars were parked either side of the white ute. As Celia inserted her key and opened the door they heard raised voices and saw a man in handcuffs being escorted from his unit.

Sergeant Barnes was shoving him into one of the police vehicles. Harry glanced at Celia, 'Some action here. Looks promising, I'll be back in a minute.' Celia heard the bip as Barnesy locked the car and stood on the tarmac. As Harry approached, another officer emerged from the unit carrying a sports bag. He locked the unit door and turned towards her. She recognised the young constable who had picked her up on Windmill Road earlier in the day. Was it only today? Celia thought it seemed an age since then.

CHAPTER 13

2004 — Back on Track

A rainbow cast its arc across the bay as Celia left the motel and hoisted her backpack onto her shoulders. The blisters on her heels gave her no trouble as she walked to the hospital.

Her phone rang as she approached the entrance. It was Charlie.

'I hear you've had a hairy time.' he said. Celia laughed.

'You could say that.'

Charlie told her the other reason for his call. A letter addressed to her had arrived. 'The envelope tells me it's from the council.' he said.

'Open it for me, Charlie, tell me what it says.' She could barely hear him but she gathered that the council suggested she attend their next meeting which would be in the New Year.

'That sounds hopeful, thanks Charlie.'

The pesky reporter and her sidekick were pulling into a parking bay. This time she was ready. Celia greeted them. Once more they accosted her with questions.

'I'll give you some details about the rescue but I'll need to check with Andy first. I suggest you wait in the foyer until I return.'

After speaking with a person at reception Celia left her pack and hurried to find Andy's room. He was sitting in a chair reading the paper. A huge smile broke across his face when he saw her.

'Hello, it's Celia, isn't it? I've been trying to remember what you looked like.'

'Well, you're looking a lot better today. How are you feeling?'

'Thanks to you, lass, I'm feeling pretty good now, ready to get on out of here.'

'The media would like an interview. They're waiting at the reception desk. What do you think?'

'Do we get our photo in the paper?' Andy asked.

'Yes, if you want.'

'Ok with me, something to show the folks back home. Will they send me some copies?'

'I'm sure they will, I'll tell them to come to your room.'

When the media left, armed with the relevant details, Celia asked Andy about his family.

'I have a teenage boy in Scotland. My wife and I divorced a couple of years ago.'

'I'm sorry to hear that, about your marriage...'

'Well, you know, it's not so bad, we get on alright. I've been seeing someone. It's all good. You must promise me that you'll come to Scotland in the near future. I'd love to see you, and I'd happily pay your plane fare.'

'That's very generous, Andy, but I couldn't accept...'

'Yes, you can,' Andy interrupted. 'I can well afford it, believe me. I'm involved in a successful family business. I'll tell you more when you come. You did a wonderful job organising my rescue. I'm more than a wee bit grateful.'

'What's happening with you from here?' Celia wanted to know.

'A colleague from Melbourne will collect me, he's driving down tomorrow. Could you give me your phone number so we can keep in touch?'

They exchanged numbers and Celia told Andy she would continue the walk from this end, as she had a few days before she needed to return for work.

'Hopefully I'll reach Cape Nelson lighthouse without any further drama.' Andy was most apologetic when he realised he'd inadvertently caused a disruption to her walking plan.

'No need to be concerned Andy, it worked out well. Harry came over from Appleton last night, which is exactly what I needed. By the way, I contacted the Walker Liaison number and advised that your tent was still at the camp. You might like to follow that up and let them know you're still in the hospital. I'll send you the number.'

'Thanks, Celia, we'll talk again soon. All the best.'

'And to you Andy.'

Celia gave him a kiss on the cheek and left to resume her walk. She would restock her food supply then visit the Portland Information Centre. Once she had registered her presence on the track she continued to Point Danger Coastal Reserve, passing the aluminium smelter. Taking a short side trip as her guidebook suggested, she was impressed with the spectacle of Australia's only land based Gannet colony.

The white tip of Point Danger was the work of around six thousand birds, coating Lawrence Rocks with layer upon layer of droppings. Celia was quite happy to view them from a raised embankment at the edge of the rifle range. How incongruous. A rifle range? 'Whose idea was that?' she spoke aloud, as she set off to find the Enchanted Forest.

*   *   *

Harry sat at his computer that evening researching the criteria for application to the Police Search and Rescue unit. He'd been thinking about it since the rescue of Andy McConnell. At least his Sergeant was enthusiastic. Barnesy had slapped him on the back this morning when Harry broached his intention; his way of showing encouragement, telling Harry he was made of the right stuff.

Applicants had to be below the rank of sergeant. Tick.

'Who would've thought,' he chuckled to himself. His lack of ambition had proved to be a bonus. He'd been drifting in the last few years. It was time to get serious. He wondered how Celia would react to the idea. A recognised certificate in Recreational Diving Competency, he read. Ok, I can do that.

He'd known a bit about diving in his youth. It would be sensible to join a gym too. He didn't think his morning run would cut it. He was under no illusions, it would take considerable effort to be accepted into the fourteen week training course and there was no guarantee he'd be successful.

When Harry spoke with Celia that evening he said nothing of his intention to apply for the SAR, he'd wait until Saturday and tell her in person at Cape Nelson. As he had guessed, Portland was the closest place to enrol in a SCUBA diving course. Harry contacted the dive centre and booked his first lesson on Saturday before he was due to meet Celia.

Summoned from home on Thursday morning, Harry left a half-eaten omelette to join another officer at the scene of a suspicious fire at a laundromat. He found Constable Clare Cheung at the rear of the property. Looking very pleased with herself, she held up a fancy button.

'Stuck in the wire security door.'

'Well spotted, Clare, a nice find.' Harry took photos of the damage and popped the button into an evidence bag. 'According to the fire crew who attended in the early hours, there's no doubt this one was deliberate.'

Later in the morning Harry sat at his desk eating a muffin and checking Council records.

'The affected building's registered to a Mrs Georgiou. Another Greek name,' Harry mused. 'We'll see what comes out in the wash.'

'Ha, ha,' Kieran's tone was ironic. Clare just rolled her eyes. The laundromat business was operated by a family named Patel.

Harry answered a call from Charles. 'Fancy a meal out tonight?'

'That's a very sensible suggestion, thanks, Charlie.'

They decided to meet at a small restaurant, specialising in mouthwatering steaks. Christmas decorations were manifesting all over town, which prompted them to discuss plans for Christmas lunch. Harry invited Charles and said he would also ask Eula to celebrate the occasion at his place.

'Thankfully, my parents will be spending a couple of weeks in London at Christmas, catching up with Tim, my brother, who's working with a cruise line company in Europe. I want to provide Celia with plenty of distractions, but meeting my parents is not one that she would relish just yet.' Harry smiled as he slid his knife into the steak that had just arrived. 'Cuts like butter,' he remarked, washing it down with a glass of full-bodied red.

Charlie agreed that it would be a difficult time. 'So much has changed in her life, I can't imagine how it will be for her.' he said.

'Yes, Celia mentioned that her friend, Beth, is likely to spend some time with us, and the Paynters will be here as well. They're expecting…I hope that it's not going to be too confronting, she seemed fine about it when they told us. By the way, did you see her photo in the papers?'

'I did. Quite the celebrity, isn't she! She called me this morning. I guess she'll be staying with you over Christmas. You'll have a full house, so in light of that Beth is welcome to stay at my place. She might want to meet me first, although I remember her, she was Celia's bridesmaid.'

'Right, that's a good idea, thanks. I'm sure Celia will let her know you're not a wolf.'

Harry gave an update on Charlie's enemy number one.

'No doubt you've already heard… it was Carruthers who'd booked into the Retro Motel. Celia was right. His prints were on file. He's been charged with the murder of Lauren's sister and a list of other offences including the attacks on you. Apparently he was jealous of your relationship with Lauren, sick bastard. He's confessed to causing wilful damage at your place, hoping to get a reduced sentence. It'll be a long one, in any case.'

'And longer still if Lauren goes ahead with allegations of sexual abuse against him,' Charles added. 'I had suspected something of the sort but I didn't want to believe it.'

'I'm sorry, Charlie, nasty business. Even so, the baby may still be yours.' Harry said.

'Yes, it's possible, I suppose, but I may never get an answer on that. Where are you at with Schofield?' Charlie asked.

'He's been deemed fit for trial, but no date has been set,' Harry said.

'It's a strange feeling for me, as I'll be the main witness. I hope it doesn't drag on. Celia will also be required to give evidence unless he pleads guilty.'

They could hear a group of diners at the next table hypothesising on the fire at the laundromat, as people do about such events. Harry spoke quietly to Charlie.

'Clearly deliberate. I reckon we've got a lead. Clare found something at the scene that might relate to the arsonist.' Charlie was leaning forward, relishing the fact that he was getting details straight from the horse's mouth.

* * *

Sand blew into Celia's eyes as the the wind started to whip up. Signs to the Enchanted Forest proved hard to locate. She was beginning to doubt that she would find it. At last she stumbled upon a long flight of shallow timber slats in the sand, leading down to a sunken hollow, the result of a landslip in the long distant past.

From the feel of the pervading atmosphere and the avenue of Moonah trees she knew she'd found the right place. Here the air was still, and smelt of damp mulch. Drooping, feathery branches reached out from either side of the path as if competing for her attention.

Lichen-covered rocks rested where they had been tossed, like green marshmallows flung from the hand of an ancient deity. In this cathedral of nature Celia reflected on the events that had forced her from the life she had known.

Further ahead she could hear excited chatter. Very few people had been walking in her vicinity since she'd started her trek. It was too close to Christmas, she supposed.

Three children were exclaiming at the antics of a large frog on the edge of a small bog. They called to her, eager to share the fun. Celia stopped to look.

'He's a very handsome frog. Do you think he'll turn into a prince? We're in the Enchanted Forest, you know,' she said. A small girl started to giggle while her two older brothers crouched at the edge of the bog, staring into brackish water.

'No, he won't.' She spoke with a hint of disdain. 'Mum says he's a Pobblebonk. When he croaks he sounds like a banjo. We heard him...and he does.' She giggled again. Their mother was taking photos and spoke to Celia.

'He sounds amazing. Now my boys want to play the banjo, would you believe.'

Celia told them it was a great idea, wished them a good day, and walked on, imagining...that could be me one day...finding funny frogs with my children. The Moonah trees whispered to her, their leaves swishing softly, the sound of them shushing her fears, their branches propelling her along.

As she considered the future Celia sensed a layer of sorrow loosening. She would not only endure, she would climb the mountains ahead and enjoy the exhilarating slides on the other side, determined to enjoy the blessings that had come her way.

At the end of the one kilometre forest walk she climbed up another lengthy set of steps and faced into the wind. There were three lookouts to pass, each one providing breathtaking views to Cape Bridgewater. A short walk took her to Mallee camp.

There she prepared for the night on one of the raised earth platforms built to accommodate tents; a method used to minimise impact on Aboriginal middens and other artefacts. She lay in her sleeping bag listening to the noises of the night.

In that moment before sleep she had the weird sensation that the ground was pulsating to the feet of dancing tribes. She could hear didgeridoos in the distance and the rhythm comforted her and carried her into the dreamtime.

Sitting on the earth platform at first light, Celia contemplated the next step in pursuit of her objective: to see the theatre used to its full potential.

Andy McConnell gave Celia a call early on Friday morning to check on her progress, and told her they were featured in the newspaper. 'How embarrassing, I hope it's a blurry photo.'

'It's a very nice photo,' Andy replied. He told her he was returning to Melbourne the following day and would keep in touch. 'Now, remember my offer, Celia, I'd be very happy to see you in Scotland.'

On the spur of the moment she asked Andy whether he would be interested in a project, a possible investment she had in mind.

'I would like your advice on this.' Celia outlined her idea.

'I'm interested. We'll have a longer chat about it when you get home. And the offer of a trip still goes, investment or not.'

Harry rang as she walked toward Trewalla camp in the late afternoon. He told her he was going to a planning meeting for the music festival at Sally's place.

'You can let Sally know that I'm happy to help. Can't wait to see you tomorrow. Don't forget my clothes, Harry.'

'Yes, your clothes are coming.'

Before retiring for the night Celia planned her route to the Cape Nelson lighthouse. She decided to follow the sea cliff nature walk. That way she would avoid covering a section of the same ground twice.

As she left the camp next morning she saw a pair of red-tailed black cockatoos chomping noisily. Her attention had been drawn to them as slivers of nuts dropped in her path. Behind the birds a spectacular sun sat low in the sky, a brilliant red-orange glow. The surrounding clouds bunched like maids in waiting, their puffy white skirts edged with pearly pink lines, sharply defined at each side. Words from the old proverb came to mind. *Red sky in the morning; shepherd's warning.*

During her schooldays Celia had learned that the collective noun for a flock of cockies was a crackle...a crackle of cockatoos. It had a delicious ring to it. Her classmates had repeated the catchy phrase until the class was in stitches, all except Beth, who sat stone faced, while the teacher imitated the bobbing head of a cockie. It made her laugh out loud just thinking about it.

Her pack had lightened as her food supply diminished. She ate another chocolate bar and strode along the sea cliff, feeling satisfied that her body was growing stronger.

On the opposite side of the bay she knew there was a viewing platform where you could watch a seal colony. Celia was feeling pleased with herself; her walk was almost done and soon she would meet Harry. It was just under three hours to Cape Nelson Lighthouse.

Not wanting to arrive too early she took a long lunch break, looking out over Discovery Bay in the hope that she might spy seals at play but today a mist shrouded the bay and the seals stayed hidden.

CHAPTER 14

2004 — Enchanted Evenings

The weather was turning blustery ahead of an approaching storm as Celia hurried on from the lighthouse to the lightkeepers cottage. She could see Harry's car there. He would be wondering where she was. She saw him stepping out from the front door, looking for her. She waved and called to him. He ran towards her, nearly knocking her over in his hurry to remove her backpack and dance her to the door.

'This is more like it,' he said, kissing her cold ears and the tip of her nose. 'I hope you're not doing that again anytime soon.'

'No, the next time, you'll be coming with me. Something magic happens out there, something shifted in me, I felt it. We need to do the whole walk. I've only had a small taste of it.'

Harry had laid out a smorgasbord of succulent finger foods. The smell of freshly baked bread wafted through the kitchen.

'Oh, this is just fabulous, Harry, you've outdone yourself. How long have you been here?'

'The bread was provided by the owners, a nice touch. I did arrive early though. I had an appointment in Portland...with a dive school.'

'Whaat!' Celia was incredulous. 'What have you been up to, Harry Bolitho? I wondered why your fingers were all pruny. I thought you'd soaked in the bath for too long.' Harry grinned as he opened the wine and poured two glasses. 'Sit down, and I'll tell you.' He took a deep breath and launched into his plan for a change in career.

'Wow, that's some change, Harry, I don't know what to think… and this idea came to you because of Andy's rescue?'

'Yep, I don't know why I didn't think of it before.' Celia was trying to process the implications of this news.

'I would have to agree with Barnesy, you've got the right temperament for it.' Celia was frowning. 'It could be too dangerous. I don't know if…well anyway, we'll see.'

'How so, dangerous?' Harry countered, 'when simply going for a run was bloody dangerous. If you work in SAR the risk is minimal, the team has your back. There are strict safety measures in place, and the training is very thorough.'

'Mm, yes, I see what you mean.' Celia raised her glass. 'Here's to your success. I think you'd be great in that job.' Harry's glass clinked with hers. 'Thanks for bringing a delicious spread. I've got something to tell you after dinner.'

The food was good. Accompanied by the freshly baked bread, rollmops, sushi, cheeses, pickles and sliced meats released their gastric juices. They ate quickly, hungry for each other.

'We'll come back for more,' Harry said, as he took her hand across the table. Other juices were at work. Outside, the storm was reaching its full force as they snuggled under the down-filled doona.

'And what did you want to tell me?' Harry asked. Celia sat up in bed.

'Yes, I was coming to that. When, and if, my ideas for the theatre work out, Andy might be willing to donate. I'm thinking I would raise some money, starting with what I can spare from the sale of my house in Bannockburn, then there's some shares my father left me over ten years ago. I'd almost forgotten about them. They weren't going anywhere at the time. Maybe the value has increased. My financial wizard will know what to do.'

'You need to see the theatre,' Harry said. 'The worst of it is at the rear, most of the stage area, the roof and half the seating is wrecked, if I remember rightly. The front and the foyer are intact, but smoke damaged. It will still cost a packet to renovate.' He sat up then and leaned into her embrace as she chattered excitedly. 'Lots to think about.'

'Yes, it is, and stop licking my ear. I'll ask Charlie if he's interested. He's got a good business head on his shoulders. Involve the community, anyone with a spare grand might want a stake. Andy is offering a trip to Scotland. He tells me he's a man of substantial means. Imagine that!

Harry's eyes widened. 'Oh, yeah. Forgive me if I'm just a bit sceptical. Is he fair dinkum? You don't know him from Adam.'

'Oh, yes, I'd say he's genuine.' Celia grinned. 'No need to be jealous. He's fat and forty something, and he has a partner.'

'Ok, you're talking too much,' Harry said, and pulled her down under the doona again. 'Now where were we?' Celia laughed and tickled at the hairs on his chest.

'When can I see the theatre?' she asked him.

That prompted him to tell her about the fire at the laundromat, but Celia was more interested in his progress report on the meeting for the Appleton Music Festival. Her mind was brimming with ideas. She thought the festival might showcase bands and performers of all stripes; rich pickings for her grand plan.

'Another fire,' she said, abstractedly. 'I hope the weather's not like this for the festival. I was lucky that I didn't get caught in any storms on the track. It's a pest having to retrieve my car tomorrow, let's hope this downpour moves on soon.'

The storm did move on but the damage was evident as Harry drove Celia to Nelson. Trees had been uprooted and the SES crews were out in force clearing the roads. On the return journey Celia was following Harry when she saw a Ford Explorer towing a caravan coming towards them. As it drew closer the van started to sway. Celia held her breath, anticipating the worst. Miraculously, it swayed to the left, away from Harry at the critical moment. The driver slowed and pulled off the road. A minute later Harry was on loudspeaker. He told her to switch her phone over.

'We don't want the police picking you up.'

'Oh, funny, I think they already have. That was close, Harry. Accidents happen in the blink of an eye...don't I know. I thought you were going to be slammed, I'm still shaking. Watch out for falling trees. I'm getting paranoid, the wind's still strong.'

'We'll take it easy, better safe than sorry, although there's not much you can do if a tree's going to take you out.'

'Stop it, Harry, please.'

It was a relief to arrive at Harry's place. Celia jumped out of her car and hugged him, not ever wanting to let him go. Loving someone was painful sometimes. The uncertainty of existence. Celia again felt that sense of the unpredictability of life.

When they entered the house Celia went to the bathroom and promptly squashed a wayward silverfish under her boot. 'Oh, whoops, I shouldn't have done that.' Jethro came to investigate, licking at her feet. It took a moment or two before she realised what he was after.

*   *   *

Eula wanted to catch up. She was very keen to hear about Celia's adventures on the Great South West Walk. Celia called on her aunt later that afternoon. While she regaled Eula on the restorative powers of the walk, not withstanding the interruption caused by Andy McConnell, Eula sat sewing buttons on a vest. She said it belonged to Guy.

'It'll be the last time I'll be doing this. I told him he can do his own mending from now on. I'm not his wife.' Eula sounded fed up.

Celia spoke to her aunt about her plans for the theatre. At first Eula was doubtful.

'Do you realise how challenging that will be?' she said, a frown forming above drawn brows.

'Probably not!' Celia laughed. 'I need to find people who will guide me through. I'm going to inspect the damage tomorrow, and I'm calling on our local member of Parliament as soon as he returns from Melbourne.' When Celia explained her efforts so far, Eula was a little more intrigued.

'I might be persuaded to help out if the Council gets behind it. Will it go to auction, do you think?'

'Maybe, let's hope they're not going to be too greedy.'

Trade at The Ice Cream Shop was brisk in the week before Christmas. The side garden was a popular spot for friends and colleagues to hold their Christmas break-ups. Celia was placing reserved signs on every table when Members of the Haymakers

Club filed in. They preferred to dine indoors as the weather was not yet warm enough for old bones.

Brianna was taking orders from a group of four when the door opened and Marcus McFadden entered the shop. Brianna's eyes followed him as he took a seat at the front window. Her lingering look was not lost on Celia as she worked the coffee machine.

Mavis was waving from a nearby table. She stood and broke into song, her voice rougher than the crackling on a roast pig. 'Deck the cells with boughs of holly. Fa la la la la lalalala. 'Tis the season to be jolly. Fa la la la la lalalala. A festive night sinks into folly, Fa la la la la lalalala.'

The diners clapped and cheered as Mavis took a bow. Celia shook her head, as if to dislodge the strident sound. She had a lot to do today. This evening Charlie was giving a Christmas Eve supper. Celia had promised to give him a hand. Guests were not expected until seven o'clock. Some, like Harry, were working, and hoped to be there for supper at nine.

Liam and Sandy arrived at Harry's in the late afternoon. While she was helping Liam unload Ruth's bed a padded disc under the mattress caught on the roof rack and came adrift. Instantly she recalled what had been niggling her since she saw Eula. She rang Harry.

'It may be nothing,' she said. 'When you were talking about that second fire, remember, the one at the laundromat... did you mention something about a button? Right...ok, thought you did. A fancy one. Can you describe it to me? Egyptian?... an embossed head, a pharaoh? Yes... well, I'm going to tell you that Eula has recently added three buttons of that design to her sewing box, taken from a vest belonging to Guy.' Celia heard Harry swear.

'You're kidding me!' Harry shouted.

'I kid you not.' Celia heard Harry swear again. His voice was loud in her ear.

'Guy Stoltz, eh, well, it could be him, from what you're telling me. Let me think. It's going to be awkward to get a search warrant tonight, but that's what we'll need, and the buttons from Eula's sewing box. Do you know where he's living?' Celia said she didn't. Harry said he would ring Eula.

'Wait a minute, Harry, he's coming to Charlie's Christmas party tonight.'

'Good, that's helpful, I'll plan around that. Charm him, Celia, say nothing to the other guests.'

Aunt Eula was with Charlie, plating up sandwiches when Celia returned. She'd spoken with Harry and brought Celia up to date with the little that she knew.

'Guy lives in a flat behind a Greek lady's house in Church St. A Mrs Georgiou, I think her name was. I dropped him there once when his car was being serviced. Harry knew the name.'

Sally and Trevor Doyle arrived a few minutes after seven. Yvette was next. Every time the doorbell rang Celia tried to still the butterflies rollicking in her stomach, as she summoned a convincing display of Christmas cheer.

Marcus McFadden and Guy Stolz arrived at the same time. Celia outdid herself, linking arms with them and kissing them both on the cheek. She ushered them to Charles' sitting room and introduced Guy.

Eula managed to keep smiling at everyone while she carried a tray of canapés around the room. Charlie filled glasses from the punch bowl and went to fetch wine and beer. Celia brought in plates of sliced ham and potato salad for the table and saw that Guy was engaged in animated conversation about American basketball with Marcus and the Doyles. At five past eight Charles spoke to his mother and informed his guests.

'We're just off to collect some food, won't be long.' Celia walked with them into the yard.

'Be as quick as you can, get those buttons to Harry. I'll hold the fort until you get back. Tell him to get himself here pronto.' When Celia returned to the guests Guy was still busy being the centre of attention.

It was a moment that no-one present would ever forget when Harry marched into the party in uniform and confronted the suspect.

'Guy Stoltz, I'm arresting you on suspicion of committing the crime of arson at a laundromat in Baker Street. You do not have to s...' Guy turned and flung his arms across the table, scattering food and drink in all directions, spattering anyone in the firing line as he made a bid to reach the door. Constable Kieran Huntley was already positioned there and blocked his exit. Harry stepped over the mess and swiftly handcuffed Guy's flailing wrists.

The Doyles held on to Yvette. Celia stood transfixed. Was this her Harry? She hadn't seen him in action before. All eyes were riveted on Harry as he recited the charges again before Guy was led away, remanded in custody until further notice.

The assembled company remembered to breathe, breaking into feverish babble, recounting every detail, as if to confirm that it wasn't some trick.

Celia fetched a brush and pan. Charlie and Eula came in from the yard. Marcus found clean glasses and poured everyone a much needed drink. Charlie was really cross, his sitting room was covered in food scraps, broken glass once again and sticky alcohol.

Many hands made light work of the clean-up and it helped to settle the nerves. Celia could feel the collective shock, they wanted more of the story. Except Eula, who said how humiliated she felt, having formed a friendship with someone who was a fraud, and a criminal to boot. She told Celia how thankful she was that the relationship hadn't progressed to the next level.

'I was deciding whether to sleep with him,' she said, when Charlie was out of earshot. 'I didn't tell Charles that. It's not the sort of thing that sons want to hear, is it?' Celia had to laugh.

Sally and her husband left to escort Yvette the short distance to her house. Marcus said he would stay a while with Charles. Eula looked pensive and wanted solitude. Celia gave her a hug as she left to drive herself home.

The police station was abuzz when Celia arrived. Work had not slowed even at this hour. She was directed to a back office where she found Harry trying to locate a solicitor for Guy Stoltz.

'It won't be tonight, I'm having trouble finding anyone sober enough. Looks like the alleged firebug will be here for a couple of days.' He walked down the corridor to the cells, beckoning Celia to follow.

'Happy Christmas, Guy,' Harry called out, as he slid open the grille and passed a bottle of water through. Celia drew in a sharp breath when she saw the holly sprigs above the doors. A drunken voice in the next cell started singing a lewd version of Jingle Bells. This was the first time Celia had seen Harry's workplace. Tonight had shown her a different side to him. She was a little in awe of the way Harry handled himself in the job.

'Tell Eula I'm sorry,' Guy shouted over the inebriated singer, as they walked back to Harry's desk.

'Eula must have made an impression. Fancy the bugger being among us all these weeks,' Harry said. 'It beggars belief.'

'I'm pretty sure he didn't stalk Eula, it was just a chance meeting. There was no way he would have known she had a connection to the police when he met her. How long will you be, Harry?' Celia asked him.

'Not too long, I should be home soon after midnight. Barnesy will have to chase up the search warrant tomorrow. I'm damned sure Guy's connected to Ariti, we just need the proof.'

'Okay, I'll go home and tell our visitors what a fun time we've had.'

....

CHAPTER 15

2004 — Reflections and Vexations

The laughter of children playing in the street woke Celia on this Christmas morning. Their cries transported her, and her head swam with images of Eddy and Clive on Christmas Day last year, when they were still alive and no-one knew what sorrow the future held.

For a few moments she could see them clearly. The wheel of Eddy's new trike dipping off the back patio and Clive making a grab to rescue him before it toppled onto the ground below.

'Good save,' she'd called. Eddy's giggles echoed in her mind. It was a beautiful memory. She blinked away her tears. Today she must make new memories that would sit in harmony alongside the old. Liam knocked.

'I've made a cuppa.' He came in and sat on the edge of the bed. 'Harry's gone to work for a couple of hours.'

'I guessed he had, I vaguely remember.' Celia sighed. 'He'll be tired later. Yesterday was a demanding and eventful day to say the least. Wish you'd been there, Liam, we could have done with you. Where's Sandy?'

'Still in bed. How are you travelling?'

'I'm doing okay, sometimes it's a tough gig. That's the way it will be, but I realise I'm lucky. Blessed with the best friends anyone could want and I've got Harry. Soon I'll be enjoying your new baby. How long now?'

'Mid March, we think. Being a father's a daunting prospect, you know.'

'Don't think too much about it, get plenty of sleep and go with the flow.'

'You mean changing nappies and mopping up vomit.' Celia gave him a hug. 'You'll enjoy every minute of it.'

Sitting down for Christmas lunch with the people she loved gave Celia other things to think about. The day was warm. Charlie and Eula were looking hollow-eyed after the exposé the previous evening. Harry was back in time to slice the turkey breast. Celia passed the warmed plates around while Charlie sliced the beef. Sandy was keeping an eye on the vegetables and stirring the gravy. Eula asked Harry if Guy was still in custody.

'Yes he is, and he's ready to talk, I'll tell you what he had to say when we've eaten. He wants you to know that he's sorry.' Eula grimaced, Celia and friends tittered derisively.

'Eula, do you think he knew I was a member of the police force?'

'I think so, yes, I'm sure I mentioned it.'

'If he knew, I'm thinking maybe that's why he turned up the night of the garage sale, getting some kind of perverse pleasure, flaunting himself right under my nose...here I am, the man you're looking for, and you haven't got a clue. He was such a complacent bugger.' Harry shook his head. 'Celia put paid to that.' He bent and kissed her cheek.

Everyone needed a nap after lunch and urged Harry to hurry up with the latest.

'Guy was certainly doing the dirty work for Ariti, who'll be arrested when they locate him. Investigators were able to connect the dots this morning when they searched Guy's flat. To add grease to the wheel Ariti hasn't paid him, owes him thousands of dollars, apparently. He may plead guilty to lighting both fires to get a reduced sentence. It'll depend if a judge accepts the deal or modifies it. He could reject it. We won't know until the courts get back to normal. Guy will be deported eventually, the D's are checking his work visa. That's a joke, which work would that be?'

'What about the Greek woman?' Eula asked.

'Oh, she's in this, up to her baklavas,' Harry quipped. Sandy pleaded for them to stop laughing. She said it was the most entertaining Christmas lunch she'd ever had but her pregnant bladder couldn't take any more. A fresh round of hilarity followed as she hurried towards the bathroom.

In the late afternoon Celia gathered everyone around the fragrant pine tree, its Christmas lights twinkling in loops. With a flourish Celia presented her gift to Harry. She watched him rip the wrapping, waiting expectantly for his reaction. Harry opened the box and drew out a black velvet vest, complete with cord lacing.

'I love it,' he said, and immediately tried it on. 'I wonder where that idea came from.' He waltzed Celia to the hallway and back.

'It's stunning,' Eula observed. Charlie and Liam loved it too, they both wanted one.

'Oh, man, that looks cool.' Liam turned to Sandy. 'Can you make one for me?'

'I could, but it won't be anything like that.'

Eula gave everyone a plant with name tags displayed on large buttons attached to the pot. Wine and spirits were popular, as always.

Celia hadn't received anything from Harry. She was at the sink rinsing glasses when Charlie tapped on the window. He was asking her to come and join him outside. 'Merry Christmas, cuz,' He gave her a kiss as he handed her a large box. Harry came through the carport wheeling an aqua and blue electric bicycle. A matching helmet was in the box.

'Happy Christmas, sweetheart.' Celia could only utter inadequate words of appreciation. 'Oh, wow, this is...oh. I don't know what to say, you two have certainly been on a mission. It's wonderful, thank you, both of you.' Harry pressed her to hop on.

'Try it out for size, we'll need to adjust the seat.' Celia looked nervous. 'I might be a bit rusty.'

The others had come to watch and gave a round of applause. Jethro darted in front of her as she wobbled from the carport to the driveway. Turning to Harry, Charlie shook his hand.

'Brilliant, I think we've earned a star for the scrapbook.'

Before meeting Beth on Boxing Day Celia went for a spin on her new bike. Harry was out on a run. This morning he'd mentioned taking her to visit to his parents when they returned from their trip.

The prospect didn't thrill her, she supposed it had to happen sooner or later. She told him she preferred later.

She stopped near a playground and sat in the sun. The year was almost over. She had witnessed events that she could never have foreseen when she'd first arrived.

Meeting someone like Harry had been the last thing on her mind. His love had steadied her. When she was floundering in seas that threatened to swallow her she had been cast on firmer ground. In the coming year she would set her compass to steady as she goes.

It was time to give Frank a call. Celia related the complicated coincidences concerning Aunt Eula and her new-found friend. 'Tell Magda she has a rival in the realm of crazy story telling.' She could hear Frank still laughing as she ended the call. Celia turned up the throttle. Feeling the motor kick in she sailed on over the next rise. She was getting the hang of it.

Close on lunchtime Charlie sent her a message to say that Beth had arrived. Celia replied, asking if they would like to come for lunch. Charlie rang her, his tone was apologetic.

'Hi, um, Beth says she's really in need of sleep, she's gone upstairs to lie down, so we won't come for lunch, if that's alright.'

'Oh, well, I suppose that's fair enough. What about you, do you want to come over? Or we could make it for dinner this evening.'

'Dinner will be fine with me, I guess Beth will be happy to do that. I'll talk to you when she wakes.'

He went on to tell her about the major news item that he'd heard on the radio. A massive tsunami had wiped out places in Sumatra after an earthquake erupted in the Indian Ocean. The aftershock sent giant waves slamming into nearly a dozen countries, all the way to Thailand.

The power of nature...freewheeling, formidable, oblivious to the lives that swung precariously on its coat tails. You never knew what it was going to sock you with from one minute to the next. She shook her head and rode home to prepare a party.

From the moment she walked in the door that evening Beth displayed the affected manner of a spoiled princess. Celia bristled, feeling that old animosity. She watched Beth parading about in her sleeveless silver-grey caftan, the side splits revealing her slender legs, as she flirted with each of the men in turn. Her black hair, thick and shiny, swished back and forth at either side of her cropped fringe.

There was a brittle energy about her as her fingers twirled through her hair. Celia saw her behaviour as camouflage, covering a still-bleeding wound. She saw Harry's eyes slide sideways for a second, as if to say, *what have we got here?*

In reply to Sandy's question about her work, Beth answered that she'd received a promotion. When she returned to Canberra in the New Year she would be working for a Government minister. Celia wanted to prick the bubble of her self-centred conceit.

'I'm not at liberty to say which one yet. It's all a bit hush hush, confidentiality agreements, you know.'

'Sounds like a big skip up from the typing pool,' Charlie remarked.

'Yes, Charlie. I imagine it'll be like moving from the familiar faces in the fishbowl to the piranha plunge pool.' Beth shrugged, looking thoughtful. 'Not sure if I really want this job.' She picked up Harry's cat, and sat, leaning her head on Charles' shoulder. Celia saw red.

The following day Harry drove to Portland for another lesson at the dive school, taking Beth and Celia along for the ride. Celia thought it was a good opportunity to catch up without other company around. The humidity was making her feel sticky. Beth looked cool in white capri pants. A pale pink sleeveless top accentuated her smooth, creamy skin. They sat at a cafe table outdoors in the shade, waiting for their order.

'Charlie and I slept together last night.' Beth came straight out with it. Celia felt the shock waves reverberating through her skull.

'What! Oh, Beth, what have you done?' She could feel the anger, red hot and rising. 'This is trouble, Beth. You don't even know Charles. He's not the type to treat that as a one night stand. Is this the way you handle your own hurt? Taking it out on another man? You come here for five minutes and then vanish back to… to…' Celia was going to say, the piranha pool where you belong… 'to Canberra.' Exasperated, she drew in a deep breath and exhaled. 'Leaving us to patch up the damage.'

Beth said nothing. She sat, gazing out along the street, chewing her bottom lip. On the return trip she stretched her feet across the back seat and continued to stare through the side window. Celia knew that Harry had noticed the moody silence. How could he not?

She asked him about his lesson, then suggested he play a disc. He placed one into the sound system, Celia nearly choked… there was Willy Nelson, singing. *Help me make it through the night.* Oh no, bad choice, Harry. She couldn't say that out loud.

'You weren't to know,' Celia said to him when they were alone. Beth had stepped from the car outside Charlie's house, muttering a goodbye.

'If you'd asked me to guess what the chill was about… well, bugger me… don't think I would've picked it. Bad form.' Harry paused. 'Could happen again tonight.'

'Yes, very likely… now the wick's been dipped.' Celia's bawdy sarcasm amused Harry no end. She started laughing. 'Let's not dwell on it. If she hadn't jumped in so soon…oh, I don't know.'

Harry started singing. *'let the devil take tomorrow, for tonight I need a friend.* Now if you look at it like that, then…' Celia butted in.

'That's all very well, if it was someone other than my cousin. He's been hurt enough.'

'They might be good for each other,' Harry mused.

'Huh, maybe...but she won't be around to find out.'

Beth called into The Ice Cream Shop on Monday morning to say goodbye. Her manner was more subdued today. She stood pulling at a stray thread on her sleeve and kept nodding as Celia tried to make small talk.

'Harry seems nice,' she said, when Celia had stopped talking.

'And Charles is lovely.' It was Celia's turn to nod, she didn't want to pursue any further commentary on that subject. 'He says he's coming to visit me in Canberra.'

'Is he now?' Celia walked her to the door. 'Go carefully, Beth. I'm sorry you're not staying for New Year. Give Gwen and Nathan my best wishes. I'll see them in February when I come for the memorial.'

As Beth walked away, Marcus McFadden approached from the opposite direction. 'Morning, Celia, is Brianna working today?'

'Not today, Marcus. Why do you ask?' She gave a knowing grin.

'I was going to invite her to come with me to your New Year party.'

CHAPTER 16

2004–2005
— A Regrettable Mistake

Fine layers of dun coloured dust covered everything, clumping in every crevice after a willy-willy swirled through the town on the morning of New Year's Eve. Harry was hosing down the back patio. The water pressure was as feeble as a puppy's piddle.

Everyone was likely to be doing the same job, he thought. His muscles ached from the stress of his extended exercise regime. The hose jerked in his hand as the pressure suddenly increased. Liam came from the house with a straw broom. Jethro slipped past, his fur standing on end, clogged with grime.

'Catch that cat, he's not coming to a party dressed like that,' Harry laughed.

Retrieving the cat, Liam sat holding it while Harry searched for a rag. He came back with an old tea towel and the pair of them endeavoured to clean up Jethro's fur.

'I've spoken with Celia, and she's keen.' Liam's tone prompted Harry to look up. 'Sandy and I would like you both to be godparents to our baby.'

'Ooh, that's big,' Harry replied. 'We're not big on religion, does that matter?'

'Neither are we, for us it's about decency. Having the same values, you know, that sort of thing.' Harry stood and rubbed his aching thighs. 'Right, let's do it. I imagine you've spoken with your families. We'll talk about it closer to the time.' Harry suddenly felt older. Maybe it was his aching body, but Liam's request had nudged him towards a realisation that serious things were about to happen. He needed to adjust.

* * *

The New Year's Eve celebration welcoming 2005 had been hard work in Celia's estimation. She was feeling at a low ebb. It wasn't just because of the willy-willy, or the ghosts of New Years past, or the tensions which had flared at odd moments. She was tired, medicating herself too often. Recurring feelings of loss had shadowed her after Christmas.

When the household packed up in the early hours everyone was more than ready to hit the sack. Celia collapsed on the bed next to Harry and tried to distract herself from dark thoughts. On a note of false brightness she guided the conversation.

'Did you see the look on Marcus's face when Brianna arrived with Kieran?' she asked him.

'I didn't realise she knew Kieran.' Harry replied.

'She didn't, that was just it. She had simply arrived at the same time. They met at the front door.'

'Oh, I missed that, now I get it.'

'Yes, she didn't get the calls from Marcus. She'd lost her phone. Misplaced it two days ago, found it in a bathroom drawer when she got home and sent me a text. Everyone seemed to be at cross-purposes tonight until they all kissed each other at midnight. Poor Charlie looked miserable. Eula fussed over him, wondering what was amiss, which didn't improve his mood.' Harry pulled her closer.

'I noticed. And I didn't get my massage. I suppose it's too late now.'

He had also noticed her sinking spirits yesterday, asking if she was feeling okay. She thought she'd reassured him sufficiently.

'Yes, it's late, but not too late for this.' Celia slid her hands down onto Harry's hips. 'I'll give you a massage in the morning, we can sleep in, it's New Year's Day and you're on a late shift, aren't you?'

Liam was packing the car ready to leave after lunch. Celia called everyone to the table. She was pleased to see that Sandy looked a little less washed out as they sat down for a meal of left-overs. The doorbell chimed. Celia jumped at the unfamiliar jingle. Harry had installed it just after Christmas.

'I'll go.' Celia rose from her chair. When she opened the door Dominic Romano was standing there.

'Happy New Year, Dom.' She took his arm awkwardly, trying to avoid his double sided kisses. As she led him into the house her phone rang. It was Andy McConnell wishing her a Happy New Year. She stepped outside to hear him. He told her to check her email, he'd sent her an outline of a business plan.

When Celia came back, Dominic looked at her. 'I was just saying that I'm interested in the old theatre.' Celia's heart jumped.

'Why would you want it, Dom? It needs a lot of work.'

'I heard a whisper that it might be on the market soon, but you're right, I haven't got the sort of money it would take to buy it and finance a rebuild as well. I spoke to Charlie about it. He's not prepared to go halves. He said he had enough gremlins disturbing his sleep at night. A sizeable bank loan would upset more than his work-life balance. He told me to come and see you.' Dominic gave her a puzzled look.

At the mention of Charlie and his 'gremlins' Celia struggled to keep a wry smile off her face. She realised that her poor cousin would have been caught on the hop, not wanting to divulge that she had already embarked on a plan of her own.

'Mm, that might be a tad ambitious,' Harry commented. Celia realised he was being diplomatic as he looked at her with raised eyebrows. She was in two minds about telling Dominic she'd made a move or two in that direction herself. Maybe she should show her hand. She didn't want Dominic, with his crazy ideas, being the one who called the shots. She quickly formulated a reply.

'Yes, Dom, you're right. It is an asset going to waste. I'd like to see it become a home for performers, plays, musicals, that sort of thing. I've already made my own enquiries and I've secured a couple of investors. Charlie is coming over this afternoon to discuss that very thing. You can stay if you want. I'd be very happy if you would like a stake in this venture. I'd certainly welcome some extra capital.'

Instantly she could see her that her statement had taken the wind from his sails, his perplexity was evident as he looked at her.

'Right, mm, I see. Sorry I can't stay for the discussion, let me know how it goes.' Dominic rose from his chair. Celia escorted him to the door. He hesitated on the porch for a moment, then turning to her he spoke again.

'I've decided on a new theme for the restaurant, you were quite right,' Dominic admitted.

'The other idea was too scary, so I'm thinking of going with the Harry Potter books.'

'Aren't they pretty scary too? Perhaps I'd better read some.'

'Well, yeah, but the kids love 'em. Sorry I didn't get to your party last night, I had a full house, the place was jumping.'

Harry had to leave for work and Sandy and Liam were going home.

'Sounds like the new year is showing a lot of promise,' Liam said. 'We might be tempted to move here.'

'Will we still be here though, that's the question.' Celia replied, as she hugged them goodbye. 'If Harry is accepted into the Search and Rescue course, things might change.' Celia suppressed her qualms, worried about what these changes might mean; the vague threat she felt if Harry's job took him away from her.

* * *

High temperatures at the end of January sapped Celia's already-depleted energy. The town was in a constant state of anxiety as fires broke out in nearby bushland. A hot dry wind stalked the town, sucking at the curled, brittle leaves of the street trees. The Ice Cream Shop was the cool place to be.

Mavis had come in just on closing time and was waiting for Celia to scoop her choc chip and mango ice cream into the cone. She wanted a double header.

'There's no relief from this heat, is there, dear?' She went on in her sing-song voice. 'Fire, water, earth and air. A fall from grace, a loss of face. Knock, knock, who's there?' Celia had given up trying to fathom any of the rhymes that Mavis chanted. 'Take care, Mavis.'

Returning to Harry's place on Friday evening, Celia hoped that the cool change was not far away. She was exhausted, and a black mood of misery was eating away inside her. Harry had organised his leave and they were planning to set off early tomorrow. She was intending to collect the ashes and give them to Frank but the thought of carrying out this task filled her with despair. Right now all she wanted was sleep.

The painting of Eddy and Clive didn't sit well at Harry's place, she wasn't comfortable with it hanging anywhere here. She would give it to Frank for safekeeping. She sat staring at it until she lost all sense of time.

In two weeks the anniversary of their deaths would be acknowledged by family and friends at the Botanic Gardens in Geelong. She called Harry but he was too busy to talk.

Celia stood feeling rejected, shivering under a tepid shower, gulping at the alcohol in a plastic cup and studying the pills in her other hand. Horrific scenes from that day last year, that indelible day when Eddy died, had been playing out in her head at intermittent intervals for weeks. This mountain was pitted and barbed. Her spirit was crumbling.

Increasing the pressure she splashed water at her face, slapping at her forehead, but the images stayed. How do I push past this gargoyle of grief beckoning to me?

The shower roared. She saw Clive's face, his features distorted in the droplets on the glass. He was shaking his head, his lips mouthing the words, 'No, no.' She felt lightheaded and stepped from the shower towards the door. The pictures faded and she was falling, falling ... into the darkness... not being, not seeing.

*   *   *

It was almost seven when Harry opened the front door. He'd been delayed, tidying up loose ends before going on leave. There were no lights, no homely noises, no music. He remembered the call from Celia. All his senses told him something was wrong. As he ran through the house he could hear water running. Steam was fogging the bedroom.

He found Celia lying face down, the lower part of her body on the tiles in the ensuite, her head and shoulders on the bedroom carpet. Checking for a pulse Harry's brain was in overdrive. He tried to count, too faint.

His eyes fell on the bottle of Jim Beam on the bedside cabinet. It wasn't quite empty. He couldn't remember where the level had been. Oh, God, he didn't have enough hands. He grabbed the bedcover and threw it over her inert body. As he turned the water off he saw a cluster of pills on the base of the shower.

Taking his phone from his pocket he called Triple O. Waiting for the operator to answer, Harry tried to figure what had happened. Within a minute he was giving the details.

'I suspect an overdose, I'm looking for the pack... wait, I've got it.' He read out the brand name and dosage. Five minutes, they said.

'Stay with me, Celie, stay with me, girl.' He kept talking to her, searching for a pulse, holding her.

Slip slidin' away, slip slidin' away,
...the nearer your destination...

The song rolled on in Harry's head. He was sitting beside a hospital bed, crying his eyes out, as he watched Celia take in ragged breaths. The hours passed and Harry dozed until he heard Celia call his name. She seemed to be asleep but suddenly her eyes opened. and she looked at him. One hand flew to her lips.

'I've done it now, haven't I?'

'Done what?' Harry asked her, his voice croaky with sleep. With an effort he rose from the chair and stroked her head. The feeble light of dawn showed through a side window. It was Saturday morning, he'd been here all night. Celia was staring up at the ceiling.

'I didn't take all the tablets...Clive stopped me. You might not believe me but I saw him shaking his head...I did! I saw his blurry face through the water dripping down the shower glass. I was descending into the same deep pit. He didn't want me to follow.' Harry was listening. Her voice faded.

'I rang you earlier, but you were too busy. You'll be angry now, Harry.'

'I'm not angry, I'm tired, and I'm sorry...sorry I couldn't talk. You need to rest.' Celia spoke. 'What's happened to my head?' Her hand touched the dressing.

'I think you slipped on the tiles, sweetheart, and it seems your head hit the door jamb... right on your temple,' he told her. 'The mark was covered by your wet hair. When the ambos arrived, we noticed the swelling. It wasn't bleeding much,' he said, almost to himself. 'Your right eye is starting to bruise.' Celia sat up quickly,

'I feel sick,' she moaned, and promptly vomited all over the bed. She started to cry.

'Go home, Harry, she sobbed. 'Go home.' He pressed the call button, pulled back the soiled bedding and went to the bathroom to find a clean towel. A nurse arrived and left again to fetch linen and a heated cover as Celia shivered uncontrollably. Harry held her and wiped her face with the damp towel. 'I'm not going home just yet, I'll go in a little while.'

* * *

Three days after Harry had found her unconscious on the floor, Celia was discharged from hospital. Today she was drinking tea with Aunt Eula on the back deck.

'Charles is going to Canberra tomorrow for a long weekend,' Aunt Eula told her.

The bruising around Celia's eye was turning yellow. 'This is not a good look, is it?' she said, pointing to her cheek. Celia was feeling ashamed. Her actions had brought distress to the people she loved.

'I tipped the tablets down the shower drain. I had no intention of dying.'

'No, I don't think you did. Go easy on yourself.' Eula smiled at her. 'Considering the year you've had to live through, I think you've been remarkable, Celia, I'm not ashamed of you, quite the opposite.' Celia reached out and put her arms around Eula. 'Will Harry ever forgive me?

'You know he will. It's not a matter of Harry forgiving you, you need to forgive yourself, I think. Can you do that?'

'I'm not sure. Harry's so good it makes me feel worse. What about Charlie? He was very upset when he saw me.'

'Yes, he was shocked. He had someone else to worry about though, rather than himself, which was a good thing.'

'Harry didn't get to visit his parents. We won't be having a memorial. I need to see Frank and Magda but I'm attending counselling sessions for a while. I've made a mess of things.'

'Messes can be cleaned up,' Eula said, matter-of-factly, brushing her hands together.

* * *

From their perch in the pines the tawny frogmouths gazed

down on Harry as he left his driveway and ran out into the road, ready to start his morning fitness routine. He was still trying to come to grips with the impact of Celia's actions. Was it a suicide attempt? It sounded so damning.

He felt again that punch in the gut...that sickening shock which had hit him when he realised she had thought of taking pills, washed down with whisky. Her behaviour was so unexpected. He should have returned her call that night, but how was he to know...pointless to dwell on the 'if only's', he thought.

When she told him that dying hadn't been her intention, that all she wanted was to erase the horrors plaguing her head, he was inclined to believe her. He could understand that.

Harry sat at his computer later that day and submitted his application to join the Search and Rescue Unit. He had debated with Celia about going ahead, but she was adamant that he must, she wouldn't hear of him quitting on her account.

'I know it's a punishing schedule, but you're not using me as an excuse. Keep going Harry, I'm fine.' He had obtained his diving certificate, and told Celia his fitness levels were improving.

'I'm a gym junkie now. Why don't you join me? It does wonders for boosting your endorphins.'

'I'm thinking about it. Sally says workouts are great for your happiness factor. You're sculpting the body of a Greek god, Harry, an impressive piece of eye candy,' she told him, as she stroked the toned muscles in his arms. Harry laughed. 'Don't get too carried away.'

'I mean it, you can carry me away anytime, let's go to bed. Sex activates your endorphins too. I'll give you a massage,' she said in a teasing singsong voice. Harry's eyes lit up.

CHAPTER 17

2005 — Moving Tributes

In February, Celia presented her proposal at the first council meeting for the year. The Mayor took her aside after the meeting and quietly advised that the time frame was unpredictable but Council members had been impressed by her vision and would do whatever possible to bring it to reality.

He went on to explain, as best he knew, he emphasised, that if the purchase had been enabled by the proceeds of crime... well, he gave a superior sniff, then the Council may be allowed stewardship for the benefit of the community.

It was a difficult matter to clarify until Ariti was found and brought before the courts. 'Our insurers are very eager to know how that would unfold,' he said, moving his head close to hers.

Breathing his sour breath into her face he gave a hearty laugh. Celia flinched, but felt she should laugh too. She saw one hand ferreting about in his trouser pocket and her antenna went on the alert until he produced a worn packet of steamrollers and proffered one, prattling all the while about the complexities of the criminal justice system, and state and federal government bodies. 'We will all just have to wait and see,' he said. On that note he clasped her hand, bade her goodbye and good luck.

Celia resumed work at the Ice Cream Shop and made herself available as a relief teacher again. The students had only just returned after the summer holidays.

On the anniversary of Eddy's death Harry had done his best to comfort her, taking her out for dinner and dancing the night away at one of the town's hotels, the only one with a live band, and popular for their Latin flavour.

Celia gave way to the music, her mind firmly on the rhythms of the tango, the samba and the cha-cha. Clive's anniversary would be in a few days and Celia thought she would be better off at work. She could forgive him now. She believed he had prevented her from following the same fatal path. Surely it meant that he regretted leaving her in such an untimely manner. She wondered if she had been in his thoughts as he drove himself over the edge of that cliff. Too late, he couldn't change the outcome.

Frank and Magda came to stay. Harry drove the four of them to the ocean, where they sent lighted candles out to sea, placing them on the waves in garlands of flowers. It was a beautiful evening and they joined hands and raised their arms to the stars. A very moving tribute and impossible not to shed a tear.

*   *   *

Charlie had returned from Canberra. Harry was on late shift this week and Celia took advantage of the opportunity to speak to her cousin, explaining to him, as best she could, the reasons that led her to contemplate taking pills. They were having a drink at the Cosy Cat Bar. Charlie put his arm around her shoulders.

'You know I'd be devastated if anything happened to you, Celia. Why didn't you call me?'

'I didn't think, I'm sorry, my head was in a horrible place.'

'Okay, but if the going gets tough, promise me you'll talk to Harry, or me, or Sally, you've got a few people who'll drop everything and be there for you.'

'I promise. I know the triggers, and I know you can't be a servant to grief forever. I'm feeling strong again, and Sally is training me in business management. Tell me about Beth and your visit to Canberra. I'm worried about this little liaison.'

'I can see why. You've known Beth for a lifetime. She is complicated, but we get on surprisingly well, she was much less flighty. I saw a more responsible attitude while I was there. You were very annoyed with her, I know, she told me. She seemed happy enough to continue seeing me and she's coming at Easter. We might go to the coast.'

'Maybe she wants to prove me wrong. Beware of that motive Charlie, I don't want to see you hurt, or stressed. I can only wish you good luck with Beth.'

*   *   *

At a meeting of music festival organisers Celia sat with Harry and volunteered to help out in the Green Room. Dominic Romano was present and whispered to Celia that the Council had been generous with funding and were developing a website listing various performers. Tonight Dominic was offering Capers Restaurant as another venue on the music festival program. She had to hand it to him, he never misses an opportunity.

Hearing Dominic's offer Sally quickly followed suit. She

thanked the selection panel who had been hard at work choosing performers, and suggested providing a children's circus for the younger age group.

'Touché, Sally,' Celia whispered. A local councillor, appearing slightly tipsy, arrived in time for supper and hurriedly updated the various committees on funding arrangements, campsites, garbage collection, advertising and insurance matters.

Six days before the start of the festival, Celia was sitting with Harry on the deck. They were enjoying a lime soda after a training session. During the last two weeks she had been attending gym classes with Harry but she sensed the easy closeness of their relationship had suffered. Celia drew in a breath and broached the subject that had disturbed it.

'Do you trust me, Harry?' she asked. 'Are you frightened that I might do something stupid in the future?' Harry hesitated for a second.

'Well, I admit... the thought does linger at the back of my mind. What if it happens again, when might it happen? I find myself asking those questions. I wouldn't be human if I didn't. I can only say you've got to talk to me, Celia, if you're feeling at all sad or lost, don't leave it until the last minute. I know you had a life, a husband, a child, before you met me, and I don't feel in the least threatened by that. You can talk to me about that life, you can talk to me about them, it's part of you... and now, it's part of me.'

Celia's eyes glistened. 'I asked the question because it's the hardest thing I have to live with right now. Not grief, but the knowledge that I damaged the trust you had in me. I wouldn't want to risk that again, it's a horrible feeling, so, yes, you can be sure I'll talk to you if I ever find myself in that dark place.'

He took her in his arms. 'Let's dance to that. I told you we were good together.' They went inside and Harry chose Norah Jone's latest release, *Feels Like Home.* They waltzed. Celia thought she would like Harry's house to feel like home.

'How about we start making babies soon?' Harry whispered in her ear. 'And another thing, you said Rohan is planning a visit in a few weeks. I think it's time we asked him to design an engagement ring for you. Are you ready for that?' Celia whirled him around in a state of exuberance.

'Yes, I think I am.' Finally she felt reconciled with the niggling reservations she had wrestled with since meeting Harry. Her laughter echoed through the house and startled the cat into wakefulness. Jethro scuttled towards the cat door and sped through to the peace and quiet of the garden. It was the happiest she had felt since Harry first made love to her last October.

While they were preparing dinner Celia answered the door bell. She was astonished to see Robert Schofield standing there, leaning on a very flash racing bike.

'Hi, Robert,' she exclaimed. 'What a lovely surprise, come in.' Robert engaged the stand and followed her to the kitchen where Harry was chopping tomatoes. Celia introduced them and asked Robert to stay for dinner. 'I want to hear all your news,' she told him.

He was quite the confident young man and told them he was studying animation and woodwork in Melbourne.

'Wow, that's an interesting combination,' Harry remarked.

'Yes, I've got a gig at the music festival. I want to thank you, Celia, for helping me when I was injured. You were a good teacher and you sorted my father out, remember.'

'As if I could forget,' Celia said.

'Yeah, of course, sorry Harry, about what my father did to you. I was coming to that.'

'Never mind that, Robert, you're not to concern yourself, it's great to meet you. I appreciate your sentiments,' Harry said. 'Let's hear your showbiz news.'

'Three of us are putting on a puppet show as part of the children's entertainment. We've been writing different scripts in Drama class for young people like...to do with what's happening in the oceans, in the bush, you know, rubbish everywhere, like how to make friends, problems at home, social media stuff. We try to keep it fast and funny. Two other students have been making the puppets and the sets with me. We've called ourselves the Ad Hoc Rock Puppet Show. We've already performed in schools in our area.'

'I'm excited to hear this. I did hear a whisper that you had auditioned.' Celia put her hand on his arm. 'You've been working hard. That's wonderful, Robert, I'll make sure I get to a performance.'

'You'd better be there,' Robert said emphatically. As he was leaving Celia mentioned her ideas for the old theatre.

'It might take a while to achieve, but a venue for performers needs talent like yours. Mind yourself on that bike.'

Freewheeling down the driveway Robert let go the handlebars and gave them a cheeky two thumb salute. Harry put his arm around Celia's shoulder.

'I feel for the boy, It's hard for him, knowing that his father's facing court. The case is not likely to be heard for months. How are you feeling about it?' Harry asked her.

'I'm fine. We're not the ones on trial, but I'll be relieved when it's over.'

'With a bit of luck, if Schofield's in his right mind he'll plead guilty, and that will save everyone a lot of hassle.'

On her morning runs the following week Celia observed three marquees arriving in readiness for the Festival. Bystanders watched with interest as teams of workers started erecting them on the parkland. Food and variety stalls started to appear on the perimeter. A merchandising outlet snuggled at the rear of the marquee housing the main stage.

Harry was in charge of Police Liaison. He had enlisted members from other stations in the shire to undertake regular patrols, some of whom she could see were already on duty.

On opening night Celia sat with Sally listening to the rich baritones of Tony Larocca. His familiar voice took her back to the first time she had heard it, waking her as it swelled up from the fruit shop. Tonight he took centre stage in Gilbert and Sullivan's *HMS Pinafore*. Members of the local Operatic Society joined him in the performance.

Now, there's a group who would undoubtedly support a dedicated performing space, Celia felt sure.

Sally hosted a wind-down at The Ice Cream Shop early on Monday evening, 'as opposed to a wing-ding,' she said. 'Everyone's too tired for that.' Celia was offering visitors a plate of sausage rolls when Marcus appeared, asking after Brianna. She had to shout over Seamus and the Old Salts, who were playing sea shanties in the summer garden.

'I gather you two are on the same page at last.' Celia led him away from the noise.

'I think so, I thought she was dating Kieran. I wasn't being very smart. She's off to Uni in a week and where the thorny path of life and love takes us...well, it's anybody's guess.'

'Give it your best shot, if that's what you want, and talk a lot, no more mixed messages,' Celia said, tapping on the back of his hand. Marcus took her hand and raised it to his lips in a gesture of gallantry.

'You're right, Celia, I'll keep it in mind.'

Robert Schofield was with a group at the far end of the garden. She managed to get his attention and he stepped away to greet her.

'Great work, Robert, the audience loved your show. I think you've found your calling.'

'Yeah, I'm lucky, knowing what I'd like to do. You'll be the first to know if I get a call from the Disney Corporation.' He gave her a cheeky grin.

She patted his arm just as her phone rang. 'Oh, my friend's having a baby. See you soon, Robert.'

Liam's voice bounced with joy. Sandy had given birth to a daughter.

'We'll be there as soon as we can. Yes, okay, I'll bring a list of names, bye.'

Mavis was approaching. 'Changes are a'coming, resist them if you dare.' Celia wasn't sure if she wanted to hear more, but Mavis continued her recital in her raspy voice.

'Keep the home fires burning, be it here or be it there, new life is a'stirring, it can happen anywhere.' Celia stood there fascinated, as she took in Mavis's words. The dear lady is an old soul, she thought, rebooted as a modern day seer, if you could believe that psychic stuff.

Charlie was sitting with his mother at one of the tables. He'd been part of the Occupational Health and Safety team and still wore his hi-vis jacket. Celia approached them to relay Liam's news but was upstaged by Dominic doing a victory dance as he tapped his way across the crazy paving.

He'd been lucky to score a gig in the comedy line up, replacing a no-show at the last minute. Ever the showman, he put one foot on the bench seat and leapt up onto the table, his stance the epitome of self important zeal.

While Dominic amused them with his witty one-liners Aunt Eula rescued the rattling plates and coffee cups teetering on the edge.

At the end of his antics Dominic wanted to know how Celia's plans were shaping up for the theatre restoration. 'I'm starting to think it might really happen, Dom. There's a rumour that it may be seized, or it may go on the market, but until a buyer is found our local council will work with state government regarding restoration costs. We can apply for a grant to establish a theatre company but if all else fails we'll need to explore other options.'

CHAPTER 18

2005 — Double Dealing

When Dominic left the Cafe garden Celia noticed a folded paper under the table. Opening it she saw the Council logo above Dominic's name. It was a letter in answer to his expression of interest to purchase or lease the fire damaged theatre for the purposes of establishing a reception centre. The letter assured him that his inquiry would be given careful consideration.

Celia frowned. Hurt and dismayed, she realised the extent of his duplicity. It was a low blow...the deceitful bastard. A lightning rod of anger blazed inside her.

Charlie was heading into the Cafe. She would tell him how two-faced his friend really was, but at the last moment she stopped short; bit her tongue and swallowed her anger. Hold your fire, she thought. She smiled warmly and took his arm.

'Your garden is looking lovely these days, Charlie. I'll collect my orange tree soon, but I'd like to know if you have a preference. I'm intending to buy a replacement for you.'

'I'm glad you've resolved your concerns about living with Harry. I miss you, but you don't need to buy me another tree,'

Charles protested.

'Shush, I'm doing it, don't argue,' Celia told him. 'Now, we need to speak to interested parties who are concerned for the future of the theatre. Sally has already shown interest and I'm sure Percy would love to be involved. A venue to showcase the region's talent will be a winner, Charlie. My chat with the Mayor gave us cause for optimism but action from Council depends on a miracle. If we don't succeed with this building we'll have to take over Sally's Cafe garden and build our own!' Charlie caught some of Celia's passion and promised to distribute flyers asking for expressions of interest.

News of the birth meant another trip to Geelong. Harry had worked all weekend and was not due back in the office until Thursday. Time to seize an overnight stay. They could visit Sandy and the little, as yet nameless mite, and take Liam to dinner. There would be no opportunity to see Ruth, that would have to wait.

During the trip Celia told Harry about Dominic and his deceitful behaviour. It was the first opportunity they'd had for meaningful conversation since the close of the Music Festival. Harry said nothing at first. He took her hand and held it to his lips. 'You'll find a way to put a spanner in his works, sweetheart. I thought he was a ratbag...now I'm thinking he's just a rat. I feel like taking a spanner to him myself but I don't want to be had up for assault. I'll let you deal with him. Let me know if there's anything legal I can do.'

Celia promised to lend a hand when Sandy's mother grew tired of fulfilling a grandma's obligations. The high jinks of the matronly hypochondriac had been a source of mirth over the years. Sandy looked well but Celia felt sorry for her, a minor problem had kept her stuck in her hospital bed.

'Hmph! All she's likely to get are flowers and a box of chocolates for her trouble. Isn't that right, Liam? Enjoy your dinner.' Celia remarked.

'Don't make me feel guilty, Celia, I'm sure most new fathers feel guilty at a time like this. I'll make it up to her when she gets home.'

'I know you will. Sorry, perhaps I'm being a bit harsh. Harry is raising his eyebrows, they speak volumes, you know, those eyebrows.' Celia tossed her head and turned towards Harry, pursing her lips in a gesture of mock defiance, then quickly changed the subject.

'Have you decided on a name yet?'

'We really like a couple on your list, Celia, maybe Verity, or Trudie.

Harry called out to her from the study on Wednesday. Celia hurried from the kitchen, wondering what had happened. Here it was, an email confirming Harry's acceptance into the Search and Rescue course; fourteen weeks of intensive work.

A letter containing the course outline would arrive in the next few days. He was required in Melbourne at the beginning of April. What will this mean, Celia asked herself. Where will Harry be when he's finished the training. She had no doubt that he'd pass. The questions shied through her head like tossed coconuts, even as Celia congratulated him.

'I'm really pleased for you.' She kissed him tenderly. 'Your hard work has paid off. Are you excited?'

'Yeah, I suppose I am. I'm letting the news sink in. There's a few things to think about…and talk about. But first, let's have a drink.'

While Harry went to choose a cold bottle, Celia took two glasses from the teak cabinet and placed them on the coffee table. Jethro crept up to Celia's feet as she seated herself on the sofa. He squatted there for a minute or so, narrowing his eyes, until, all of a sudden, he looked up.

Eyes wide, he held her gaze, as if to say…Hey! I've got a few questions too, y'know? Celia thought his inquisitive expression was hugely funny and laughed until her nose ran and tears wet her cheeks. Harry returned with a chilled bottle of Prosecco. He looked at Celia.

'What's so funny?' She pointed to the cat. 'He is,' she said, still in fits of laughter.

'Oh, did Jethro say something? Sometimes he does that.'

Harry kept a straight face as he poured the wine. Celia burst into fresh peals of laughter, rolling on the couch, trying to control herself. Harry could no longer resist. They both rolled onto the floor, laughing together in the joy of the moment.

During the next two weeks arrangements were finalised. Harry would stay at his parents' house for a short period. He felt sure he would need his own space in a matter of days, he told Celia. On occasion he would come home or meet Celia at Frank and Magda's house.

She was pleased that Harry's acceptance into the course would afford her the opportunity to visit her mother and Frank, taking the ashes as she'd intended. She wasn't pleased that she would be separated from Harry for much of the time, although she knew that Harry's family were very pleased about it. His younger brother was due to return from Europe at the end of May. Harry rarely spoke of him. Celia thought their relationship had been fractured by distance.

She would remain at home in Wombat Glade until it was time to assist Sandy with her new baby routine. Aunt Eula and Charles agreed to share the care of Jethro and keep an eye on the property when she was absent.

Celia habitually referred to this house as Harry's, although he'd asked her to think of it as her own. She still felt like a visitor, until Rohan came to stay and brought with him a fat cabochon sapphire, surrounded by diamonds.

'Once again, you've produced an eye-popping sample of your talent, Rohan, it's magnificent,' she told him. Celia had fun modelling his latest pieces while Rohan took photos to send to his agent in Europe.

With the ring on her finger, and her increased contribution to household expenses, Celia felt more comfortable living in Wombat Glade. Negotiating at length with Harry, this last wrangle helped her to regard the house as a shared nest. She was relieved when Harry recognised the importance of that and finally accepted her terms.

By an odd coincidence, Easter Saturday fell on the 26th of March and presented itself as the most convenient time to celebrate an engagement, a week before Harry was due to leave. Celia had the feeling that, once again, a wily universe was at work. Her marriage to Clive had taken place at Easter. These two significant events would now be inextricably linked.

Celia was at a loss to understand the how and the why of this. Both were happy and meaningful occasions, celebrated at a sacred time in the Christian calendar. Even though her religious affiliations had changed, Celia still believed in a greater power.

She could only conclude that it was best not to think, not to ponder too long on the whys and wherefores. She figured that the lesson to be learned here was one of acceptance. We can't discard the past, she thought, it informs the future and I'm at the beginning of a new journey.

The celebration was held at Dominic's restaurant, much to Celia's chagrin. Both she and Harry realised it would be taken as a direct snub if they chose to hold it elsewhere. Besides, there was not much 'elsewhere' to be had in Appleton, apart from the pubs. The Ice Cream Shop wasn't quite right.

'It's just as well I haven't confronted Dominic yet, or mentioned the matter to Charlie,' Celia remarked, talking to Harry as guests arrived. Beth sat with Charles. Celia watched as he wiped a crumb from her lips. Harry nudged her as his parents walked in the door. The moment of reckoning was here. They looked as apprehensive as Celia felt. Harry whispered to her.

'Relax, they're all heart, you'll see.'

She wished she had met them earlier, as she felt herself swept up in their embrace. Aunt Eula came forward to greet them. When Harry made the introductions, she clasped their hands, nodding and smiling as she led them to their seats.

Celia stood, looking around at everyone who had stretched out a hand to steady her; loved and nourished her through the months of adjustments and uncertainty. Her speech was ready. She had so many to thank and much to be thankful for. Celia clutched her notes in her hand, walked to the podium and took the mic.

'You all know my story, the sorrow that threatened to drown

me.' She paused, taking a long breath to calm herself, then continued, her voice stronger. 'But I stayed afloat, and I'd like to thank those special people...and they're here tonight...those wonderful people who carried me through dark country when I first arrived. My cousin, my aunt, my stalwart friends, and my beautiful, patient Harry. Forgive me if I don't name all of you, let me just say...I love you... your names are etched into my heart. And a special "thank you" to my old friends, Sandy and Liam, who helped me survive until I got here.'

When Harry was ready to leave for Melbourne the looming separation was affecting them both. 'I promise you, I'll be fine.' Celia assured him. 'I've got work to do. Tomorrow, I'm meeting with people who are keen to discuss the fate of the theatre. I plan to do more bike riding while there's only me to cook for. I'll see you in a few days, it's not like you're going off to war, let's be thankful for that.' Harry calmed down as she walked with him to the car.

On the weekend of Trudie's christening Harry joined Celia at Sandy and Liam's house to play the godfatherly role.

'We managed. The days just flew by,' Celia told him. He gave a disgruntled snort.

'Hmph, they might have, for you. The week seemed interminable to me, I don't know which was worse, bootcamp or staying with my parents...felt like I was fifteen again.'

Celia laughed. Yes, maybe her week had been more enjoyable, but she didn't say that.

'I can't help thinking that godparents are irrelevant these days. What do you think, Harry?' Celia asked him when they were alone.

'Yes, Can you imagine if you took the side of a rebellious teenager...end of a beautiful friendship. Ritual and reality...two different things.'

On Sunday afternoon Harry entertained them with stories of his torturous training regime. They responded with much laughter and not much sympathy.

'What are you moaning about, man?' Liam said to him. 'Look at your body, I'd kill for a body like that.' He pulled up his sleeves to show his puny white arms.

'You could start with some push ups,' Sandy told him. 'Or join the pram brigade and jog along the waterfront while Celia and I do some serious retail therapy.'

Liam took her up on that. Sandy gave him a hug. 'You'll do,' she said.

Celia returned to Geelong soon after Trudie's christening when Sandy's mother said she needed respite. Harry had told her he would be posted to Geelong if he completed the course successfully. He'd explained it was customary to send members of the SAR to major policing centres to gain experience. Secondly, while deployed on SAR work their absence could be covered more easily.

Celia had been a little disconcerted to hear this, but his next words had given her a small measure of reassurance. He'd learned that his home patch was currently under review. Pressure was mounting from various quarters for the South West to be adequately manned. Celia thought perhaps this had given further weight to Harry's application.

While helping Sandy adjust to first-time motherhood, Celia

decided to look for a suitable unit. She called a couple of agents and inspected one possibility.

Located near a park, it was a generic one of four with two bedrooms, freshly painted throughout. Good enough. Celia was aware that discussing Harry's situation had helped her secure the rental on a month to month basis. The agent was happy to grant her a lease if she signed the agreement, effective from the coming Saturday.

'Oh, well, why wouldn't he be happy?' she said to Sandy.

'At least there's a lawn at the front.'

Sally was finally planning a week off and Celia must now make good on her promise to run the shop. The added task of sifting through job applications was another new experience for her. She had never been in a position to interview anyone for a job.

How would she begin, she wondered. Perhaps she should consult with Eula, she'd started a plant nursery when she was first married. Harry had been no help. They were at Frank and Magda's house when she asked him for his thoughts on the procedure.

All he'd said was, 'Watch out for people with pink-rimmed eyes, they're either aliens or drug addicts.'

'You're a shocker, Harry Bolitho, I should report you to the bias police.'

Magda had the best advice. 'Go with your gut,' she said, although she had clenched her hand over her heart.

Frank's approval of Harry was evident and Celia told him she was touched by his generosity regarding her new relationship. The ashes and the painting of Eddy and Clive were left with Frank for safekeeping. The painting had moved him deeply.

'I'm surprised at the liveliness that Yvette has captured, it has a feeling of joy about it,' he told her. 'And it brings a smile through my tears.'

Celia whittled the ten applications down to four and finally chose a motherly woman in her mid fifties named Annika, who was an expert with Dutch poffertjes.

An inspired choice, Sally had later told her. 'Annika's poffertjes are a big hit.' It was Celia who then suggested a name change.

'The menu is reflecting more than ice cream, Sal, and the outdoor dining area is a real winner, maybe you need a name to match. We've had requests for small functions; birthdays, anniversaries and business lunches.'

Always ready to embrace new ideas, Sally had been quick to respond. She suggested a competition among family and friends to brainstorm a new name. It was Marcus McFadden who came up with the winning entry. *'Piccalilli Parlour'*, with the by-line below. *Light meals and ice cream delights.*

For his trouble he received a bottle of wine and a complimentary dinner for two at Dominic's restaurant. Marcus was moving to Melbourne in the name of love but assured Celia that distance would not be a barrier. He would still be able to look after her financial requirements if her theatrical venture ever got off the ground.

Before Celia took her own extended break from work at The Ice Cream Shop, Mavis made another of her baffling declarations. With hands on hips she raised her gravelly voice.

'Sikhs and beaks and winter blues, tongues that speak conflicting views...,' Mavis trailed off, as if fearful of divulging any further veiled prophecies still brewing in her head. Celia swept a hand through her hair and stared, watching Mavis hurriedly depart.

Not long after that unsettling announcement Celia packed her car with the essentials and moved to the partly furnished unit in Geelong. Liam had scrounged a double bed and a trestle table. She transferred money and sent him off to IKEA to buy flat-packs.

Harry came from Melbourne for a night or two when his schedule permitted. Unfortunately, he was not there when Celia welcomed Charles and Eula for a weekend stay.

She had no spare beds so they'd brought their own blow-up mattresses. Celia felt humbled by the nurturing that Eula lavished on her, not least by way of her culinary contributions. Celia remarked on the number of large people who mooched around in the nearby shopping mall.

'Beefy men in checked shirts and beanies, women in tight lycra, bra-less and broadbeamed. It made me realise I could be heading the same way, indulging in too many chocolate sundaes at Piccalilli. It's time to take action. Healthy salads for me before my hip handles get beyond the breadth of Harry's hand, so please, Aunt Eula, could you keep that in mind next time you visit.' Eula shrugged her shoulders.

'We could all do with losing a few kilos. Charles, you're looking a mite too chubby these days.'

'Speak for yourself, mother dear,' Charlie replied, while he helped himself to a second slice of fruit cake. Aunt Eula chose to wash the dishes and suggested that her son could do with a walk.

Celia spoke with Charlie as they strolled around her new neighbourhood. She told him she suspected she might be pregnant.

'Celie, that's great news, I hope you're right...' he trailed off, a concerned look on his face.

'I'm sure it will be fine, Charlie, don't look so worried. Just keep it to yourself for the moment. I'm planning to keep up my running routine. There are some lovely green spaces quite close by, though I really miss the parklands in Appleton.'

'How is Beth these days? I presume that you two are still commuting?'

Charlie sighed. 'Yes, but not often enough in Beth's opinion. I try to make it once a month, but it's a challenge.. I think she's hooked on the drama of the political environment, even though she denies it.'

'Beth's in denial about a lot of things, Charlie, she has no clear picture of who she is or what she wants. You might have to wait for her to grow up.'

'Oh, I'll wait. I'm a patient man.'

The change in location had the advantage of situating Celia closer to Summerleigh. Her mother's health had declined in the last twelve months, she no longer recognised anyone.

Celia was there for Ruth on the day she died. She sat with a multitude of emotions in Ruth's room on a wintry day in June, thinking about her mother's difficult life and trying to process these matters of life and death. The child in her womb would never know this grandmother.

It had been truly surprising for Celia to watch Harry's reaction when she told him her pregnancy had been confirmed. He was completely overcome, he could say nothing as he swept her up, burying his head into her ear, until she complained.

'Hey, you're drenching my shirt, and dribbling down my neck.'

He had laughed at that as she handed him a box of tissues. Gwen was kinder to Celia after her move to Geelong, helping her with funeral arrangements while at the same time making it clear how dutiful she had been in Celia's absence. Frank and Magda came across on the ferry for Ruth's funeral and Harry was given a day's compassionate leave. They were thrilled that Celia was pregnant. The sad occasion of Ruth's passing provided the chance to reconnect with her brothers and their children. Her pregnancy lightened the mood and gave everyone something to talk about.

Heavy rain woke Celia one grey Sunday. She was enjoying her mid morning coffee when someone knocked at her door. Celia answered the knock, still in her dressing gown. A small Indian boy stood in the doorway staring up at her. He introduced himself. 'Hello, madam, I am Dilip Singh.'

Rain bounced off the eaves onto the scrap of cloth covering his thick black top knot. He thrust a container into her hands.

'My mother wishes you to have this curry.' He looked up at her and smiled, then rummaged in his backpack and located a package of naan bread. 'And this too. Welcome to our block.'

With that pronouncement he gave a sudden little bow, as precise as his accent and scurried away before Celia had time to complete a thank you. She would call on his mother as soon as she made herself presentable.

The lady who answered Celia's knock was the most beautiful woman Celia had ever met. Her skin was flawless, and her lustrous brown eyes reflected an intelligent presence. Her knee length skirt was a bright floral and she wore a pink finely knitted pullover, the lower band sitting snugly at her slim waist. Celia felt dowdy in her faded jeans and polo top. Before she had time to speak Dilip's mother reached out to her in a modest embrace and introduced herself.

'Hello, you're my new neighbour, I know, I've seen you these past few weeks. My name is Jassi Kaur, K-A-U-R, I always need to spell it. Please, come inside, we'll take tea, if you would like.'

The boy took Celia's hand as she finally managed to say her own name. He led her into the sweet smelling living room, the fragrant aroma of curry blended with incense burning at a small shrine against the far wall. Celia wandered over for a closer look. Jassi brought tea and spiced cookies on a tray.

They sat at the dining table and Celia asked about the significance of the shrine. Jassi explained to her the finer points of Sikhism.

'We pay homage to our founder, Guru Nanak, and the more well known Guru, Gobind Singh, who formalised the Sikh religion. It's founded on the principles of freedom, equality and justice and we believe in one God.'

'Oh, I see.' Celia was unsure how to respond until she remembered a boy at university. 'I had a friend once who told me every Sikh is a Singh but not every Singh is a Sikh. You said your surname is Kaur, how does that work?'

'Yes,' Jassi said. 'All females are named Kaur, part of gender equality. Five hundred years ago Gobind Singh freed us from the rigid caste system. All Sikh males were to adopt the name, Singh, meaning lion, and women use the name, Kaur, meaning princess.

'Oh, wow, that's so enlightened,' Celia replied.

Jassi continued speaking as Dilip played with Lego blocks at her feet.

'The men wear turbans,' Jassi appeared to enjoy enlightening

Celia, 'which were once worn only by the elite, but the Guru wished us to see all men as noble.' She gave a satisfied smile.

Celia was intrigued that such wisdom had come about so long ago, yet in this modern twenty-first century women still did not have equality.

'I like the sound of this, Tell me more.' They were interrupted as a tall turbaned man came through the front door. Jassi introduced him.

'This is my husband, Dev.' She smiled affectionately up at him. 'He's been working at the Gurdwara today, preparing food for those in need. Everyone is welcome, needy or not.' She gave a little laugh. 'People love our cooking, you must come.'

Dev shook Celia's hand and took a seat at the table. Addressing her, engaging her with his soft brown eyes, he made her feel special. 'Please, come and visit us here at home too, any time.' Celia felt the warmth of his nature wash over her. 'I'd love to come. Thank you.'

Celia explained why she was a recent neighbour and promised that she would bring her partner next time, when she hoped he would be here on a more permanent basis.

This family was a delight. Celia looked forward to seeing them again. She suddenly recalled the words Mavis had recited and realised perhaps it wasn't 'seeks' that Celia thought she had heard, but possibly Mavis had meant 'Sikhs.'

Not wanting to overstay her welcome Celia left her newfound friends in the early afternoon and walked the few paces to her unit. Before she could insert the key into the lock she heard a loud thud from the other side of the tall hedge forming the boundary.

A male voice was groaning. Celia hurried out onto the footpath and turned left to investigate. Looking down the next-door driveway she saw a middle-aged man in overalls standing on the top rung of a ladder, his hedge clippers had fallen onto the concrete below. Celia walked to retrieve them.

'Are you okay?' She passed the shears up to him.

'I'm fine,' the man replied in a terse voice. 'Just got a cramp in my thigh.' Celia nodded. 'Right, I'll be off then.' The man's tone had been distinctly hostile. She decided against introducing herself and walked quickly back to her unit. Celia couldn't help but wonder why someone would be trimming a hedge today, when showers had soaked the suburb since early morning. His hedge was glistening with recent raindrops. Celia had the impression he was up there for a good sticky beak, checking out the new tenant who was closest to his property.

CHAPTER 19

2005 — Birds and Bullies

Time was hanging heavily on Celia's hands in this small space. Apart from the usual chores there was only limited planning to mull over while the theatre was a ruin.

At the end of Harry's course he was posted to Geelong, as expected. Celia felt a surge of pride at his graduation, putting her fears about his new role to one side, happy that he was now able to resume normal life with her. Order and routine restored once more.

Constable Clare Cheung was staying in the house at Wombat Glade for a nominal rent. Sending a report on Jethro's wellbeing she confessed to being in love with the cat.

'Yes, he does have that effect on people,' Celia replied. 'I really miss him.'

Celia hated being away from Appleton. She wanted to be on the spot in case there were developments concerning the future of the theatre. In answer to her emails the council kept repeating that it would be a lengthy procedure. She had missed the last meeting with the lobby group. Charlie had attended and called to give her an update.

'Things are at a stalemate,' he said. 'If Ariti could be located and an arrest made, then there's a chance that the State could acquire the property, as you said. It's getting very frustrating, there are others who have also registered interest for their own purposes. It's going to be dicey, who wins and when.' Celia replied in disgust.

'Fat chance of finding the bugger, he could be anywhere. I bet he has a bagful of boltholes to bunker down in, he'll be laying lower than a legless lizard. And the time it's taking allows more punters in on the action.'

The following week Celia dropped a note into each of mailboxes at the front of the property, inviting her neighbours to a barbecue. As she stepped away Dilip Singh almost knocked her over. He tore into the driveway followed by two boys on bikes. He hid behind Celia. She could feel his fear as his breathing slowed.

The bikes came to an abrupt halt and the boys stared at her, obviously surprised. They couldn't have been more than eight or nine.

'Are you friends of Dilip?' she asked, and gave them a friendly smile, knowing full well they were not. The boys looked down at their sneakers, avoiding eye contact.

'Dilip, would you like an iced cordial?' Celia asked him. He looked up, nodding shyly.

'How about you two? I have some chocolates, it would be lovely if I could share with you.' Celia waited. She could see they were tempted, both uncertain what the other would do.

Celia pointed to her flat. 'I live just there.' She started to walk, holding Dilip's hand.

'Dilip will help me bring a tray. Would you do that for me?' He nodded again. 'Yes, madam.' The boys laughed. Celia turned her head towards them.

'We could sit over on the grass.' The boys stood holding their bikes as she opened her door. She heard them move behind her and turned to watch. Dumping their bikes on the edge of the lawn they sat cross-legged in the centre and whispered to each other.

Inside her unit she spoke to Dilip. 'I know they were trying to scare you. We'll just be friendly to the boys, there's nothing to be frightened of now.'

Bird calls filled the space as Celia laid out a rug and served cordial. Dilip offered the chocolates on a paper plate. 'How about we introduce ourselves? You can tell me...' A large black bird took their attention as it pooped on the grass in front of them. They all laughed. Celia took advantage.

'Lots of birds in this garden today, boys. Look, there's a little yellow honeyeater, can you see some more?' Dilip pointed to a black and white butcher bird, trilling to a mate.

'They're all different.' Celia was going into her schoolmarm mode. 'Red beaks, black beaks, yellow beaks. So, can you tell me what they have that is the same?'

Dilip piped up.

'They all have beaks.'

'That's right.'

'And feet.' The taller boy looked pleased with himself.

'And wings,' said the the smaller one.

'Yes, all different, with many bits the same too. Now, tell me your names, we all have different names, different bodies, but lots of bits are the same, just like the birds.'

Two of the neighbours that Celia already knew had replied to her invitation: Jassi and Dev, and a guy who'd introduced himself as Fletch, a tradie who reminded her of Clive. The fourth unit appeared to be unoccupied. Sandy and Liam would come with Trudie.

Outside the shopping mall Celia sat in her car, checking over her shopping list. The car radio was playing softly. Her ear picked up the sound of a favourite song introduced to her by her mother. The songs of Leonard Cohen had interspersed the fluctuating moods of her early teen years. Celia had preferred U2, Coldplay or the Red Hot Chilli Peppers and had been scornful of her mother's taste in music.

Birds seem to be unusually influential in my life lately, she mused as she turned up the volume and listened to the lyrics of *Bird on a Wire*. To Celia the song symbolised her own struggle. In the first months of her grief she had been conscious of living on a wire, an unsteady tightrope beneath her feet, threatening to topple her. Unlike the bird she had no wings...and suddenly Harry had come along to hold her, to catch her when she stumbled.

Today she felt a release from that unsteady high wire existence. The sharp edge of her sorrow was becoming smoother, like an aged river-stone; diluted to a gentle rill of tender remembrance. Celia turned the key in the ignition and the engine roared to life.

On the day of the barbecue the weather stayed favourable but the nosy neighbour next door decided to be a noisy one as well, the sound of his motor mower roared, disturbing their the peace. Dilip covered his ears.

Celia was quite sure the horrid little man was being deliberately vexatious. Perhaps she should have invited him. Maybe she would. Gesturing to Harry she pointed to the hedge and then to the table. He caught her meaning and nodded.

'It's not too late, is it?' she shouted, as he moved closer.

'We'll give it a shot,' he said, and together they walked around into the man's driveway. Waving and calling failed to attract his attention. He kept staring determinedly down at his rowdy mower.

Perhaps he really is deaf, Celia thought. She crossed the short distance between them and tapped his shoulder. He flicked her arm away impatiently. Harry strode across to him as Celia stepped back. 'Hello there.' Harry spoke loudly, 'I'm Harry, we've come to invite you over.'

The man glared defensively from one to the other, hesitated for a second, then gave a cursory kick to the mower as he reduced the throttle.

'This is Celia, we'd be very happy if you'd join us for a...' The man interjected,

'I won't be joinin' you for anythin', thanks all the same, got work to do.'

'Oh, that's a shame, maybe another time then.' Celia tried on her widest smile. 'Lovely to meet you, er...' but of course, she didn't know his name.

Harry and Celia walked back to their giggling guests. Liam turned away from his peephole in the hedge and laughingly commented. 'That went well.'

'Yeah, I thought so.' Harry grinned at him as he pinched a sausage from Liam's plate.

A short time later Jassi held her hand behind her ear and leaned into the group.

'Listen, can you hear that, no mower noise.'

Celia hoped the man had gone inside and couldn't hear their raucous laughter. Harry brought out his guitar and performed a few of his favourite melodies. When he launched into the iconic Men at Work number, 'I come from a land down under, where women glow and men chunder,' Dilip laughed so hard he cried, but he wasn't sure what 'chunder' meant. Harry put it delicately 'Well, you know when boys eat too many lollies, sometimes they...' He rubbed his belly and screwed up his face.

'Oh yes, oh yes.' Dilip got it.

On Monday evening Harry flopped onto the couch after work and put his arm around Celia.

'I know what's been eating our crabby neighbour,' he whispered. Celia turned towards him, frowning.

'What. You do? How come?'

'Mmm, that grabbed your attention,' he teased.

'Come on, tell me what you're talking about.'

'He turned up at the Station today, asking for me. Very subdued, he was.' Celia was frowning.

'Go on.' .

'He knew I was with the Police, said he saw me in uniform.' Celia was nodding, thinking the nosy old bugger wouldn't miss a trick.

'Right, and?'

'He's been scammed, chasing love online and losing a bundle. His depleted bank account trumped his embarrassment. He didn't get what he paid for...and whadda ya know...' Harry grinned. 'The little lady was a no show...three times, and he still didn't realise she probably didn't exist. Poor bugger. The Feds will deal with him.' Celia was making sympathetic noises. 'He's lonely, Harry. Do you know if he works?'

Harry kissed her cheek and ran his hand over her baby bump.

'He said he specialises in bespoke carpentry and fancy plaster finishes but he's not getting much work at the moment.'

'Mmm.' Celia looked thoughtful.

'It's tough, and he's getting on a bit. Did you get his number? He could be useful to know down the track.'

'I can ask him, we're mates now, his name's Renzo, why do you want to know?'

'Really? Renzo?' Celia looked amused.

'Yeah, short for Lorenzo, I'm guessing.' Celia answered his question.

'The theatre came to mind. The lobby group keep me in the loop, they've sent photos of the smoke damage in the foyer.'

In late September Harry was notified that he would be returned to Appleton, probably sometime in November. Celia had been away from home for three months. Another two months in Geelong, away from the town she'd grown to love was a frustrating prospect. Not least because her pregnancy would be well advanced, but also because she was itching to get on with matters concerning her grand plan. She wanted to be with the people close to her heart. And some that were not.

'Keep your friends close and your enemies closer, isn't that how it goes?'

'Yeah, something like that.' Harry answered absently. He was studying a training manual and told her that he would be joined in Appleton by another graduate after Christmas. During the past two months they had worked together, winching fishermen from boats in trouble, locating injured hikers who'd fallen from steep cliffs. The most recent call-out involved abseiling to reach a woman wedged in boulders in the Grampians.

'That was a tricky one,' Harry told Celia. 'When we reached her we had to send for the right equipment from a quarry fifty kilometres away... a heavy duty mallet and stone cracking chisels. That's why we were there all night, working by headlamps. It was slow progress, we wrapped her in a blanket and covered her with a tarp as best we could to protect her from flying chips.'

Celia shuddered at the thought of it. She knew Harry loved the job, the challenge of it, but she was ambivalent about it and Harry became more precious to her every time he returned from one of these missions.

Tonight Celia was hungry and impatient, trying to enlarge the waistband on a pair of trousers. Dinner was simmering in the crockpot and Harry was late. Too hungry to wait, she set aside her sewing and moved awkwardly to the small kitchen, her ankles feeling stiff and puffy. The moment she put spoon to bowl she heard the front door open.

Harry came striding across the room. He greeted her, kissing the back of her neck, excitedly spinning her to him. Removing the bowl from her hand he placed it on the bench.

'Time for that later. I've got something to show you.'

'Can't it wait, Harry, I'm starving. Where have you been?' Taking her face in his hands Harry chuckled.

'You'll never guess. Come with me, my love. Wait 'til you see. This'll make you smile.'

With a sigh, Celia swallowed two mouthfuls of the thick minestrone and joined him in the spare room. The computer murmured and the screen brightened as Harry slid himself from the only chair and gestured to her.

'You'll need to be sitting down.' he said, gleefully. He knelt and rapidly tapped at the keyboard.

'Barnesy sent this.' he said, as he adjusted the screen. Celia stared hard and focused on the words in front of her. The article was written in English but looked to be from a French publication.

'In a small bay off the coast of Corsica a yacht with Greek registration sailed into trouble and foundered on a well known stretch of saw-toothed rocks. When maritime safety officials boarded the vessel they discovered the captain, identified as Dimitri Ariti, had suffered a fractured skull. At this time he was travelling on an Australian passport, although officials seized several fake documents in the process of their search. He and his crew have been detained in Corsica, pending further investigation. An Interpol alert had been issued, Australian police sources confirmed. His cargo included five kilos of cocaine and further amounts of other illicit drugs were found secreted in the vessel.'

The article's headline read, *'Coke on the rocks!'* Celia could barely speak for laughing, cackling like a mad woman. 'Oh, that's hilarious! How crazy is this?' she spluttered.

In its mysterious way the ocean had tossed up their quarry into splendid view like a slug in a green salad. Harry's eyes gleamed.

'The tide is turning!' he exclaimed. extending the palm of his hand to her. She slapped him a hi-five and he jumped up, exuberantly punching the air.

'He'll be extradited, eventually.' he said. Celia was shaking her head.

'Divine intervention, no less. My faith's restored.'

They sat over dinner, marvelling at the peculiar forces that ebbed and flowed in their own good time.

'The wheels of justice need a squirt of lubricant to bring this bugger home,' Harry predicted.

The news that Ariti had been flushed out by the foibles of nature gave Celia the most delicious sense of poetic piquancy, so palpable she could almost taste it.

Trying to sleep that night her thoughts alternated between Ariti's downfall and the preparations she needed to make for her return home and ready for the birth. Harry would soon follow.

She had planned to call on Renzo, her now more amenable neighbour, according to Harry, but decided a visit from her might embarrass him so she left him a friendly note instead.

Jethro purred with pleasure when Celia arrived home on the following Monday. Eula was there, helpful as always. Celia breathed a sigh of contentment.

Sally hosted a private baby shower at Piccalilli Parlour. The party was well under way when Mavis arrived apologising for her lateness. She presented her gift. When Celia opened the box a child sized tiara blinked at her from its bed of satin lining; a shimmering silver adornment, arrow tipped and dotted with amethyst stones.

'Oh, it's beautiful, Mavis. A girl! I'm having a baby girl?' Celia stared at Mavis. 'How can you be sure?'

'Sterling silver with fine stones aglow, wouldn't spend the money if I didn't know. Wild and free, bold and curious, sometimes furious, this little Archer will be a she.'

Celia was dumbfounded. Loud clapping and whoops of joy resounded through the room as Mavis's gift was passed from hand to hand.

The fate of the damaged theatre was still unknown. Celia was sitting with a group of supporters at the last meeting for the year and feeling the frustration. The prolonged delay was causing further deterioration inside the building. Lamenting the lack of progress, the group voted to hold a public protest at the end of January if the council didn't start to implement a clean-up.

Two days after Harry's birthday he was required to take part in a three day bivouac. It was only three hours after his departure when Celia felt the first contractions. She called Charlie in a state of disbelief.

'This is not going to plan, Charlie,' she screamed, as another contraction sent her into a panic, and sent Charlie speeding to deliver her to the hospital. Baby Nancy plummeted through the birth canal three weeks early.

Harry had missed the birth. Celia knew just how disappointed he'd felt. It was something he deeply regretted, but nobody could do a thing about it...a contrary universe orchestrating their lives, as Celia told him more than once. Now it was a fractious new baby orchestrating their lives. Nancy suffered with colic until Celia discovered *Infants Friend;* the mixture was a godsend.

Much to Celia's surprise, guitar music; in particular, Spanish Flamenco, suffused Nancy's body with rhythm. Celia watched, fascinated, as Nancy lay in her cot nodding her head back and forth in time with the beat. Her little fists balled up and bounced on her covers. Nancy's fondness for rhythm prompted Celia to ponder a future for her in the dramatic arts.

CHAPTER 20

2005–2006 — Kinetic Energies

On Christmas Eve a storm broke as Harry and Celia were decorating their tree. Thunder rumbled before heavy rains filled the gutters to overflowing. Jethro took refuge under the couch. Celia was sitting on the floor untangling the Christmas lights, quietly reflecting on the changes that the year had brought.

'It's been quite a year for us. You have a new job and we have a baby girl. I still find it amazing. When I came to Appleton I never would have guessed that I'd feel joy again.' Celia looked up at Harry. 'Even in my saddest moments, losing my mother, thinking of Clive and Eddy, in spite of it all, I feel privileged. It occurred to me only recently that the fire at the theatre was a fortunate thing for me. If it hadn't happened I doubt that I would have met you. Is that a weird, incongruous thought?' Harry contemplated her words for a moment. 'Not so weird, I can think of a more wretched one. We may have eventually met in the aged care home without ever knowing what could have been.'

'Oh, Harry, that's a disturbing and dreadful thought!' Celia threw up her hands in mock horror. She reached out to him. He pulled her up from the floor, embracing her, whispering words of gratitude in her ear.

'Thank our lucky stars we found each other when we did.' he said, as he placed a glittering star at the top of the tree.

Christmas lunch would be a subdued affair this year. Charlie and Beth arrived on time. When Celia asked,

'What have you done with my lovely aunt?' Charlie said, 'Oh, yes, of course.' He said he must have muddled the arrangements, he thought his mother wanted to drive over. Hurriedly they left again. Charlie seemed to misplace his wits when Beth was around, Celia thought, but she was thankful for a brief respite and turned the oven temperature down before collapsing into her favourite chair while Nancy slept.

She drifted on waves of fatigue, not quite asleep, her thoughts taking her back to her time on The Great South West Walk. How long ago that seemed, when her loss was still raw and she was an angry traveller.

Walking in nature had given her a deeper understanding of the hugeness and wonder of things outside of herself. She wanted to do that walk again; a much longer version next time in the company of Harry... and Nancy too, when she was older, and could walk on her own two feet.

Harry had been called out in the early hours in response to major flooding along the highway and Celia wasn't sure that he'd be back in time for lunch. She stirred from her sleepiness. Harry's voice was calling her. When she managed to drag herself out of the chair it took a moment to locate him. He was under the carport, calling to her through the kitchen window. She stumbled to the back door and saw that he was almost naked.

'Didn't have you pegged as a flasher, Harry,' she admonished, pokerfaced, just as Charlie drove up and flashed his headlights. Eula, Beth and Isobel scrambled from the car, their laughter ringing in the rafters.

'Bring me some dry clothes please, sweetheart, I'm drenched to my underpants.' Harry entreated. Feigning false modesty he made a grab for the mop, the nearest thing at hand, and held it strategically in front of him. That sent the onlookers into shrieking hysterics. Harry ran with the mop to hide in front of his car. Charlie led the chase. Celia ran to gather some dry clothes.

They were still giggling when they sat down to eat, wanting to know about Harry's morning.

'I fell out of the dinghy, yeah, SES volunteers were manning it, we were pulling a bloke into it. He'd come off his motorbike. Water was flowing fast, the force of it washed him down the road and into a drain. I reckon the side of the dinghy deflated and I tumbled out. That's my story.'

'Sure, Harry, we believe you.' Charlie winked. Eula piped up over the laughter, 'Seriously, of course we believe you. Why wouldn't we?'

On a hot and steamy morning at the end of December Nancy was having fun in her bath tub. Celia splashed the barely warm water over her tummy. As Nancy's eyes locked onto her mother's face Celia smiled at her precious baby girl. Her thoughts rebounded to the events around this time last year when she had been hospitalised after that fateful shower. She shook her head to cast off the memory.

Beside her on the bathroom cupboard her mobile rang. Quickly she scooped Nancy onto the change table. Her hands were too damp to answer. She saw that the call was from Harry and grabbed a towel. She managed to answer when it rang a second time.

'Hi, I had wet hands and the phone didn't like it,' she said. Harry spoke.

'Glad I got you. I'm likely to be late tonight. Dominic Romano is stuck in a creek bed with a boulder pinning his arm.' Before Celia had time to process what Harry had just said he went on.

'His new girlfriend is with him, they were camping up near the Big Shot lookout. We're on our way to the site now. The para's are just ahead of us.'

'A boulder? Oh, my God, Harry! I don't wish him any harm, do what you have to do. I'll wait for further news.'

A cobweb above the bathroom window drifted across the glass, agitated by the movement of air as Celia flicked open the towel and patted Nancy dry. Celia pondered the cobweb, its broken strands reminding her of the tenuous relationships that existed between human beings. She was startled from her thoughts of love, friendship and betrayal by the ringing of the front doorbell.

When she answered the door the aroma of cinnamon and apple wafted through the hallway. Aunt Eula had brought morning tea. Celia made a pot of coffee. She gestured to her aunt to take a seat. As Nancy suckled contentedly at Celia's breast she shared the news of Dominic's accident.

'We'll have to wait for details. I imagine it will be a late night. I'll call you in the morning. Charlie probably hasn't heard, could you let him know?' Eula nodded as she cut into her freshly baked slice. She laid the knife aside and set a plate in front of Celia.

' I met the girl, Dominic's new girl I mean, only about a week ago. She seemed a capable sort.'

Celia confided her disenchantment with Dominic of late and the reason for that.

'I hope he's okay, but if he's in a creek bed it doesn't sound good. I don't think he's aware that I know what he's been up to, competing with me on the sly for control of the theatre. It gave me a nasty feeling, and it needs to be discussed out in the open.' Eula was nodding her head in agreement.

'If he survives,' Eula murmured. Suddenly her voice rose, 'That boy confounds me sometimes. Impetuous, never stopping to consider the outcome. Well, a boulder seems to have stopped him now, I wonder what he was doing for that to happen.'

After lunch Celia napped on the couch. In spite of a gnawing concern about Dominic on two counts; his well-being and the resentment she harboured towards him, she managed to fall asleep.

She was woken when Charlie's car pulled into the carport. Celia guessed he'd heard from Eula.

'I've been trying to call you.' he said, anxiety creasing his face.

'Sorry, Charlie I was asleep.' Celia brewed more coffee and brought the remaining apple slices from the fridge. She told him she'd not heard anything further but he seemed in no hurry to leave. He said there'd been another surprising development that was likely to impact his life big time. 'What are you saying, are you sick?'

'Oh, no, nothing like that.'

'Well, hurry up and tell me before Nancy wakes.'

'You know I'd given up the paternity thing.' Celia sat up straight in her chair, her eyes fixed on his face.

'It came right out of the blue,' he said. 'A resemblance to me in her daughter's features and hair colouring...her brother-in-law in gaol for the next fifteen years. According to my lawyer, Lauren couldn't handle the thought that her child might be the result of rape by that murderer, so she took a punt. And lucky for all of us that she did. Isobel is my daughter.' Celia jumped up and ran to him, both of them too overcome to speak.

When Charlie recovered himself he said that Isobel would be coming to him every weekend, more often if Lauren wasn't coping. His daughter was now three years old and Charlie had to make up for lost time.

*   *   *

Harry was driving the patrol car at breakneck speed along the highway, siren blaring. Next to him the second member of the Search and Rescue Unit sat clutching the strap of his seatbelt, his chest heaving with a mixture of exhilaration and the fear of looming disaster.

He breathed out through pursed lips when Harry suddenly slewed to the right to take a side road, hardly more than a track and a rough one at that. It was impossible to maintain any decent speed as they dipped and flipped in and out of the desiccated potholes impacting their progress.

'You ok, Jace?' Harry asked him.

'Fine, I'm fine,' Jace replied, somewhat defensively.

'Do you know Dominic?'

'Not really, I've seen him at his restaurant. Do you reckon he'll be alright?'

'We'll soon find out,' Harry said as he drove up a steep slope and sailed down onto a more or less level strip of land.

A tent and a couple of caravans were visible in the distance. An ambulance was parked close to the camp area. As they headed across the field a woman in shorts and T-shirt scrambled from the edge where the land fell away. She stood for a moment outlined against the sky then ran towards them.

Harry stopped the car and lowered his window as she drew level. Breathing in ragged gasps she introduced herself.

'Hello, I'm Grace, Dominic's friend.' Harry introduced himself and Jace.

'I gather the paramedics are with him. What's his condition? Do you know?' he asked her.

'Not great, they've given him pain relief, he's barely conscious, dislocated shoulder, possible broken ribs, almost certainly a fractured left arm. Could be more than one break but the boulder has trapped his arm, they can't shift it. Luckily there's not much water in the creek.' Harry thanked her as he edged the car forward.

'Wait,' Grace called out, 'the path down to the creek is to the right. Be careful, that's where Dominic slipped, trying to retrieve my undies. It's all shale and stones. He dislodged the boulder on his way down and it followed him.'

They heeded Grace's warning, picking their way down the incline and across the shallow creek to join the paramedics. Harry took in Dominic's ashen face. Thermal blankets had been wrapped around him. An inflated pillow held his head above water and away from the stony creek bed. He appeared to be out to it, which was just as well, Harry thought.

'We'll need a tractor and rope to move this bastard,' Harry said, 'the rock, I mean.'

'Yeah, the quicker, the better,' one of them replied.

'Jace, get back to the car and radio in for a take on the nearest farm. Tell them to inform the SES. We need them here as well. See if they've got a heavy vehicle with enough grunt.'

It was after midnight when Harry arrived home. Celia was tucking Nancy into her cot. She looked up expectantly as Harry entered the room, fearful of what she might read in his face.

'Dominic's in bad shape,' Harry said and breathed a deep sigh. Whether from relief or exhaustion Celia couldn't tell. Probably both, she thought. She pulled him close.

'I've made soup. Come and sit down. Tell me the worst while I warm it for you.'

'Thanks, I'm ready for it.' Harry sat at the table and described the scene.

'It got complicated. The tractor arrived on our side of the creek. Access was too steep. The SES firetruck arrived on the opposite side but it took an extra half hour for the tractor to get around there. The business of roping that bloody boulder and moving it was a nightmare. I can't begin to describe the noise. Engines revving to the max and Dominic screaming blue murder. It was gut wrenching. In the end they managed to raise it enough for the paras to get Dominic out from under..' Harry sighed again and ran his fingers through his hair.

'Here, have your soup, just tell me...where is he now?' Celia asked. She placed her arm around his shoulder and kissed his cheek. She could feel the tension in his tired muscles.

'He's here in the hospital on a morphine drip. I've just come from there. They'll be sending him to Geelong for surgery when his condition is stable. He's conscious, more or less, and kept repeating that he wants to see you.' Celia frowned. 'Is he delirious?' Harry smiled.

'Who knows?'

Celia was sending text messages updating Charlie and Eula. 'You need a massage,' she said, when she'd finished.

Dust motes danced in the cast of a moonbeam shining from the high bedroom window. An owl momentarily diffused the moonlight as it flew close to peer at the inhabitants. Harry murmured with pleasure as Celia smoothed the fragrant oil into his tired muscles.

'When should we go? she asked him.

'Go where?' Harry was almost asleep.

'To see Dom, of course.'

'Oh, before he's moved to Geelong, too far to make a special trip there at the moment...so early tomorrow would be best.'

The visit to Dominic didn't eventuate in the way they'd planned. Nancy woke early, pale and sobbing. Something was clearly not right. Celia took her temperature and watched as the indicator climbed above normal range. Celia called the Medical Centre to book an appointment. Quickly she warmed a bottle for Nancy. It was seven minutes to nine and the day was not starting well.

Nancy was sleeping in her carry cot as Celia headed home. Her temperature had returned to normal by the time they left the clinic. The doctor concluded that Nancy very likely had an ear infection. She advised Celia to apply warm and cold compresses with mild pain relief if necessary. Celia pulled over and called Harry.

'I was about to call you,' he said. 'We can see Dominic, if you want. Patient transport won't be available until later.'

Celia's face registered her shock when she saw Dominic. She stared open mouthed. His pale face was the colour of a dirty snowball. Propped up with his injured arm on two pillows and his shoulder strapped, he looked a sorry sight. Purple and black bruising was creeping up his neck. It made her wince.

He opened his eyes as Harry placed Nancy in her carry cot beside his bed. Celia quickly rearranged her face into what she hoped was a convincing smile.

'Well, just look at you,' she said.

'Hi Celia, Harry. I'd rather be looking at you two. Don't think I want to know what I look like. Thanks for coming… and Harry, it goes without saying I'm grateful to you and the guys, getting me out of that cold creek. Lifting that bloody rock off me, don't know how you managed it. Thought I was a goner. Bloody good effort. Now, before those ambos arrive, I need to man up to you, Celia.' Dominic took a sad, shallow breath. They could both see he was hurting.

'I was a sneaky bastard, I applied to the council for the lease on the theatre and I'm really sorry I did that, going behind your back, it was a low act. When I was lying there, pinned under a rock like an insignificant insect, my life didn't appear very worthy. I didn't like the way I was living it.' Dominic looked down and twitched at his sheet with the fingers of his good hand.

'Yes, Dom, I've been waiting for you to tell me about that. I'm pleased you've finally come clean.' Celia took his hand in hers and smiled reassuringly. 'Seems that boulder brought you down to earth in more ways than one.'

Nancy stirred in her carry cot as the paramedics entered the room. 'How did you know?' Dominic asked her.

'A story for another time,' she told him. Poor Dom, he looked as tired as a worn-out rug and just as flat. He raised his good hand in a feeble salute as they wheeled him away.

*   *   *

In the beginning Charlie told them he hadn't been sure how this new person coming into his life would impact on Beth. Their relationship had been turbulent, made the more difficult by distance. He had come to rely on Celia to help him navigate the upsetting disturbances.

'It's just so unpredictable,' he would tell her. Very often, Celia tried to dissuade him. On one particular occasion she had quizzed him, 'If Beth is continually making your life a misery, Charlie, why do you persist?'

'I can't resist her, Celia, she's cast a spell over me.'

'Rubbish, Charlie, maybe you like being unhappy. Do you like being a martyr?' Her sharp rebuke hit home.

It was not long before Charlie confided to Celia that he was seeing a counsellor. He would not be taking trips to Canberra for the time being. Beth's trips to Appleton were few, while Charlie focused on learning to be a good father.

Everyone had been elated when Charlie told them he was the father of Isobel, and no-one more so than Eula.

'A grandchild!' She was so thrilled. 'How extraordinary!'

At first, Isobel was a girl of few words. Charles and Eula spoke to Celia about it, they thought she was too quiet, troubled perhaps. They were mistaken. Within weeks she was exhausting them with her constant chatter. Her many questions often left them floundering for an answer, and her obsession with doing cartwheels was mesmerising.

*   *   *

Finding the right time to marry Harry was proving difficult. Andy McConnell was waiting for them to make the trip to Scotland.

Celia's pregnancy had been too advanced to contemplate plane travel in the September of 2005, the time she had nominated as a possible marriage date. Plans were now firming up for an April wedding.

Three weeks before the appointed day Celia had not found a suitable outfit. She was about to order an ensemble from the tailor who had made Harry's vest, but a lucky find at Marvellous M Vintage Clothing saved her the trouble. She was out for a stroll, pushing Nancy in her pram, when she saw a beautiful cream sleeveless dress with a matching short jacket displayed in the window.

Mavis told her that it had come from a design house in Adelaide where it had never been collected. When she took Harry to see it he was impressed.

'Yes, that's the one, it's perfect, the tiny seed pearls around the neckline are just enough,' he assured her. 'It reminds me of something that Jackie Kennedy might have worn.'

'You would think that, wouldn't you, retro man, but yes, I think you're right.'

A small tuck in the side seams of the bodice was all that was needed, and voila! Problem solved. A cream pill box hat with matching seed pearls stitched here and there, and a pair of low heels with a pearly patina completed her wedding attire.

They were married by a celebrant, a plump lady in crumpled linen, at their home in Wombat Glade. Celia finally felt comfortable saying that: our house, our place. Bradley didn't make it from the west, but Gwen and Nathan were there. Harry's parents and his brother travelled to Appleton for the occasion. They stayed at a B&B as the Paynters were with the Bolitho household.

This time Sandy was Matron of Honour. Celia had been curious about Harry's well travelled brother, Tim, the once troubled youth; a loose canon, according to Harry. Tim acted as Harry's best man.

She thought he was friendly enough in a constrained sort of way, and slightly effeminate. She suspected he might be gay. Harry had never mentioned it. She wondered if the thought had crossed his mind. Surely he would have said.

Beth had arrived from Canberra the day before, vivacious as ever, although Celia noted that Charlie had a wary look about him for most of the day, as did Jethro.

The catering for a light luncheon was shared between Sally and Eula. Dominic had insisted on supplying the wedding cake. The guests dined at Capers restaurant later in the evening. Officers from the Appleton Police Station had increased in number and there were five attending, including Sergeant Barnes, who took part in a 'roast', an exaggerated litany of Harry's most notable exploits and humiliating moments.

Sergeant Barnes recalled the time when Harry had slid down a muddy embankment in pursuit of a suspect and they both ended up sinking in quicksand at the edge of a lake. The suspect, later proving to be an innocent greyhound trainer, plucked his whistle from his top pocket and used it to attract the attention of a local farmer.

This story prompted loud clapping and roars of laughter. On a more serious note the guests applauded when they heard how Harry had talked a distraught young man out of electrocuting himself astride the top of a power pole near the Anglican church. 'Harry nearly toppled over the edge of the cherry picker,' Barnesy said.

He ended with the details of the latest complicated rescue, saying, 'As a result of Dominic's gallant gesture, running helter-skelter down the bank to retrieve his girlfriend's underwear, he ended up squashed under a boulder, scuppered like a trapped salmon in a cold stream.'

Dominic's girlfriend looked a little uncomfortable as Barnesy brought his comments to a close. Grabbing her hand Dominic brought her to the front, directing his gaze to her, 'No hard feelings.' he said as he kissed her cheek. Several guests nudged each other and giggled knowingly.

'Oh, that was not what I meant, you bawdy lot.' Bursts of clapping and laughter echoed around the room. Dominic raised his hand. As the applause faded he thanked his rescuers for his survival and gave an exaggerated bow.

Celia was touched when Robert Schofield took the floor and lavished praise on her for the help she had given him after his accident. His career as a performer and puppeteer could only have come about because of the confidence that grew from Celia's belief in him, he said. And he was confident, she could see, as he stood there addressing the audience. He was a young man going places.

While coffee was being served Celia took Dominic aside, asking if she could have a word. He took her arm. 'Bring your coffee, we'll go to my office where it's quiet.' When they were seated Dom looked at her expectantly.

'I was wondering if you'd consider joining forces with me.' Celia stated. Dominic sat back in his chair and raised his eyebrows in surprise.

'I know you wanted the theatre to become your next big catering adventure, but I'm convinced that Appleton needs a showpiece, a stage for a variety of entertainment, our own theatre company to bring plays, musicals, comedy... that's where you could shine, Dom. It would embrace the whole community. I haven't forgotten it's going to be a slow process but I'm determined to give it my best shot. If we present a united front to the Council it won't be so easy for them to sideline us and we need to scare off the opposition. I can see an opportunity for you to hold intimate dining experiences in one of the rooms adjoining the foyer. In the other you could install a kitchen. They're quite large.'

Celia saw a flicker of interest in his eyes now. She put it to him that he could promote local product.

'Cut a deal with the wineries in the region, the fruit growers, cheesemakers, truffle snufflers, artisans in the foodie world. No doubt you know some of these people already. Take it to the next level, cultivate your clientele... business owners, community groups, sporting clubs, anyone who holds meetings. And anyone else who fancies themselves as cultural elites. They'd love it. There's just a couple of things I would stipulate. The first: run any interior decorating ideas past me.' Dominic burst out laughing.

'And the second?'

'We draw up a formal agreement between us.' There was a short silence as he contemplated her serious face. He breathed out and scratched his head.

'Mmm, I can see you've given this a lot of thought. I'm blown away by your generosity, Celia, knowing the selfish thing I did.'

'I'm not being generous, Dom, I'm being practical. I'd like you to work with me because you've got skills that would be of benefit to me. The playhouse that I have in mind will require catering too, not just on opening nights but during rehearsals for our own members and visiting performers when cast and crew, even parents, could do with a salad, wholesome snacks or hot soup and a sandwich. You don't have to give me an answer now, there's plenty of time for you to think about it. If there's any chance we can pull this off, two heads are better than one.'

'Thanks, Celia, It's an appealing proposition. Can I ask if you've forgiven me?'

Celia smiled at him. 'We'll see about forgiveness. I'm warming to the possibility. If you want to talk further about my suggestion, you'll have to wait until we come back from Scotland.'

CHAPTER 21

2006 — Manna from Heaven

Nancy proved to be immune to the discomforts of air travel. When she wasn't sleeping she guzzled her milk and crooned to the dull thrum of the engines. Singapore was an experience never to be repeated in Celia's view. Acrid smoky fumes polluted the air. In the oppressive heat fetid body odours intermingled with sundry spices. All the smells on the street conspired to unsettle Celia's last meal.

In contrast, Scotland was a whirlwind of wonderful times with Andy. Celia knew now how he could afford to be so generous. His family were whisky barons, the malt had permeated their nostrils, and their purses, for generations. Andy lived in the hamlet of Whim in a fortified manor house, a three hundred year old burnished stone building, with sentry boxes on each corner of the wall surrounding it.

The broad sweeping staircase at the entry led to four apartments, tastefully furnished in the best Scottish tradition, each one with a bedroom fit for a queen and a bathroom to match. In the sitting room next to an open fire Celia relaxed into one of two deep leather sofas where you could sit and take in the view.

Gazing across to the Pentland Hills Celia felt she had returned to a different time, imagining herself as a player in a Scottish drama. Yes, surely she had been cast in an episode of 'Monarch of the Glen'.

Andy took them to Edinburgh, forty minutes away. A visit to the University and to the Castle was followed by a tour through two distilleries part owned by his family.

It was heady stuff! The smell was enough to send Celia tipsy. The tastings sent Harry past tipsy to the verge of inebriated. There were gift shops and cafes, even a small theatre showing the history of the establishment. Celia was inspired. Talking to Andy that evening gave her a rush of ideas for her pet project. He assured her his money would be ready when she needed it.

'If my plan gets off the ground.' Celia gave him a dejected look.

'We've got to believe it will,' Andy replied, as he gave her a reassuring hug.

Celia couldn't wait to get home. Dominic was keen to have further discussion.

*   *   *

Soon after their return to Appleton Celia traded her Corolla and purchased a four year old station wagon. She felt a pang of nostalgia parting with her trusty old car. It had been a constant and solid presence in her life for ten years. She thought fondly of countless journeys, driving and dreaming, the fun of picnics and parties through carefree student days. How proud she'd been, loading a new baby into its embracing warmth. How sad she'd felt travelling alone towards an uncertain future in Appleton.

Shaking the past from her head she collected her new car from a dealer's garage where child restraints had been fitted. Slowly she nudged out onto the highway, pointing the immaculate Toyota Tarago in the direction of home where Harry would be waiting to inspect it.

During their time in Scotland Celia had spoken briefly to Harry about his brother. Harry had shrugged indifferently, acknowledging they hadn't been close in recent years. Celia thought she detected a hint of regret in his response.

Tonight she decided to broach the subject of Tim again. Over dinner Celia mentioned that she'd like to get to know her brother-in-law.

'Maybe you could ask him to visit us again. It could be a chance for you to spend time with him. I think it would be good for both of you.' Harry nodded.

'Yes, I haven't seen much of him.' After dinner Harry extended the invitation.

'Tim sounded keen. He said it would give him a break from the parents' domain.' Harry reported. 'He emphasised how good that would be for everyone.

The winter was interspersed with childhood ailments; Nancy sniffled her way through chilly days and grizzled through teething troubles and a case of flu. Even Harry was laid low. Somehow Celia avoided catching the nasty germ by avoiding him.

Harry's home remedy was to cover his head with a tea towel twice a day and breathe in the vapours of Vicks over a steaming bowl.

'Nothing snuffs the flame of romance quicker than a dose of the flu,' Celia said, giggling as she ran a hand under his dressing gown and up his bare leg. Harry turned, the tea towel flopping over his eyes as he reached out to grab her.

'Come on, baby, light my fire,' Harry sang in a husky voice. Celia dodged.

'Sorry, we'll have to let it smoulder this week.'

'Pfff,' Harry blew a miffed snort of defeat. 'The week's only just begun,' he wailed.

'Yep, that's right.'

*   *   *

The elusive Ariti had been returned to Australia. Celia conscientiously monitored every article concerning his arrest. His trial on several charges was scheduled to be heard before the end of the year.

A report printed in today's paper thrilled her. Strong evidence presented by Guy Stolz at his own committal hearing had turned suspicion into bold allegations.

Jumping from her chair she sent messages to members of the lobby group and called Dominic. That night Celia and Harry entertained supporters at home. With boisterous hilarity over too many drinks they took turns in reading the article aloud.

Guy had given explicit examples of the crimes he'd committed under instruction from Dimitri Ariti. He was quoted in the byline. 'There's no bull about it!'

Roaring in defiance Guy swore that Ariti had ordered him to burn down two properties in Appleton owned by his boss. Braying like a bloated donkey he dropped Ariti right where the state prosecutors wanted him.

A month after Guy's testimony a conviction for drug trafficking put Ariti behind bars for the foreseeable future. Arson charges were expected to come before a court at a later date.

Celia was sitting with Charlie at a hastily convened gathering. He told them that a city law firm had been advising Council. She listened in confused silence as the debate on ownership rights turned into pointless argument. Would the town benefit from the proceeds of crime? Disentangling the labyrinthine legal wrangles might take some time.

Whether in light of these developments or not, the Council decided to start on the clean-up of the damaged theatre. It had been almost three years since the fire and so long with no action that Celia was beginning to think her approaches to Council would come nothing. Was it worth the effort, expending time and energy on a long shot?

Dominic thought it was. After their third meeting he accepted Celia's terms. She watched him sign their private agreement, a little incredulous that he'd capitulated with barely a whimper.

Their roles would intersect when the need arose, Dominic primarily in charge of food, with his comedic abilities put to good use where appropriate.

'You're happy with that?' she asked him. He voiced his approval. 'I am, and I rely on you to curb my impetuous nature.' She wasn't quite sure how to take that glib remark.

'Are you ready to share responsibility for the faint chance of wrangling a performing animal with more tricky tentacles than a deformed octopus? We haven't won the war yet. Maybe you think we won't, is that why you're so agreeable? I'm just wanting to double check.'

*　*　*

On the long weekend in June Harry and Celia took a short break in Mornington, staying at a cottage with Frank and Magda. It was the right time to scatter Clive and Eddy's ashes. They had chosen a quiet cove on Ticonderoga Bay.

Celia and Frank embraced each other as tears flowed. Stepping towards the water's edge holding the remains of her loved ones Celia could only think that she really was living in an alternative universe.

They were not here... they couldn't be, Clive and Eddy were at home in Bannockburn, weren't they? She was here, thrust into a parallel life. Everything was an illusion. The feeling lasted several seconds until Celia finally handed a container to Frank, who removed his shoes and waded in, tipping the ashes onto the waiting waves.

It was only then that Celia followed his lead. Harry and Magda wiped their eyes as Frank stepped from the sea and walked to Magda, hugging her close. Celia stood in the shallows, staring at the horizon, silently giving thanks for the love she'd known.

It was almost a year since Ruth's death. Three significant people gone from her life. As it was and as it is now Celia realised that love is everything. Harry gave Nancy to Frank and went to her. Celia took his hand, thanking him for being in her life.

The morning had been mild but now a chilly breeze blew as they hurried from the beach and travelled the short distance to the Portsea Hotel for lunch. Nancy was a very helpful distraction. She sat in her high chair examining the crumbs that had dropped into the scoop of her rubber bib.

Her fingers couldn't quite reach in. The adults watched with interest as she pondered the problem. In a moment or two she grasped the sides of her unyielding bib, tipping it up in the direction of her mouth. It was hilarious to see.

'I think she might be a bright little spark,' Frank remarked.

On a quiet Sunday afternoon in August Harry was dozing on the couch. Celia left her chair, moved his legs and made a space for herself.

'We really should start thinking about an extension to the house, what do you think, Harry?' Celia asked him. Harry roused himself.

'Somehow I knew you would be toying with that idea, because I'd been thinking of saying the same thing to you.'

'That surprises me. I'm glad we're on the same page. We're hard pressed to accommodate visitors, we need another bedroom. The back deck could be reduced, we don't use all of it.'

'That's the logical spot, let's get some plans drawn up, builders are always busy, we'll be lucky to see it by Christmas.' Celia gave Harry a peck on the cheek.

'You're an angel,' she told him.

The land sloped away on the right hand side at the back. Celia wanted to utilise this and build a small nook below a new room. She thought a trapdoor with pull down steps would be nifty. Harry was considering cost and wanted to leave it open for storage. Celia called him an unimaginative troglodyte.

'So my angelic qualities have suddenly evaporated, lost my place on the page, have I?' Harry pulled a puzzled face. Celia screwed up her nose in answer to that.

While they were in the midst of these discussions a pleasant surprise came by way of Celia's trusty financial adviser who, in answer to her query, found that the shares her father had left her had finally born fruit. Amounting to almost fifteen thousand dollars they had doubled in value. This tidy sum would certainly help with the cost of the renovation.

Harry arrived home one wintry night in a state of high excitement, prompting Celia to ask if he'd had a pay rise.

'More exciting than that. A gift from the Gods.' he declared. 'A crew repairing the roof of the theatre found melted plastic canisters wired to a beam, and they didn't store reels of film. Oh, no.' Harry paused for dramatic effect. 'Charred passports, thought to be fake, old foreign currency, charts and receipts dating back years were addressed to Ariti. These roofing guys are local, they know the story and reported what they'd found. The prosecutors will be in a feeding frenzy when they see this stuff. What a hoot! Smoked out by his own sly conniving.'

Celia's eyes opened wide as she took in Harry's startling news. 'That's awesome! I wonder why he left them there. Surely this adds weight to the evidence from Guy Stolz.'

'I'm guessing he thought the canisters would burn, or he forgot they were there. Good thing either way, it might speed up proceedings when the arson case gets to court.'

Celia was hopeful about whether it would, but somewhat stressed if renovations on both her projects got under way at the same time.

She found out soon enough that this would not be a problem. Just as work was scheduled to start on their extension the builder called in. The man was nervous, the fingers of his right hand balling into a fist, curling in, then out again. Something was amiss.

'Sorry, mate, I'm really sorry about this.'

It was a Saturday and Harry's day off. He stood waiting for the man to explain. Celia walked in from the yard holding a bundle of dry washing. The body language of both men alerted her that something bad was going down here.

She stood watching, as the man stammered a confession. 'I… um,' he sighed deeply. 'Well, thing is, I'm bankrupt, yeah well, being declared…bankrupt.' What can you say to that, Celia thought.

She glanced at Harry, who was very slowly nodding his head. The builder squirmed, looking as shrivelled as a pricked sausage on a hotplate. More apologies spilled out as Harry stared at him. Celia dropped the washing onto the sofa and started to fold the towels. It seemed like an age before Harry spoke. 'Good luck, mate.' The unfortunate man headed for the door. 'Thanks for coming in person,' Harry said as he saw him out.

'Oh, boy, we're going to be in a pickle now. I'll make some calls.' Harry looked around for his phone. Celia was about to utter a few chosen words of disgust when the doorbell rang.

She marched up the hallway to open the door, sighing in frustration. Two young men stood in front of her, dressed in smart black pants, white shirts and ties, their wide toothy smiles plastered to their faces.

'Oh, God,' she said. 'It's the Mormons.'

'Yes, hello, we'd like to discuss with you today the wonders of God's creation.' The speaker waved a pamphlet at her face. Celia replied.

'I'm in the middle of my own creative hell right now, so unless you are experienced builders in bricks and timber, I suggest you be on your holy way.'

'Unfortunately, er, no, but we can build you a stairway to Paradise,' the other guy said brightly, trying his luck.

'I'm not quite ready for that yet. I must away now and deal with my earthly stairway. Goodbye, have a nice day.' Celia closed the door. She could hear Harry laughing.

Out of the blue Celia's brother, Nathan, came to the rescue, not in person, but by suggesting a recently qualified friend, prepared to work on the build if he could be accommodated. Charlie obliged, his bed-sit utilised again.

Harry's brother, Tim, arrived at the end of August and stayed longer than planned. Tim's technical skills surprised even himself, he said, as Harry and Celia expressed their admiration and suggested he start on preliminary work before the new builder was due.

It had been a time of adjustments and disruptions. Celia revelled in every dirty nappy, and every whiff of baby vomit. She thought it miraculous that she'd been given the chance to be a mother again. The joy of it was intoxicating and to share this remarkable life with Harry was very precious to her. He'd slipped into fatherhood as smoothly as a bird rises in the air.

That sense of wonder, reawakened while trekking in nature, stayed with her. Problems on a new build might be frustrating but not greatly important if you viewed them from a different standpoint.

As Nancy's blonde curls grew more abundant Celia was reminded of Eddy. At ten months of age she had become a toddler, pulling herself up from the floor with the help of her rocking horse. Her parents nearly missed this milestone, as they argued playfully one Sunday over who was cooking lunch. Nancy let out a triumphant squeal and they turned just in time to see her totter around the horse.

'Well, aren't you the clever one.' Harry had grasped her chubby hand. 'You've set us another challenge.' He looked at Celia.

'We'd better child-proof the place, quick smart, she'll soon be running riot.' Nancy swayed on the end of his arm, giggling as her legs gave way and gravity brought her to the floor.

In the latter part of the year Celia was reminded again of the day when Harry had been shot by Alan Schofield. They hugged each other with relief when he was finally brought to trial, pleading guilty to the charge. It meant they were not required to give evidence.

Harry read from the transcript, summarising the gist of it… Schofield had decided to take the advice of his legal counsel…the judge recorded in his summary that the defendant had shown no signs of remorse. Perhaps because he was heavily medicated, the judge concluded.

Schofield received a sentence of ten years. Celia felt sorry for Donna and the children. In an email to Robert she asked him to pass on her best wishes.

On the streets of Appleton Christmas lights winked and glowed. Shiny red bows and snowflake motifs paraded over brightly lit shops brimming with the commerce of Christmas.

Coming into the council building for the last meeting of the year Celia was struck by the greyness of it; the elves had not worked any magic in here. An indifferent mix of greys on walls and cabinets cast a pall of gloom throughout the room. Lit by suspended fluorescent tubes the light played mostly in the wrong places except for two bulbous globes which shone down over heavy timber tables. The former courthouse still carried an air of censure about it. Taking a seat next to Dominic she whispered that the place could do with a make-over.

After the formalities were dealt with Celia listened attentively. The councillors were displaying a burst of congeniality, calling for tenders to refurbish and repair the theatre. Dominic and Celia locked eyes in surprise.

Celia thought of Renzo. A voice broke through her thoughts.

'And now to the final matter on this evening's agenda.' The Mayor was addressing the chamber. Next to her Dominic fidgeted in his seat. Celia's eyes were on the Mayor as he rose from his chair and stepped into the light.

'I would like to propose a motion regarding the much disputed use of one of our major assets, our beloved theatre. Our town councillors are committed, as always, to listening to the voices of our residents.' Cynical sniggers and muttering from the gallery greeted this last statement. The Mayor glanced towards the source.

'I can't deny it has taken a considerable time to resolve this issue. In fairness, the matter was beyond our control. However, recent changes to previous circumstances have impacted in our favour. Reports detailing these changes are available for your perusal. The property in question has been languishing in limbo for far too long. Tonight I'm delighted to tell you it will be administered by local government into the future. I move that this property be used to accommodate a wide range of artistic endeavours, a place where our youth can learn all facets of stagecraft and performance, where visiting productions can enrich the community and where a proposed local theatre company will have a permanent home.'

A small woman stood, raising her hand to second the motion. The Mayor shook out a large handkerchief and blew his nose before continuing.

'In relation to this last intention, interested parties are asked to contact Ms Celia Bolitho who has led a tireless campaign in the advancement of this admirable initiative. Other staffing considerations will be evaluated once the building receives a certificate of occupation.'

The Mayor declared the motion open for discussion. When the votes signalled victory Dominic leapt to his feet and planted kisses on Celia's cheeks. This time she didn't try to dodge. An excited crowd was lining up at her elbow, eager to register as members. She saw Percy Hendricks in the queue behind Sally.

As she waved goodbye to Dominic and Sally, Celia did not know what to think. After the long months of waiting, the outcome of the evening's proceedings was overwhelming. Twenty-two names and phone numbers were written on a clipboard that Dominic had filched from a nearby table. Her mind was in turmoil as she placed it on the passenger seat beside her and laughed and cried all at once.

'How do you start a theatre company?' Celia asked herself. Reality started to take hold. University days and school plays had given her only a cursory knowledge of the requirements. There was a mountain of work to do.

Charlie had not been present at this auspicious meeting. When Celia called him his excitement was contagious and she began to feel that she could go the distance.

It was getting late when Celia arrived home to her own quiet celebration with Harry. Several messages were pinging on her phone. Tomorrow would be time enough to deal with them.

Harry was dozing peacefully on the couch as she entered the lounge. He woke with a start when Celia noisily deposited two mugs of hot chocolate onto the coffee table.

'How goes it?' he asked, stifling a yawn. 'By the pleased look on your face I'd say you have a happy tale to tell me.'

'I don't know whether to laugh or to cry,' she said, before launching into the surprising results of the meeting. When she'd finished her blow-by-blow report Harry gave a gleeful chuckle and slapped her thigh.

'This is going to be a lark, where do you plan to start?'

'A brainstorming session with you... not tonight though, it's bedtime.'

Celia couldn't sleep. Her brain was galloping back and forth over the hurdles she imagined she would have to contend with. All the knowledge she didn't have, all the mistakes she would be likely to make in her ignorance. Where to find the right people with the right experience who did have some clues, and how to enlist them to help her.

She thought of the few already in her sights, like Andy McConnell, but he was in Scotland. In this regional town she thought her options might be limited. Celia finally fell asleep thinking she'd bitten off way more than she could chew.

Replying to her messages next morning Celia found one from a high school drama teacher who had experience in theatre and was offering to help. She arranged to meet him after Christmas. Other messages from a playwright, a fiddle player, a Celtic dance ensemble, and a cluster of music and dance teachers lifted Celia's spirits. It might not be as difficult to find the right people as she had imagined.

CHAPTER 22

2006–2007 — Significant Steps

In the week prior to Christmas Celia was enjoying Eula's company. Her aunt was ready to add a dash of spice to her life in the coming year and had booked herself a two week cruise to New Zealand. Her townhouse would be available for visitors.

'It'a win-win, my house will be ship-shape when I return,' she told Celia.

'What makes you think that?' Celia smiled. The house in Wombat Glade was in no fit state to accommodate the usual crowd over the holiday period; the extension was still a work in progress.

The new builder was due to return at the start of February. Celia had put her teaching job on hold when her pregnancy had become obvious. The school said they would welcome her back whenever she was ready. It was nice to know but there were too many other competing interests to allow her to return just yet.

Christmas Day was spent at Charlie's this year where the only discordant notes were in Celia's head. Her thoughts scurried from one consideration to the next. The holidays were an irritation for her, bringing work on all fronts to a standstill.

At the end of December, pleased that she could take one small step forward, Celia met with the drama teacher at Piccalilli Parlour. She was greeted by a slim man with an open, friendly manner. Giving Celia a few practical starting points he advised that she share the vision she had with all interested parties to determine whether they were in accord.

'A clear vision is the first step. Is it to be a profit making concern or not? Either way, how do you ensure funds?' Celia smiled and kept the perplexity from her face but she could feel the frown inside her.

The only clear vision Celia had was to see performers on stage. How they got there was about as clear to her as a pot of boiled cabbage. With an effort Celia took her head out of the cabbage pot and tried to concentrate.

'Call for nominations to form a committee, job descriptions for key roles, and choose a name. Estimate start-up costs, get a legal person or an accountant to handle registration, membership and insurance, all the tiresome technicalities. It's not mandatory yet, but if there's one money man or woman hanging about with thespian leanings all the better. Oh, and think about marketing and merchandise. Design a logo.' He ended by saying he would love to become a member. Celia grasped his hand, hoping she didn't appear too desperate.

'Oh, please do, I'm so grateful for your help. Thank you,' she said, as she walked him to the door.

Sally joined her, curious to know what Celia had gleaned.

'I have gleaned that I need that man on board. I wish you'd been sitting in to take notes, Sal. Here's what I remember,' she said, and spoke aloud, trying to remember each point and scribbling on a napkin.

'Ok, I'll draft a newsletter to send to the people on your list. It's given me an idea, I can install a notice board in the shop. Piccalilli can be our headquarters until the Arts Centre is ready. Make sure you delegate jobs, it looks like there's heaps to do.'

'There's a few jobs to keep me busy over the New Year holiday,' Celia admitted.

Harry was at home with Nancy today and Celia wasted no time enlisting his help. He suggested she take advantage of new software.

'We'll work on the record keeping. A free spreadsheet's available.'

'Ugh.' Celia shrugged. They both knew it wasn't her strong point.

'What do you know about web design?' she asked, changing the subject.

'Not much, I'd like to know a lot more. Kieran's the one to ask. He follows whatever technology has to offer.' Celia added Kieran to her recruitment list.

In answer to her update Andy McConnell called her early the following morning. The man's generosity made her cry, and it had all come about because she had helped a snakebite victim. Any decent person would have done the same. The remarkable serendipity of it never failed to astonish her.

His donation would go a long way in meeting some of those start-up costs. She had not even managed to take in the business plan he'd sent. She would handball that to Charlie. Celia was already thinking of merchandise, visualising little plastic apples filled with sweets…That would be the fun part, but she was getting ahead of herself.

Katherine flew in from Perth after New Year, taking advantage of Eula's empty house. Kath and Celia sat at Piccalilli catching up.

'Alex is not keen on the state of marriage. That doesn't bother me so much, but I'd like to have kids. Time's running out, and he's not keen on that idea either.' Celia sensed trouble brewing in this relationship.

'Maybe you need a break from each other, seems like you've hit a stalemate. Take a long holiday, time apart might help you decide if he's a stale mate, or not.'

'Ha.' Kath smiled at that.

Frank and Magda joined Katherine for a few days, bringing with them the painting of Clive and Eddy. Harry had encouraged her. 'It can hang in the new extension and Nancy will learn about those events from the past as she grows,' he'd said. 'She'll come to know about her brother and his father, who died before she was born. It's an important story to tell our children.'

'Our children?' Celia had caught the twinkle in his eyes.

'Yes, we'll have room for more now.' He laughed as she buried her head in his shoulder.

Every year Celia dreaded the month of February when she had to face those two significant dates. It was never an easy time. At least this year her mind was focused on two big projects. The new extension was starting to take shape, power connected and plumbing in place, or so Celia thought, until Tim arrived to help with painting, and discovered that hot water had been plumbed through the toilet cistern.

'I couldn't believe it when I pressed the flush. Steam wafted up from the bowl. I touched the cistern, and it was hot!'

Celia arranged a chat with the plumber, who came quick smart to remedy the situation, explaining that he'd given that job to his son, an out-of-work roof plumber who hadn't grasped some major distinctions. That young guy had certainly had a spaced-out look about him, Celia recalled. She'd had the impression at the time that he was a fan of the wacky tobaccy.

Over dinner that evening the story amused Charles and Beth, who had come to see the new work. Beth looked thoughtful as she flicked a light switch.

'What about the sparkie? I hope his work isn't faulty. That could be deadly. I'm thinking of the words, "skill" and "kill". Not much between them, is there. What do you make of that?' Nobody knew what to make of that. Charlie thought it had potential to be part of a slogan for the Apprenticeships Board.

*   *   *

Celia was not surprised that the Appleton Music Festival was now an annual event. This year she was looking forward to seeing Harry take part as lead guitarist in a Fleetwood Mac tribute, dressed in knickerbockers and his favourite vest over a white full sleeved shirt. He gave her a preview in his sexy gear one evening after rehearsal.

'Oh, boy,' she declared. 'You're making me go weak at the knees.' Harry had lifted her then, and carried her to their bed.

'In that case, we'd better keep you off your feet.' He was in his element. 'I've always wanted to do this.'

'What, the Fleetwood Mac thing, or racing me off to bed?' Celia waited expectantly while Harry hung his outfit inside a suit bag.

'Oh, there's no question.' Harry grinned as he leapt naked, onto the bed. 'What do you reckon?'

Sally spoke to her about a return to work.

'I'm missing you, Celia, have some mercy and come back,' she pleaded, 'I've had a lengthy period of staffing problems. Unless you have something else in mind.'

'No, I haven't Sal, not at this stage. I've been bogged down in kid's stuff, furnishing and painting the new extension and replanting around it. The ferns you donated are starting to look quite lush. It is time for me to get out of the house. Nancy could do with a few playmates. Now that Isobel has started school she's in danger of becoming a bored, selfish brat.'

It had been a difficult decision to place Nancy in child care. Celia had become hyper-vigilant, afraid that some dreaded mishap would occur when she wasn't watching, just as it had with Eddy. It was not helpful to either one of them and Celia knew she needed to be less intense about it. She returned to work at Piccalilli and hoped that Nancy didn't catch mumps or chicken pox just yet.

Progress had been a long, slow and stressful business since Celia first thought of her aimless ideas for the fire-damaged theatre back in 2004. She marvelled that her modest musings had morphed into a major undertaking. A new performance space was rising from the ashes. On a fine Saturday morning in September Celia was at the entrance to the newly named Appleton Arts Centre with Sally, Charlie, and Dominic — chief fundraiser, marketing manager, and business partner, respectively. Two members of the advisory panel arrived to join them.

'I think we're ready to launch the Harvest Theatre Company,'

Celia told them. It had taken two months to decide on a name. She felt indebted to her diligent team of supporters, the most surprising being Renzo Korlecki, the once crabby neighbour in Geelong, who right now was walking towards the group as they stood in the foyer.

In answer to Celia's letter, sent after that critical council meeting last November, Renzo had followed up with a phone call apologising for his previous behaviour, telling her how touched he was that she'd thought of him.

In his next conversation he said he'd written a letter to the council which led to an interview with a very positive outcome. Initially the council had contracted him to work on the fine plaster friezes throughout the building. More recently Celia learned that an offer of a permanent position in their maintenance department had followed.

On hearing this news she immediately thought he would be the perfect fit for the set manager she needed. After extending her congratulations Celia expressed the possibility to him, explaining the responsibilities of the role. He was thrilled.

'I've got a new lease on life!' he'd shouted. They both thought it was hilarious that he would be in charge of the venue, which he already was, the set designers, and maintenance, which was also in his remit. It all dovetailed beautifully with his paid job. The pair of them could not have been happier.

Dominic sauntered through the front doors carrying bolts of fabric for Celia's consideration. He was keen to start decorating his rooms. He asked Renzo if he could have a double entry door on one of them, which he planned to call 'The Salon', an intimate space for people of taste, he told them, or that was his hope. Celia smiled and refrained from comment. Renzo sighed and said he would run the alteration by his boss.

The second room would house a basic, efficient kitchen. Dominic proposed the bright idea to offer cooking classes. 'Make every post a winner, boost the takings in the off times.' Celia thought it had merit. She and Dominic were presently negotiating fees and charges with the Shire's accounting department. They were hopeful of a peppercorn rent in the start-up stage, to be reviewed on a yearly basis.

Celia gazed around at the stylish, decorative mouldings of parrots and peacocks in leafy branches, high on the pristine walls of the foyer.

'You've done a magnificent job, Renzo. What a great backdrop for art works.' Sally immediately suggested an art competition. 'That's the first thing we should do. Yvette will certainly be interested.' Charlie nodded enthusiastically.

Renzo led them through to the auditorium. Here, carpenters were sanding the pale timbers on the front wall of a new stage.

A thrill of excitement prompted Celia to skip up the steps at one side. Taking centre stage she raised her arms, shouting, 'At last, at last,' before breaking into a lively jig. The group gave her a wholehearted round of applause.

'Don't get too carried away, there's months of work ahead of us yet.' Renzo warned.

Soon after their visit to the theatre Celia joined a group of company members at Piccalilli to discuss the order of events. Aunt Eula was present, refreshed from her cruise, having been cajoled into the role of wardrobe mistress. Sally was happy with the number of entries already received for the Art Show. It was a mammoth task in itself. With Yvette's help they would start the installation as soon as Renzo gave the go-ahead.

How and what to stage for their inaugural production was the next headache. Almost unanimously, it was decided to cast the younger members in a daring dance and gymnastics performance. Not too ambitious, as it required no dialogue or awkward costume changes.

Celia nominated the Ad Hoc Rock puppets to be considered as a featured act to open the second half. There were no objections. Someone raised the all-important question of a name for the show. This could take some time. Suggestions came thick and fast. Celia prepared a shortlist. The final choice would be decided at the next meeting.

As the theatre was still a building site Charlie had suggested the old Scout hall as a suitable location for auditions and early rehearsals. For those unfamiliar with theatre productions, the drama teacher kindly printed copies of an explanatory glossary, listing the jargon that oils the wheels of every production.

She was astonished at the number of terms she'd never heard of from All Call to Dry Tech, Gel and Gobo, Paper Tech, Speed-through, Spike marks and Wet tech, to name a few. To her they sounded like the services one might receive from a Turkish Bath House. What else do I need to get my head around, she thought.

When she saw Sally print out the latest 'Harvest' newsletter and pin it to the notice board Celia let out a shriek.

'I've got a print expert under my very nose! I can't believe it didn't occur to me sooner.'

'Who?'

'Frank, of course, he could handle our print needs: brochures, posters, programs, tickets…I'll ask him for a quote. That reminds me, I need to speak to Kieran about a website.'

The Harvest Theatre Company attracted a great deal of attention, as Celia had known it would. The first little crop of hopefuls had waited impatiently for rehearsals to start after Christmas.

Each week Celia welcomed members of all ages. Older members pitched in to help with backdrops, lighting and props. Most importantly, they patched up the inevitable injuries, plumped up wounded pride, and bolstered bruised egos.

CHAPTER 23

2008 — Blast off!

In March of 2008 Renzo gave the go-ahead and rehearsals moved from the Scout hall to the Appleton Arts Centre. Celia stood on the floor, filled with pride and disbelief. She wrapped her arms around as many children as she could reach. Jubilant, she walked around in circles, embracing friends, teachers and crew.

Setting up the Art Show may have caused tempers to fray until the very moment it was launched, but when the awards were presented and Dominic plied artists and guests with champagne and savouries, everyone forgot their squabbles and congratulated themselves. It was an inspired and successful lead-in to the Company's first major production.

Celia and her supporters were kept busy handing out brochures, answering questions, and handling sales. It was marketing magic. She wished her little sweet-filled apples had arrived in time.

On a rainy night in May, Celia stepped onto the stage in a striking low-cut gown of burgundy velvet. She touched the tiny pink roses that Harry had pinned at her shoulder. The footlights emitted a dull spreading glow at her feet as a spotlight swung at half strength across the expectant faces of the audience. Coming on strong it sought her out, capturing her standing tall in its bright beam.

Speaking with passion she mentioned only a few of the tribulations that had threatened her impossible dream, preferring to concentrate on the gradual triumphs that friends and members of the Harvest Theatre Company had enjoyed to get to this day.

'Money raised from the staging of the Art Show and Music Festival has been instrumental, pardon the pun, in enabling us to succeed in this endeavour. Once again, a venture made possible through the tireless work and generosity of people here and abroad.

May I say how proud I am of our talented young performers who will dazzle you with the energy and flair they bring to this stage tonight. Welcome to "Blast Off" our first fabulous production presented to you by our very own Harvest Theatre Company.

On that note she introduced Dominic, 'your compere this evening,' handing him the mic and stepping to one side. He thanked Celia for her own tireless efforts and told her not to go away as he was about to make an important announcement. Celia staged a baffled response as Dominic played to the crowd.

She really was a little curious, she didn't know what he had in mind. She soon found out. Dominic raised his hand in a gesture commanding attention. His voice took on a Churchillian resonance.

'That singular person from abroad, that mysterious benefactor, has flown in to be with us this evening. Please give a warm welcome to our patron and guest of honour, Mr Andy McConnell.

Celia was flabbergasted and gave an audible gasp as Andy suddenly materialised in front of her, wrapping her in a warm embrace. The audience loved it, whistling and clapping as Celia and Andy stepped forward, bowing and waving, before exiting the stage.

Dominic called the house to attention once more, beckoning the Mayor, who had appeared from the wings. Celia stood in the shadows with Andy's arm around her, watching in anticipation. This time she knew what was coming.

In a shock move Dominic grasped the hapless Mayor by the scruff of the neck and shook him.

'And there are no thanks for this man.' he said, taking a firm hold of the Mayor's padded shoulder.

'This man with a shoe fetish who stole every tap and ballet shoe he could find. You'll see... our children have no shoes.' It was the audience's turn to gasp as Dominic turned the Mayor around and spanked him soundly on the backside.

'Is this for real?' a voice cried out. Dominic held up his hand again, shaking his finger. The Mayor turned to face the audience, hanging his head.

'Tell us, good sir, where are our shoes?' Dominic asked, as he tossed the microphone to the Mayor. Celia heard her daughter's voice, loud and clear.

'Shoe, shoosh!' shouted Nancy.

The microphone wobbled in the Mayor's hand. As the spluttering man attempted to speak, the lights went out and the microphone lost volume. People hurriedly flashed lights from their phones. Dominic called out from the stage.

'No need for alarm, our resident sparkie is working to restore power. The show must go on.'

His voice thundered around the auditorium. Suddenly Celia heard the sound of drumming as the stage lit up. Barefoot dancing girls and boys, holding LED lanterns on glittering poles leapt and tumbled as the poles were thrust from one to another in the midst of a breathtaking gymnastic display.

Rings of light on wrists and ankles left an afterglow as the performers whirled in somersaults, back and forth across the stage. First Nations children with painted bodies stepped forward, crouching with shaded eyes, switching seamlessly from ancient corroboree to modern creative dance while a didjeridoo sounded its own intrinsic message. The corroboree receded as clowns on stilts took centre stage.

After interval the Ad Hoc Rock Puppets served it up to the schoolyard bully, the litter bugs, the bootlickers, tattlers and lip-smarts. Celia sat with her family as the audience hissed and booed on cue. She was filled with a kind of wonder at the punchy narrative and nimble fingers of the puppeteers.

The dancers returned to the stage, gyrating in illuminated hula hoops that blinked in the dark until the lights surged and four banners of Scottish tartan unfurled from above. Celia laughed at Andy's delighted exclamations. She held her breath as concealed acrobats spiralled from the folds and wowed the crowd with banners interweaving in a first-rate exhibition of flying trapeze.

A youthful pianist played lively Scottish reels as airborne feet changed pace in a clever heel and toe routine. Hand-held clickers imitating the sound of tap shoes striking the floor were used to good effect.

As the curtain fell to thunderous applause the Mayor appeared downstage with a clutch of assorted shoes hanging around his neck; the heavy mayoral chains had gone. The crowd went wild. He shook hands with Dominic and they linked arms behind each other's shoulders, tapping their feet in a soft shoe shuffle, smirking with pleasure as they basked in the outrush of love from the audience.

The curtain rose for a second call, then a third, as the elated cast took their final bows to a spirited standing ovation. Harry, Charles and Eula clapped the loudest. Young Isobel had been up there, strutting her stuff among the dancers.

Celia turned to smile at the beaming faces of her family, marvelling at how clever they'd been, keeping Andy's visit a secret. Her thoughts flew back to the day she'd arrived at Charlie's house where destiny opened the door and the future beckoned her in.

Not long after the Music Festival this year Celia had been feeling nauseous and realised she was pregnant. When she told Harry he was just as weepy as he had been the first time. Harry had been devastated at missing Nancy's birth. Celia knew he was determined to be there for this one.

*   *   *

In the first week of May Harry and Celia were travelling along Mountside Road in a silver convertible watching the onlookers lining the pavement, waiting for the arrival of the bridal party. Tony Larocca, the fruit shop baritone, stood in readiness on a raised platform. A hum of anticipation rippled through the rows of smiling faces. The crowd moved forward, necks craning towards the sound of approaching cars. The hum gathered momentum as they jostled for position, cameras and phones at the ready.

A gleaming white Audi Cabriolet glided to a halt outside number 70. Best man, Dominic Romano, alighted from the driver's seat as the roof on the roadster rolled away. He signalled to Tony and leaned in to lend an arm to the bride. Wearing a gown of white guipure lace with three quarter sleeves Beth stepped from the car.

A wisp of pearl-studded veil snuggled into her dark shoulder length hair. On the far side the bridegroom swung open the low door and walked to join his wife. Gwen hurried along the roadway, greeting the couple with effusive kisses. Tony Larocca launched into 'Sweet Disposition', the irony not lost on Celia.

Superb, Celia thought, as she stepped from the BMW driven by Kieran Huntley. Harry reached into the rear of the car and lifted his daughter from the child safety restraint. Celia whispered to her.

'Nancy, darling, come and see Auntie Beth and Charlie.'

The child squealed as the bride and groom waltzed along the street, sweeping her up between them amidst a shower of rose petals. Tony's performance came to a close and onlookers burst into enthusiastic applause as the sun hid behind a stray cloud for a moment or two.

At Piccalilli Parlour Sally Doyle waved a greeting to the bridal party. During the last four years significant changes had come about: the outdoor area had been extended across the block and an undercover deck, complete with stone fireplace, proved popular nearly all year round.

Young staff members were checking place settings, polishing glasses and plucking at floral displays. A Scottish piper was warming his pipes at the entrance to the garden. The bridal party took up their positions on the street and two little girls stepped to the front. The piper led them in. They circled around the garden and stopped on a patch of lawn, pausing there as the pipes exhaled their last notes.

Charlie hoisted Isobel onto his hip.

'Well done, girls,' he said, addressing her and Nancy. 'You managed that very nicely.' He kissed the top of his daughter's head and lowered her to the ground as his mother came forward. Eula linked hands with both girls. Celia extricated herself from a group of gushing matrons and moved toward her daughter.

'Nancy, we're going to have some yummy food now. Go with Aunt Eula, she'll help you find your seat.' The child looked from one to the other.

'Is my seat lost?' she asked.

'No, no, honey, go with Isobel, it's next to hers.'

Nancy spied Mavis across the lawn.

'Mavis, Mavis,' she called, pointing to the silver tiara clasping her spun gold curls; the perfect picture of a sweet angel, but Celia knew she could be as awkward as a crabby aunt if she chose. Mavis waved. Celia waited.

Nancy's tiny shoulders rose as she took a deliberate breath, pursed her lips and eyed her mother. Grinning wickedly, she grasped Isobel with one hand while propelling Eula forward with the other.

Little minx, Celia thought. This time a tantrum was not the preferred option. Relieved, Celia rolled her eyes as Harry appeared at her side, raising an inquiring eyebrow.

'Everything okay here?' He placed his hand in the crook of Celia's back, giving her a gentle squeeze. The Bridal party stepped under the laserlite roof to take their places at the front table. Waiting staff moved around the tables serving seafood cocktails. A four piece jazz ensemble was playing 'La Vie en Rose' in the background. Celia called Harry's attention to the musical notations tattooed on the fingers of the trumpet player. 'How groovy is that!' Harry said.

Guests whistled and cheered as the speeches concluded. Dominic Romano, microphone in hand, invited the bride and groom to take the floor for the bridal waltz. Harry and Celia followed, trying not to upstage the happy couple. Soon the temporary wooden floor was bouncing with jiving feet.

Even Eula laughed wildly as she was whirled around by a silver-haired gentleman. Celia recognised him as the editor and owner of the local newspaper and gave Eula an approving smile. She spoke to Harry, raising her voice above the music.

'We'd better check on the girls, I can't see them.' They made their way across to the almost empty tables. An older couple were the only ones still seated.

'Have you seen the two little girls?' Harry asked.

'No, not for a while. We saw them playing with napkins then they wandered off towards the dance floor,' the old man told them.

Scanning the sea of dancers to no avail they returned to look in the narrow space behind the fireplace, moving on to search among the tables in the garden, asking all the while if anyone had seen the girls. Celia went to look for Charles. She found him inside the shop talking to Sally.

'Charlie, sorry to interrupt, the girls are missing.'

'Oh, heavens! They can't be far,' he replied, and hurried outside. Charles and Harry walked the perimeter calling for the girls.

'Isobel, Nancy, where are you?'

Dominic heard them and stepped away from his glamorous

partner to speak to Harry. Hurrying towards the band he raised a hand, signalling them to stop playing and took hold of the mic. Celia took off towards the entrance as Dominic put out an alert. Beth came from the cafe, dressed in her going away outfit and caught up with her.

By now all the guests knew the girls were missing. Mavis buzzed about in a state of agitation, not having predicted this turn of events.

There was no shortage of searchers. Harry called them together, issuing instructions and formulating a methodical search plan. One group was sent to cover the creek area, considered the most dangerous. Another group followed the laneway. The remainder fell in behind Beth and Celia as they moved along Mountside Road, each pair of eyes peel left and right as Harry had instructed.

Celia searched in front gardens, in back gardens, in shops, in side alleys. She returned to the front of Yvette's house. Celia was bordering on hysteria. Beth tried to comfort her. 'They'll show up, don't panic yet.'

She saw Yvette and Simone searching their garden and called out to them.

'Any sign?' They shook their heads.

Pictures of a terrified Nancy, interlinked with memories of Eddy, were playing an ominous slideshow on the screen in Celia's head.

'Let's go back to the cafe,' Beth suggested, as she took Celia's arm. 'That'll be where any reports will come in.'

'Yes, you're right.'

Beth stepped outside to ring Charles. They were supposed to be in Melbourne tonight, ready to depart for Tasmania. He answered, saying he was down near the creek and members of the Fire Brigade had just arrived with searchlights. Celia sat at one of the indoor tables, resting her head in her hands. Beth joined her, passing on the update from Charlie.

'Most of the guests are out searching, even Eula. The girls can't be far away.' Beth tried to sound positive.

Sally sat with her arm across Celia's shoulders, gently massaging her back, talking to her, distracting her from morbid thoughts. Celia's mind was not so easily distracted; it was sifting through certain dubious characters who lived in the town.

Voicing her thoughts she suddenly declared, 'What about that Jackie Playdough?'

'Who?' Sally looked vague. Beth frowned. Celia explained her odd remark.

'You know the one. The local kids tease him, calling him Jackie Playdough because he's forever kneading some glutinous substance; moving it through his fingers, squeezing it, stretching it. Perhaps he likes to...ugh.' She couldn't bear to think about it. 'Maybe not, I don't think he'd have the presence of mind to kidnap anyone, he always appears to be confused.'

'Oh, that one, now I know who you mean. No, surely not.'

'Then there's that sleazy charmer at the butcher's, sizing up the female population, ingratiating himself. Serving up lashings of flattery as he wraps your roast lamb. "Delicious, Mrs Featherstone, juicy and succulent, sweet as that pretty face of yours. Have a nice day."' Celia grimaced, she could hear him now, talking to Eula.

'I saw him in the crowd today. Why are butchers renowned for their patronising banter, Sal?' Sally thought for a moment.

'I'd say the culture started when butchering became a

commercial business. No longer bloodying the backyard with guts and gore. The customer was mostly the little housewife at home. You need to keep her coming back. Stroke her self esteem while you slice her bacon, hey.' Celia sniffed and blew her nose.

'Well, it's not the forties any more.' She wiped her nose again. Her ankles were puffy. She stood and moved to pull out another chair and parked her feet on the extra seat to relieve them.

'There were rumours around last year, when people thought that a paedophile had been re-housed here, and they were right,' Celia whispered. 'Harry knows him. The guy's required to report in. He'd be top of the list.' Panic started to overtake her and her head felt tight at the temples.

'Where is she, where could they be? Somebody knows. Poor little girls, some-one must have taken them,' Celia cried. Her distress was disturbing to witness. She pressed her fingers to her head. 'Where's Harry? Why isn't there any news? I need to speak to Harry.'

She sobbed as she called his mobile. Sally brought her aspirin and filled her water glass. It was now almost nine o'clock in the evening. Searchers were all over the area, calling in from time to time for respite. Yvette and Simone had just returned to the venue. They had searched their property three times, as well as all the properties along the lane. Everyone in the vicinity was on the alert.

*   *   *

Two hours... three hours...nearly four hours later, and Nancy and Isobel had not been located. It was past seven in the evening and Harry was trying not to panic. A member of the Search and Rescue unit and I can't find my own daughter, or Charlie's, he thought.

How that made him feel he couldn't possibly describe. He has registered a missing persons report. Three police officers were available. Celia would never cope with the loss of another child. Was he being melodramatic even thinking that?

Dominic and Harry met each other coming from opposite directions a few blocks away from the cafe. They were both desperate for a cigarette. Harry couldn't remember the last time he'd had one. He told Dominic he needed one now.

'Come on, I've got a pack in the car,' Dominic told him. 'It's parked at Charlie's place.'

Harry felt his phone vibrate in his top pocket. Answering on the run, he listened to Celia's frantic appeals.

'Yes, yes, I've got it covered, sweetheart. Two constables are calling on those persons of interest right now. Sit tight, we'll find the girls. I'll be back in a few minutes to brief the officers when they return. See you soon.'

Entering by the front gate they made their way along the side of the house to the rear yard. Dominic's Audi shone in the darkness. Dominic grabbed the pack and a lighter from the glovebox. Harry took a cigarette. Dominic lit it, then lit another for himself. The two men leaned against the car, taking deep drags, watching the smoke curl away on the night air.

Dominic was saying something, but Harry's ears had picked up another sound. At first he thought it was a bird. No, it wasn't a bird, more like a smothered cough. Dominic had heard it now and flicked his lighter over the car. Harry turned on his phone torch. They peered into the car. Harry saw a chubby hand poking from the black faux fur rug on the back seat. His own hands started to shake.

He reached in over the low door. Pulling back the rug he felt as though a kitten had skittered through his stomach and was scratching at the lining of his gut. Nancy yawned, squinting at the light.

'Hi, Daddy,' she said. 'We had lollies.'

'Hello, sweetie, so good to see you.' Harry tried to steady his breathing. Nestled into the leather behind Nancy, Isobel stirred, opening her eyes. She gave a sleepy sigh.

'Hello, Isobel.'

'Hello, Uncle Harry, we've been hiding.'

Harry didn't know whether to laugh or to cry. He messaged Charlie, then asked Dominic if there had been confectionery in the car... or, more importantly, any drugs. Dominic assured him that there had definitely been no drugs, only jelly beans in a seat pocket. He was deeply offended.

'And the jellies were there in case Beth's blood glucose levels dropped during the church service.'

'Sorry, Dom, just had to be sure, you know. With little kids...'

Everyone present in Piccalilli screamed when Harry and Dominic walked in, each carrying a child. Celia's heart went into a spin when she saw the foursome step through the door. She felt her heartbeat careening; racing and pounding as her frazzled nervous system took a moment to synchronise with her brain. They're here!

Celia tried to still her unruly heart as she leapt from her chair, blessed relief sweeping through her tired, pregnant body. She wiped tears from her face and reached out to embrace them all. Her words came out in a jumble of endearments.

Charlie came rushing through the side entrance. He was shaking, asking Harry a dozen questions.

'Have they been harmed? Where were they? How did you?... Did someone... ?' Harry gave Nancy over to her mother's waiting arms and put his hands on Charlie's shoulders.

'Calm down, everything's fine,' Harry told him, before ushering him to the seat next to Celia.

Isobel put her arms around her father's neck. Two police officers arrived, happy that they were no longer needed. Searchers returned as the good news spread. People gathered closer.

Sally poured drinks while they listened to Harry and Dominic relate the story of the discovery of the two girls. Celia was touched when Harry said he would never forget the radiance shining from her tearstained face when he walked in with Nancy.

Jassi and Dev came with Dilip for a day trip on the following Saturday. Isobel was staying with Eula and they had both arrived for lunch.

Dilip had grown into a sturdy teenager and today he had a surprise for them. After the meal he came into the lounge with a guitar slung over his shoulder. He soon had their attention and played a mean version of 'Down Under.' It was a special moment. He said it was Harry who had inspired him.

'I've wanted to play that song since the day it made me laugh so much I nearly wet myself.'

The little girls giggled and clapped, then everyone clapped as Harry picked up his guitar and joined Dilip for an encore.

Easter 2009

Under a glorious blue sky three members of the Bolitho family walk into the Enchanted Forest on Easter weekend. The fourth member, six month old Benjamin Edward, is dozing in a baby buggy being propelled along the track by his father.

Nancy walks determinedly in front of her parents. She is already a stage tragic, soon to make her debut in the upcoming production of 'Mojo' the story of a small egg who didn't make the grade.

Celia extends both arms to touch the delicate branches of the Moonah trees swaying and waving on each side of the well worn path… back and forth they wave. In feathery arcs they reach out and rise up in triumphant salute to the glorious sky, to the family passing by, to the tenacity of life itself. A rising breeze escalates their movement. Celia fancies she can hear the sound of rustling applause.

She recalls the day when she came upon the little family watching the Pobblebonk and wonders if those boys ever learned to play the banjo. She touches Harry's arm, smiling in delight.

'Will we be lucky enough to find a funny frog?' Celia asks him.

He stops and reaches down, placing an arm around her waist, squeezing her in a brisk embrace. Nancy bounces on her toes, jumping in circles around them.

'Oh, not again,' she says, screwing up her nose as she regards her parents. 'No more kissing today, please… I want to see Isobel and Trudie, they'll be waiting for us at the cottage. Come o-on.' Nancy crouches beside her sleeping brother.

'Benny's hungry, he wants Easter eggs.'

Benny yawns, clutching Blue Ted closer to his cheek.

www.ingramcontent.com/pod-product-compliance
Lightning Source LLC
Chambersburg PA
CBHW060536190726
48283CB00003B/744